"I never asked

He kept his eyes averted as he continued to work. "Are you asking now?"

"Yes."

"We lived around Cheyenne until I was eight. Then we moved southeast." Backing away, Rhett peered at the sky. "It's late. I need to return you to the ranch before your uncle worries."

He needed to? His choice of words struck her, reminding her that she now lived in a different place where people took the law into their own hands. If her uncle believed for one moment that Rhett had insulted her, he wouldn't hesitate to string up his newest worker.

"Let's hurry, then." Ellie leaped down from the back of the wagon. And soon they were on their way.

But for the remainder of the drive, she couldn't help but think she knew so little about the man seated next to her. Yes, he was courageous, strong and a hard worker, but what did she really know about him?

What secrets did he carry that he was unwilling—or unable—to share?

Anna Zogg has long been fascinated by the West—ranch life, horses, and the tough men and women who tamed it. Ever drawn to her Native American roots, she and her husband, John, reside in the heart of the West. Visit annazogg.com to learn more about her love of music, her eclectic taste in fiction and some very special children.

Books by Anna Zogg

Love Inspired Historical

The Marshal's Mission
Frontier Secrets

Visit the Author Profile page at Harlequin.com.

Frontier Secrets

ANNA ZOGG

LOVE INSPIRED
INSPIRATIONAL ROMANCE

Recycling programs for this product may not exist in your area.

LOVE INSPIRED®
INSPIRATIONAL ROMANCE

ISBN-13: 978-1-335-91234-3

Frontier Secrets

Copyright © 2021 by Anna Zogg

This edition published by arrangement with Harlequin Books S.A.

For questions and comments about the quality of this book, please contact us at CustomerService@Harlequin.com.

Love Inspired
22 Adelaide St. West, 40th Floor
Toronto, Ontario M5H 4E3, Canada
www.Harlequin.com

Printed in U.S.A.

For man looketh on the outward appearance,
but the Lord looketh on the heart.
—*1 Samuel* 16:7

To Virginia Smith:
writer, mentor and, best of all, friend

Chapter One

Wyoming Territory, May 1888

This cannot be the grand frontier my uncle mentioned in his letters.

As Ellie Marshall stood inside the Fort Laramie general store, she peered through the grimy window. A mud-caked soldier rode through a sea of sludge, his horse's hooves making a sucking sound with every step. A passersby on foot plowed through the muck. Ellie looked down at herself. The same brownish-red that marked the military post also stained her violet traveling gown. Grimacing, she scrubbed at the half-dried blotches on her sleeve.

Soon this will be over. Not only the ordeal of filth, but the endless hours on mind-numbing trains, followed by a bone-jarring stagecoach ride from Cheyenne. At least she was on the last leg of her journey. She closed her eyes, trying to picture her uncle's description of his ranch—lush green grasses and rolling hills spread before majestic purple mountains. Compared to this barren wasteland, his home promised to be a haven. She couldn't wait to begin her new life there. For the first few months, she planned to reacquaint herself with him, her closest family member. With his permission, she would practice medicine on his ranch. If not there, then someplace else. Regardless, grand new opportunities awaited—ones that would make all the difficulties of the journey worthwhile.

The shrill voice of Mrs. Rushton, a fellow passenger, punctured the low hum of conversation in the post. As the portly woman scolded her son, Ellie slipped out the door. She sought to escape them as well as a new passenger, Mr. Tesley, whom she had met the night before. Everyone within earshot knew the troubles the businessman had faced and recounted at top volume. His buggy had broken down and he was in a hurry to get to Casper. When he found his only travel option was the stagecoach, he let the whole post know the arrangement was not to his liking.

Standing by the store's entrance, Ellie surveyed the fort's rough log walls and primitive buildings. Beyond a massive barricade, tattered tepees dotted the hills. Try as she might, she couldn't reconcile the description of Fort Laramie she'd read about in travel brochures—an "oasis for travelers"—with the stark reality. Everywhere she looked, she saw filth, coarseness, degradation. The setting reminded her of the more unseemly areas of Chicago that she thought she had left behind.

A yell from across the yard startled her. Ellie turned to see the Deadwood stagecoach heading for the open gates. The heavy Concord vehicle with its eight-horse team creaked and jangled while travelers shouted farewells. By her count, fifteen men rode inside the coach or perched on top. Not only did the shotgun messenger tote a weapon, but so did a number of passengers. Because of outlaws?

Gulping, Ellie dabbed her forehead with gloved fingers. Though the stagecoach company downplayed the possibility of holdups, they made no promises of safe passage. Ahead of her awaited the less frequented road to Casper. Not only that, she'd be traveling in a smaller vehicle that looked like it had seen its best days a decade ago.

Taking a deep breath, she forced herself to more pleasant thoughts. Tonight, she hoped to reach Uncle Will's. Then this whole miserable journey would be a distant memory.

From the corner of her eye, she caught a glimpse of her coach as it appeared from around the buildings. She squinted at the driver who held the horses to a walk. Who was he? Pete, the Irishman who'd brought them from Cheyenne, was not guiding the four-horse team. In his place sat a lean man, dressed in buckskins. Brown hair framed a tanned, clean-shaven face. He appeared to be more frontiersman than cowboy. Gazing ahead, he seemed oblivious to her gawking as he halted the stagecoach beside her.

While living back east, she had read about wild men who embraced their own values and boasted of no ties to society. Was he one of them? Her gaze strayed to the large, sheathed knife at his waist. He appeared to have stepped off an advertisement for Buffalo Bill's Wild West show.

When he looked her way, she gaped. He had the most startling blue eyes she had ever seen. They, and his impeccable tidiness, stood in stark contrast with his rough clothing and dangerous demeanor.

When his eyebrows rose, she felt her cheeks burn. "I—I beg your pardon, sir. I didn't mean to stare."

And yet, she had. Once again, Ellie failed to curb her natural curiosity, a fault that her father often censured.

"I just traveled from Chicago." She hoped her explanation excused her inquisitiveness. "And I've n-never before seen…"

A mountain man? Frontiersman? She could think of no polite description.

His lips twitched in what might be humor. Before he could answer, raised voices inside the general store drew her attention. Two men burst through the doorway. Pete, the redheaded driver, stalked out with Mr. Tesley trotting close behind.

"This arrangement is preposterous. Unacceptable." The weasel-like passenger threw one hand in the air.

What was Mr. Tesley's problem now? Last night, he had subjected Ellie and everyone within hearing about his importance. Because of his efforts—apparently his alone—Wyoming Territory would soon join the union.

The two men stopped next to Ellie.

Pete waved toward the stagecoach. "He's the best coach gun from Missouri to California. I need him for this leg of the trip."

"You can't be serious. Isn't anyone else available?"

"No. Rhett is it."

Rhett? Ellie peered at the man still in the driver's seat.

"I don't care what name he goes by," Mr. Tesley growled, "I recognized him the moment I saw him."

"From where?" Pete glowered. "What're you saying?"

"I always figured his kind would show up again. No telling what kind of skullduggery he's been up to."

"He's no outlaw."

"Y'sure?" Under his breath, the businessman muttered, "He's got outlaw blood."

Outlaw? Ellie stared up at the man in question. The stagecoach company would not have hired a criminal, would they? Unlikely. She adjusted the tie on her bonnet. No doubt Mr. Tesley was merely fabricating yet another reason to voice discontent.

Glancing her way, the businessman chomped his gray mustache with his lower teeth. He stepped closer to the driver. "Surely you are capable of handling any problem we may encounter. Without *this* man's assistance."

The Irishman's chin jutted. "Oh, so now you're *not* afraid of holdups."

"I'm...of course, I..." Stammering, he waved in Ellie's direction. "Mind you, it's not for my sake I bring this to your attention."

She stifled a snort.

Appearing pious, the businessman steepled his fingers. "We must think of the safety of all the passengers."

Ellie clenched one fist. Was he trying to use her to justify his own bad behavior?

"I *am*." Pete's tone grew stern. "That's why we need Rhett. He can shoot the eye out of a—" He stopped when he caught Ellie's gaze. "Out of—of a knotty pine fence post."

She pressed her lips together to hide a grin.

"I don't care." Mr. Tesley crossed his arms.

"You don't seem to understand." Pete drew himself up. "Ever since gold was discovered in the Black Hills, outlaws roam the trails. But with Rhett along, we've not had—"

"Do you think it wise to frighten the womenfolk with such talk?" Mr. Tesley fairly screeched.

"Excuse me." Ellie raised her voice. The two men swiveled toward her. "Let it be clear that I have every confidence in our driver and his companion. I can only speak for myself, but this particular *womanfolk* isn't frightened."

Pete glowered at Mr. Tesley. "Frankly, I don't think it's the *women* who're scared."

As the businessman sputtered, the other two passengers—Mrs. Rushton and her son—emerged from the store. Eyes wide, the stout woman glanced between them. "Is something wrong?" Her hand clamped on the boy's shoulder.

"Not at all, Mrs. Rushton." Pete opened the coach's door. "The sooner you get settled, the sooner we can be on our way. We're already behind schedule."

"I don't care what you say, I am *not* riding with that—that…" Mr. Tesley pointed at Rhett and mumbled an inexcusable term.

Ellie's ears buzzed.

"Suit yourself." Pete straightened with a jerk. "Ladies?"

Chin quivering, Mrs. Rushton drew back and yanked her son closer.

Pete turned to her, hand extended. "Miss Elinor?"

Beyond him, she caught sight of Rhett's narrowed eyes. Was Mr. Tesley's accusations true about this man being an outlaw? Or at least related to one? Heart pounding, Ellie clenched her handbag.

Then she straightened her shoulders as she dismissed Mr. Tesley's outrageous claim. Why drive a stagecoach when one could merely hold it up? She wasn't going to condemn a man based on nothing more than Mr. Tesley's suspicions and insinuations.

Gathering her skirts, she took Pete's helping hand.

After she climbed aboard, she fought to speak in an even tone. "I saved the best seat for you, Mrs. Rushton. Does Nicholas want to sit by me or at your side?"

Likely the six-year-old would hang out the window despite his mother's protests. The only thing that had captured his attention for more than a few minutes was Ellie's watch. However, she allowed him to merely look at it since he had already broken his mother's brooch.

"I wanna sit by Miss Ellie." Nicholas wrenched from Mrs. Rushton's hold and bounded into the stagecoach. With obvious reluctance, she followed.

"I'm sending a telegram. To complain." Mr. Tesley shook his fist. "This very minute."

"Suit yourself." After securing the door, Pete climbed on top. In moments, Mr. Tesley's bags and trunk flew off the stagecoach and thudded to the boardwalk.

"You haven't heard the last of—"

"Hee-aw." Pete's call rang through the fort. With a lurch, they were on their way.

As the stagecoach settled into a rocking motion, Rhett braced his feet against the floorboards. They were well away from Fort Laramie and deep in the grassy plains. His fingers tightened around the company-issued shotgun as he kept a sharp lookout. In the many runs he'd made across Wyoming Territory, they'd experienced no trouble. Regardless, Rhett remained alert. Easy marks were what criminals preferred.

Outlaws like my father and uncles.

Nearly two decades ago, their band had terrorized this area. Thanks to the bravery of Rhett's mother, the two of them had escaped the group's evil clutches. Only after lawmen and locals had put the Walker Gang per-

manently out of business had it been safe for Rhett and
his mother to return to the area.

Unfortunate that Mr. Tesley recognized him earlier
that morning. Ma always claimed Rhett looked like his
father. That fact might have been proven today.

"What ballad are ya in the mood for?" Pete's question broke into his thoughts.

Rhett chuckled. "You pick. You know I like 'em all."

Though gifted with a fine voice, Pete preferred to
whistle instead of sing. His impressive repertoire ranged
from ditties and theater tunes to the realistic cries of
animals.

Pete began to hum, before he settled on a favorite
and switched to whistling. His anchor mustache and
beard bristled outwardly as the volume increased. Although he claimed the music calmed the horses, it also
signaled that all was well.

The day promised to be neither too hot nor too cold,
a pleasant change after recent rains. Though the short-
cut Pete had chosen was less traveled, it lacked some
of the hazards of the more frequented thoroughfare—
dangerous deep ruts and washed-out areas that would
slow their journey.

Rhett's mind drifted from the road conditions to the
pretty blonde inside the stagecoach. The cut of her plush
wrap, embroidered skirt and fancy bonnet proved Miss
Elinor, as Pete had called her, was a lady. She had traveled a fair piece, evidenced by the weariness on her face
and by her dust-covered gown. Yet despite her fatigue,
she had maintained her manners, speaking courteously
to all, including him and Pete. Most passengers merely
ignored them.

And she wasn't afraid.

Miss Elinor had not seemed troubled by Tesley's

comments. The slightest accusation that he was connected to outlaws would have had most passengers refusing to ride the stagecoach with him. Not her. She had studied him as though weighing truth from fiction. A pleasant change.

As the day grew warmer, Rhett peeled off his leather jacket. In his sleeveless shirt, he enjoyed the warmth on his arms. This was his seventh run from Fort Laramie to Casper. He had done other routes as well, but this was his favorite. Over the last three months, he had learned the road and the drill.

After intervals of heavy rain, the sun had baked the ground into hard ruts over the past several days. Occasionally the coach jerked when its wheels caught in a deep furrow, but Pete always succeeded in urging the horses to break free. Despite the occasional rough patch, the ride grew more pleasant as the afternoon peaked. As Rhett peered into the vast and brilliant blue sky, his heart swelled in gratefulness.

Thank You, Father God, for steady work. And for this friend named Pete.

Rhett considered how to pray about his encounter with Mr. Tesley. Although they'd never met before that very morning, the suspicion on Tesley's face was one Rhett was quick to recognize. Enough time had passed that few seemed to connect him to the outlaws of decades past—but one person raising a fuss could ruin his reputation for good. Had the businessman known his father? They would be of a similar age—if Rhett's father still lived.

The shuddering stagecoach snapped his attention back to the present. The momentary vibration ceased. That was no rut.

Whistling squelched, Pete raised his voice. "Feel that?"

Rhett nodded.

"Second time that's happened."

Third. But he kept that to himself. The occasional shimmying seemed different from anything he'd experienced on other runs he had made. But what did he know about the workings of stagecoaches? He had been hired to guard the passengers and the strongbox.

The Irishman's brow lowered. "When we get to Casper, I'll check it out. I meant to in Fort Laramie, but…" He grumbled under his breath. "That bigmouth sidetracked me."

Rhett's chest tightened. If Mr. Tesley sent a telegram like he'd threatened, Rhett might very well be out of a job. Then what would he do? His mother depended on his income.

"Glad he opted to stay behind." Pete's meaty fists tightened on the reins. "'Nother fifteen minutes, we'll stop for a break. I have to show you this sweet lil' spot that—"

A crack—like a gunshot—ruptured the air. Bucking like a wild mustang with a bad attitude, the stagecoach lurched to one side. For a moment it hung in space. Releasing his shotgun, Rhett hurled himself from the floundering vehicle.

He hit the ground, hard. Dirt filled his mouth. In the distance he heard screams, splintering wood, shrieking horses. He lay motionless, gasping for air.

What happened?

For several moments, the world continued to wobble. When his head finally cleared, he hissed at the burn in his left forearm.

A large twig was embedded in his flesh. Without reflection he jerked it out, grunting at the torment. Blood bubbled up from the wound. He yanked off his kerchief and bound it around his arm.

"Help!" A muffled voice called from inside the coach. "Anyone there? Help. I'm stuck."

Miss Elinor. Still alive. Relief pumping through his body, Rhett lurched to his feet and staggered toward her voice. The stagecoach lay on its side amid shredded harness lines. The horses—and Pete—were nowhere to be seen. Rhett climbed onto the toppled vehicle and jerked open the door.

Brown eyes peered up from a jumble of dark skirts and white petticoats. The boy lay on his mother, eyes closed as though in peaceful sleep. Both of them had landed on top of Miss Elinor who appeared to be the only one conscious.

The young woman grunted as she strained to shift the woman and child. "Can't…can't breathe."

Rhett knelt. "Give me your hand."

As he pulled steadily, she groaned anew. With their combined strength, she was able to extricate herself from under the pair. The moment he freed the younger woman, she shot up and into his arms. Bracing himself, Rhett fought to keep them from tumbling off the unstable stagecoach. Once he caught his balance, he steadied her.

Clinging to his shirt, she buried her forehead against his chest. Draping his arm, the warm silk of her blonde hair caressed his skin. A pleasant, but unusual scent riveted him. Lavender?

He blinked, then shoved aside the distraction. "Are you hurt?"

A deep shudder ran through her as she hiccupped. Was she crying?

Rhett craned his neck to look at her face. Eyes closed, her mouth pinched with whiteness.

"You're safe," he whispered, but she didn't appear to hear. "You have nothing to fear."

She had the look of having been pampered her whole life. Her white hands and pristine fingernails showed no sign of manual labor. Her skin appeared as soft and milky as a foal's underbelly. She belonged in a civilized city, not here. What had induced her to travel to the wilds of Wyoming Territory?

When she whimpered, the plaintive sound caused a tender protectiveness to reverberate through him. Regardless of why she was there, a woman like this needed to be safeguarded.

"Miss Elinor?"

Her eyes flew open. Her gaze finally focused on him.

He studied her, noting a bump forming at her temple. "You hit your head. Where else do you hurt?"

Eyelids fluttering, she touched the spot. "I don't—I think I'm all right."

"I'm glad." The words slipped out before he could contain them. He pointed below, to the stagecoach's interior. "What about them?"

"Them?" Brows drawn, she stared below.

She must have hit her head harder than he thought because she seemed bewildered.

"The woman and her son," he explained. "Do you know the extent of their injuries?"

"I—I'm not sure." Gasping, she grabbed Rhett's wrist. "You're bleeding."

"It's nothing."

"It's *not* nothing. I need to look at that."

She needed to look at it? Her odd phrasing took him aback.

"Later." He pointed to the other two passengers below. "They need care first."

As though to emphasize his words, a muffled whine rose. The child had come to.

After kneeling, Rhett braced his hands on both sides of the opening. "Hey, boy."

"Nicholas." Elinor's tense whisper interrupted as she crouched. "His name is Nicholas."

Rhett lowered his head through the open coach door. "Nicholas. Take my hand."

"Mama." The boy thrashed amid the voluminous black fabric of his mother's skirts. His howl followed. "I want Mama."

"Boy—Nicholas—grab my hand."

No response.

"Nicholas?" Elinor added her own plea. "Listen to Rhett. We need to get you out of there."

Still crying, the child finally obeyed. Two thin arms reached toward the sky, Elinor grabbing one and Rhett the other. Together, they lifted the boy out. With the three of them balancing on the coach's side, where no one was meant to stand, the vehicle creaked as it rocked.

"Wait here." Rhett leaped to the ground and then reached for the wailing child.

After lowering him, Elinor took Rhett's hand to jump down, as well. The second she landed, the boy wrapped his arms about her waist and buried his face against her skirts, sobbing. A bewildered expression crossing her face, she draped her arm across his shoulders.

Now that these two were safe, Rhett considered what to do next. Find Pete or try to move Mrs. Rushton?

"Do you think she's all right?" Elinor's voice quavered as she nodded in the direction of the coach.

Had she read his mind? "I'm not certain, miss."

"Please, call me Ellie." She gave a small headshake as though confused. "I need to know how she is."

That decided him. He responded with one abrupt nod. "Stay with the boy."

After climbing onto the toppled stagecoach, Rhett again evaluated the situation. How was he to attend to Mrs. Rushton? Lowering himself into the interior, he took care not to step on the large woman. With difficulty, he rolled her over by bracing his feet against one side of the coach and pushing. When he found her heartbeat, a quick exhale of relief escaped him. Although she wasn't bleeding, a bump on her forehead was beginning to grow as purple as Ellie's gown. After a quick check, he found no other injuries.

"Mrs. Rushton." He called out her name and shook her shoulder, but she didn't respond. Given how difficult it had been to turn her over, Rhett could not possibly remove her from the coach. And not without Pete's help.

After ensuring she could breathe with ease, he clambered out and balanced himself on top.

"How is she?" Ellie's tense voice drifted up from below, the boy's wails nearly drowning her question.

Rhett debated how to answer. "Alive."

"I need to examine her."

Again, Ellie's words confounded him. Then he shook his head and pointed to the boy who still clung to her. "There's nothing we can do for her right now. *He* needs your attention."

Nicholas had not stopped howling since they pulled him from the coach.

Her hand caressed his shoulder. "Nicholas, where does it hurt?" When he didn't answer, she asked again. At her insistence and in between sobs, he pointed to his head, elbow and knee. When Ellie was apparently satisfied his injuries were minor, she squatted before the boy and spoke comforting words. Like a mother would.

Was she a mother herself? No, Pete had called her "Miss Elinor," so she wasn't married. But perhaps she had a fiancé waiting for her in Casper. That would explain her traveling alone to this part of the country. Disappointment rippled through him at that idea of Ellie already being spoken for. But that would only make sense.

Before he jumped down from the side of the coach, he took advantage of the high position to view the wreckage around them. Boxes, bags and splintered wood were strewn about. He spotted his shotgun. But where was Pete? The driver had likely been pulled off the coach, dragged by the horses. Did he need help? Was he seriously hurt?

As Rhett squinted into the distance, the report of gunfire startled him. Both Ellie and Nicholas screamed. Instinctively he crouched, blade in hand as he readied himself to defend them all.

Chapter Two

Ellie watched, heart pounding, as Rhett appeared to prepare for an attack. His eyes darted to the horizon, then down at her. A chill ran through her at the tense readiness of his expression.

Two skinny arms tightened around her waist as Nicholas huddled against her. She clasped the silent, shuddering boy.

When nothing more happened for several minutes, she whispered to Rhett, "What is it?"

He squinted at something in the distance. The next moment, he stood upright and sheathed his knife. "Pete." A frown pinched his mouth. "He shot one of the horses."

"What? No." Stepping toward him, she stumbled over Nicholas and then righted herself. "I might have been able to save it."

Rhett jumped to the ground. Meeting her gaze, he shook his head. "Unlikely. Pete would know if something could be done."

"He should've let me look first." Though her experience was mainly with the human body, she might have been able to do something for the poor creature. "Don't let him shoot another horse. Please."

She expected derision at her statement. That's what she had always encountered on the faces of Chicago doctors. While she accompanied her father to assist him on his rounds, they made it clear they merely tolerated her.

But she'd heard Wyoming Territory was different and that women were more respected. She felt confident she could practice medicine here, even without her father—a dream that Chicago doctors had mocked.

Rhett's brow relaxed. "I'll find Pete and ask him."

"Thank you." Her eyes stung with relief.

He continued to study her, as though ascertaining something about her. Pressing her lips together, Ellie backed away. Nicholas, still clinging to her waist, hampered her movements. Again, he began to wail.

"Stay here. I'll be back as soon as possible." Rhett strode off.

She couldn't tear her gaze away from his retreating figure. He moved with deliberation, yet with a grace that she had never before seen in a man. Perhaps it had something to do with the soft, knee-high boots he wore and not the heavy ones most men favored.

Turning her attention to the six-year-old, she patted his back. Still he wouldn't loosen his grip. "It's okay. No need to be afraid."

Funny that Rhett had used similar phrases with her. And now she said them for not only the child's benefit, but her own. When she looked at the destruction around them, her heart quaked. She couldn't help but think of Mrs. Rushton, still inside the toppled coach. Perhaps when Rhett returned, they could find some way to help the woman.

Ellie found herself wishing she had taken time to examine the woman before exiting the stagecoach, but she'd felt so dazed, she couldn't think straight. Regardless, Nicholas needed her now. She would have to trust Rhett's evaluation that the woman didn't require immediate care.

When Nicholas hiccupped, his arms loosened, signaling the end of his sobs.

Ellie softened her voice a notch. "Want to do me a favor?"

A mute shake of the head came as an answer.

She inserted regret into her voice. "That's too bad. I don't know who I can ask for help."

A red-blotched face turned upward. "Maybe you can ask that idler?"

She clenched her teeth at the reference, which seemed to infer Rhett was a lazy good-for-nothing. Though that seemed far from the truth, it wasn't her place to reprimand the boy for his rude speech. "You mean Mr. Rhett?"

Nicholas nodded.

"He's busy right now." She sighed. "I wish I knew some brave young man."

The boy sniffed, brow wrinkled. "To do what?"

"Help me gather our belongings. And some wood. What do you think about a fire?"

His eyes widened. "You gonna burn down the prairie?"

"I hope not." She grinned for his sake.

Obviously the splintered stagecoach was unusable for further travel. That meant they would likely be spending the night in the open. If so, they needed wood. And supplies. The waning afternoon warned Ellie they didn't have a lot of time.

Anxiety for Mrs. Rushton again hounded her. But as long as the woman remained inside the stagecoach, Ellie could do nothing but worry.

Nicholas tugged at her skirt. "What's the matter, Miss Ellie?"

"Nothing." She shook the anxiety from herself. "Let's get that wood."

As the child followed her around, she kept an ear and eye out for Rhett and Pete. A couple times she caught a glimpse of the men in the distance. They tended the animals and brought them toward a clearing where they seemed to be creating a makeshift camp. The way the driver hunched, cradling his arm, warned her he too had been injured.

Pete motioned to the stagecoach. Rhett climbed inside but exited shortly afterward. After some more discussion, they righted the vehicle with the help of the horses. Again, the driver stood outside while his partner climbed back in. To attend to Mrs. Rushton? Pete merely watched from the open door.

Ellie kept drawing Nicholas's attention away from the scene, fearing that he would again melt into hysterics. Or she would. While she wanted to see if Mrs. Rushton required help, it seemed best if they stayed out of the men's way. Surely Rhett would call her over if she was needed.

In no time, she and the boy had gathered enough wood to keep a fire burning for hours. Then they assembled some of the scattered boxes and luggage. The heavier pieces she left where they'd fallen.

When the heads of the two men came together, she knew they were deciding their collective fate.

"Could you keep this safe for me, Nicholas?" She passed him her watch. It would occupy the boy's attention for a few minutes better than anything else she had on hand. "I'll be right back."

"F'sure." Eyes wide, he fingered the gold filigree as she strode away.

"It's the only way." The driver's voice sounded low and urgent.

Rhett merely nodded.

Both men straightened as she approached.

"I'm going to ride for help, Miss Elinor." Pete's mouth settled in grim lines. "Rhett'll watch over you until I get back."

She made certain not to break eye contact with the big man. "I have every confidence in Rhett. But before you go, I need to see to your injuries."

A long gash marked one cheek, the blood mostly dried. With the way he spoke in a nasally tone, he'd likely sustained a broken nose, as well. Already, the darkened skin swelled.

Pete's eyes widened.

Anticipating resistance, Ellie spread her hands. "For years, I worked alongside my father in his medical practice. I can at least bind your arm to relieve you of some pain."

"My shoulder's merely strained." His features relaxed as she spoke, but his tone remained unyielding. "I appreciate the offer, but we have little left of the day. I need to leave before dark."

Expecting that reply, she sighed in defeat. "Very well. But before you go, please move Mrs. Rushton so I can see to her care." Ellie pointed to where Nicholas sat on a log, face bent over the pocket watch. "Put her over there. I need to tend to her through the night."

She met Rhett's narrowed gaze. Was that admiration she beheld? Her cheeks grew warm when he gave her a slight nod.

"Keep the boy occupied." It was Rhett who spoke. "We'll take care of Mrs. Rushton."

Taking a deep breath, Ellie strode back to Nicholas. "Did you figure out how the watch winds itself?"

"No." Face scrunching, he extended his hand. "It's dumb."

Without responding, she pocketed the watch. "Let's go exploring. Think we can spot a rabbit?"

Chatting, she kept him distracted while they moved away from the makeshift camp. As they walked along the road, she studied their surroundings. No animals visible. And no towns or humans. Who could live out there? Scrub brush, gnarled trees and forbidding mountains met her gaze. The landscape appeared scarred by thousands of travelers over the years, but now no one was in sight. With new railroads crossing the country, pioneers could bypass the dangers of the open plains and imposing mountain ranges as they moved farther west. The center of Wyoming Territory, though, remained untamed.

Ellie stifled the urge to chastise herself for leaving the comforts of a modern city.

They have accidents in Chicago too.

Like the one that had killed her father a mere five months before. Except for Uncle Will, all her immediate family was gone. Nothing remained for her in Chicago. Her future lay here—uncharted territory in more than one way.

Not only did she anticipate a joyful reunion with her uncle, she needed to resolve a mystery. Inside her trunk, she had buried Mama's diary as well as four letters, written by her uncle to her mother. They had been stashed in a secret compartment of her mother's secretary, undiscovered until Ellie had cleaned it out a mere month ago. She had begun reading one when she realized it was a love letter. After that realization, she had put them away. She refused to intrude on their privacy.

But why had Mama hidden them? Why keep them at all?

After Ellie settled on her uncle's ranch, she would seek answers to her questions. Because both her parents were now deceased, Uncle Will would have no reason to hide the truth.

"Look, Miss Ellie." Nicholas pointed to a great herd of elk in the distance.

For several minutes they watched the graceful animals bound across the field. The elk appeared to glide across an undulating sea of grass. Ellie caught her breath. As the group moved out of sight, the crystalline blue sky deepened into azure, warning of the steady approach of evening—and all the dangers it held.

Rhett stretched, spine popping. One more glance at the campsite assured him that he had done all he could to secure it for the night. They had enough wood to hold them until morning. The freight, luggage and mailbags clustered around them, creating a wall of protection of sorts. On the other side rested some logs.

After promising to be back as soon as possible, Pete had ridden off with the best horse. Likely he wouldn't return before midmorning. Ellie and Nicholas had gathered the few blankets Pete carried aboard the stagecoach. Rhett noted the pitiful amount of food—mostly jerky and hardtack. Not only that, but they had little water.

He had foregone his share and noticed Ellie doing

the same. Taking a sip of water, but consuming none of the food, they'd stashed the remainder for later. Rhett debated scouting for a creek, but discarded the idea of leaving the passengers, especially the injured Mrs. Rushton.

The stout woman lay on her back. Ellie had made Mrs. Rushton comfortable by pillowing her head with a blanket and propping her feet on a bag. Nestling against his mother, the boy rested his head on her abdomen, eyes closed. Ellie covered them both with a thin blanket, then watched them for a few minutes.

Apparently satisfied, she turned to rummage in a small bag. After removing some strips of cloth, she tucked them into her pocket. Then she walked with purpose toward Rhett. "Let me look at your arm."

He drew back, not because he didn't agree that it needed attention, but because with all the work, he had forgotten about it.

Brow lowering, her head tilted to one side as her delicate lips pursed.

He stifled the chuckle that rose in his throat. Though he dwarfed her by almost a head, the steely determination on her face warned him that she would force him to yield.

Or at least try.

Already he had noted how Nicholas did not hesitate to obey her commands. From what he'd overheard earlier, the boy actually minded her better than he did his own mother.

But how would Ellie react when she saw the wound? He extended his arm.

Her shoulders immediately relaxed. With deft fingers, she untied the knotted kerchief. He ignored the ache as her fingers tightened around his forearm while she examined his wound.

"It's bleeding. Why is it still bleeding?" She studied the gash, muttering to herself. Her brown eyes met his, a spark of gold flashing in the late afternoon sun. After running her fingers beside the length of the wound, she hemmed to herself. "I need to check inside your wound. But it's going to hurt."

He shrugged. It already did. In the past, he had suffered much greater injuries and deprivation. By comparison, this was nothing.

"First I need to wash." Ellie turned. "I need more water. Where can I find it?"

He shook his head. "That canteen is all we have."

"But I need to clean my hands." She held up blackened palms. "They're filthy."

"We cannot spare any water."

She made a sound of irritation. "I have to use something. I can't…" She sighed, brow furrowed in thought. "Very well. I'll do without my portion."

"You'd go thirsty? For this?"

"Yes." She raised her chin. "My father believed that hands must be clean. I will not risk injuring you further."

Rhett studied her until a delicate pink colored her cheeks. With her creamy complexion, the rose only added to her exquisite beauty.

How could one so fair and delicate be so strong? He had never before met anyone like her. She was nothing like the rough-and-tumble women of the frontier. But in some ways, she seemed tougher.

"Very well," he finally answered. "But only if you allow me to volunteer my ration of water. Instead of yours."

"No, I..." A storm gathered on her brow.

Shaking his head, he waited for her to give in while she—no doubt—did the same. Minutes ticked by as she glared at him.

"Apparently, I'll have to bleed to death before you'll agree." Rhett held out his arm, red drops falling to the ground. "Well?"

"Oh, very well." She spoke with a huff.

Hiding his smile of triumph, he strode off to retrieve the one canteen.

When he returned, Ellie rolled up her sleeves and then held out her hands. "Pour some over my skin. Excellent."

When she appeared ready, he again extended his arm.

"Here goes." Without hesitation, she jabbed one slim finger into the gash.

Rhett grunted as she searched.

In moments, she murmured, "Ha." With bloodied fingertips, she held up a wedge of wood. "Here's the problem. Now your arm can begin to heal." She took another second to double-check. "Wait." Again, she felt along the gash.

He took a second to find his voice, but merely to tease. "You sure you're not getting even with me? For arguing with you?"

Pressing her lips together, she ducked her head. But she couldn't hide her grin. After retrieving strips of cloth from her pocket, she cleaned her fingers on one and wrapped his arm with another.

He studied the bandage, expertly tied as he flexed his arm. Not too tight or loose. Perhaps she was as well versed in medicine as she claimed. "Perfect. Thank you."

The smile with which she graced him set his heart to pattering in a new, but not uncomfortable way.

Ellie planted one fist at her hip. "Now I need to see that horse."

He knew which she meant—the one tied behind the stagecoach.

After shooting the one with a broken leg, Pete had taken the only uninjured animal. Of the remaining two horses, only one would likely survive. The fourth, a chestnut, had a massive gash across his back leg.

Ellie drew closer. "I know what you're thinking— that I might know something about people's injuries, but not a horse's. Which is true. But I have to at least try. Give me a chance."

Her eyes gleamed in the setting sun. If they were to do something, it had to be now while they still had light.

Rhett wanted to argue that the gelding was frantic with pain. That even he hesitated to approach the animal. In his heart, he knew that Ellie would be unable to get close enough to examine the horse, much less care for it.

But her eyes compelled him. In his heart, he knew he would not dare disappoint this determined young woman. Although he would hate to see her fail, he would hate himself more if he didn't help her try.

"Come with me." Without another word, he strode toward the back of the stagecoach.

Chapter Three

The injured chestnut looked piteous. His head, hanging low, gave him the appearance of abject despair. Despite her determination to handle anything she might encounter, Ellie's throat tightened.

As they drew closer, the horse raised its head and whickered a warning. His eyes were so wide, the whites glittered. He held up his injured leg while foam dripped from a slack mouth. Ellie sucked in a quick breath.

He's dying.

She didn't have to see the blood-soaked soil to know he wouldn't last the night. Eyes burning, she turned to Rhett. "I have some astringent powder that will deaden the pain. Then I need to stitch him up."

His eyebrows rose. "You won't be able to get near his back leg."

"I have to try. I have to at least…" She bit her lip as her eyes stung anew, hating the fact that she could never control her tears when she beheld suffering. Human or animal—it didn't matter.

Maybe I am weak and too emotional, like my father always said.

She studied Rhett's expression, expecting contempt

like she had seen many times on her father's face. But she saw only compassion.

Rhett's head tilted. "Get your supplies. I will try to control the gelding."

Nodding, she rushed to retrieve her medical bag.

Nicholas continued to doze beside his mother. Anxiety again arose as Ellie beheld the unconscious woman.

I wish I could do something more for Mrs. Rushton.

But what? She wasn't feverish. Although bruised, she had no broken bones. Ellie made certain the woman could breathe easily and had seen to it that she remained warm and dry. Nothing else could be done but wait.

Although Ellie's medical bag was a jumbled mess of broken glass and spoiled contents, she located the powder tin, a needle and long length of thread.

When she returned to the backside of the stagecoach, Rhett had positioned the horse beside it. Two ropes bound the animal to the vehicle while Rhett held a third. As she drew nearer, she heard him speaking to the gelding in a low tone.

Gulping, she stopped. Would the horse allow her help?

"Approach him slowly." Without looking in her direction, Rhett used the same hushed tone.

Ellie obeyed, scarcely breathing as she eyed the gelding. One kick from his powerful leg could break bones. Or kill.

With care, she pried the lid off the powder tin. Heart pounding in her ears, she moved cautiously closer. She froze when the horse's head jerked up. Only Rhett's quiet words and gentle hand on the gelding's muzzle soothed him.

When she got near enough, she scattered powder into the large, gaping wound. Its deadening power should work fast, but she worried about the dosage. How much needed to be applied to keep the horse from feeling the bite of the needle? She couldn't be sure—could only hope she used enough. After securing the lid, she pocketed the tin and then grasped the needle and thread.

Rhett's gaze flickered to her. He nodded ever so slightly as he continued to speak to the horse. Mouth dry, Ellie stroked the gelding's quivering flesh. She positioned herself to make use of the last of the sunlight before it slipped behind distant hills.

Perspiration broke out on her forehead as she stabbed the needle through the skin. The horse jerked, tremors passing through his body. Rhett's voice seemed to grow more riveting. Breath coming in short gasps, Ellie worked as quickly as possible, mindful to keep her movements small. Sweat ran down the bridge of her nose and perched at the tip before falling. Any remaining moisture in her mouth evaporated.

Hurry. Shadows lengthened. When the thread ran out she would have to be done. With difficulty, she tied off the end and left it dangling.

"There." She backed away, tucking the needle into her collar for safekeeping. When she glanced at Rhett, he rewarded her with a smile that made her heart leap.

With his hand still on the horse's muzzle, he nodded. "You've done well."

She was slow to respond. "Thank you."

They made a good team. Was he thinking the same? The longer he scrutinized her, the warmer her cheeks grew.

With a tentative hand, she stroked the gelding's rump. "Poor boy. He deserves only kindness."

The chestnut seemed to lean into her as she ran her palms along his ribs. Slowly, she worked her way toward his head. The longer she caressed him, the more relaxed he seemed to grow.

Was it her imagination or had he lost his dejected look?

Ellie studied Rhett. "What will happen to him? Once we reach Casper?"

His hand smoothed the horse's neck. "Doubtful the stagecoach company'll keep him."

"Would they shoot him?" Sorrow tightened her throat.

"I don't know."

"Sell him?"

Brows furrowing, Rhett shook his head. "Who would buy a wounded animal?"

Ellie stroked the horse's soft neck. "He's such a sweet-tempered boy. Can't you see? It would be a shame to destroy him."

Rhett nodded.

"Promise me," she said, holding his gaze with her own, "when you hear what they decide, you will let me know?"

He looked away, then took a deep breath. "I promise."

When she stroked the horse's soft cheek, he nickered. "There's a good boy." She scratched the spot between his ears.

While she'd lived in Chicago, her dealings with horses had been minimal. Animals were for transportation or sport. Out west, things would be different. Many, many things in her life would be. *For the better*, she hoped—and resolved.

"I'm sorry, Rhett." She bit her lip as her fingers continued to stroke the gelding. "I just realized I could've used the powder on your arm."

He took so long answering that she looked up.

"Perhaps I should've wailed more." A grin tugged at his lips. "Like Nicholas."

She giggled. "Or foamed at the mouth."

"I'll remember that next time." His smile broadened before he again grew serious. "God has gifted you with a healing touch."

She took a quick breath. "Why do you say that?"

"It's obvious. Look at this horse."

The gelding still held up his back leg protectively, but with his eyes half shut, he appeared sleepy. Even content.

"No." She backed away. "I'm not gifted. I merely have knowledge. Skills I'm not afraid to use."

If her father had permitted her to attend medical school, she would have learned more. To this day, she didn't understand his anger when she suggested it.

Rhett's head tilted. "Just because a person is educated or trained doesn't mean they are gifted. You are."

Squirming at that idea, she continued to shake her head. God didn't visit her—or anyone—with special talents. Everything she had learned about medicine, she had gleaned from her father. And with him, she was always lacking.

Not good enough, Elinor.

His rebukes still rang in her head. She failed to clean his medical instruments correctly. She needed to curb her curiosity and not ask his patients so many questions. She did not memorize enough information from the literature he recommended. No matter how she tried to please him, Father never seemed satisfied. And after Mama had died, he had grown even more tyrannical.

For seven years, Ellie watched him lose patients and most of his staff. They closed off parts of the house and let many servants go. His long, slow slide downhill ended when he stepped in front of a runaway wagon. But at least he was now at peace.

Ellie hoped.

The dark night wrapped around the four of them in the small campsite. Rhett squatted before a roaring fire, gaze flickering to their small group and beyond— assessing and reassessing their situation. Across from him lay the unconscious Mrs. Rushton. Ellie periodically checked on the woman who had awakened briefly.

The look of relief on Ellie's face assured him that perhaps the woman would recover.

Nicholas lay beside his mother, one thin arm draped over her belly. Rhett guessed him to be six or seven years old.

About my age when Pa was hanged.

Rhett would never forget his own mother waking him at night and her frantic whisper to pack what he could. They needed to flee from the infamous Walker Gang. Pa had been the ringleader. With him dead, Ma had no protection from his two brothers who were as wicked— or worse—than Pa. She often said she would do any-thing, even die, to protect Rhett from being forced to follow his footsteps. That decision resulted in years of hiding and hardship.

But ultimately my salvation.

After years of hiding, they had found their way to the home of a retired preacher. Or rather God had di-rected them there, as Rhett now believed. Ma had be-come the man's housekeeper.

Ellie's movements as she sat across from him drew his attention. She unbound her hair and raked her fin-gers through the long blonde strands as she stared into the night. The light of the fire danced across the liquid-gold tresses, enthralling him.

Many a time, he recalled Ma doing that. At the end of the day, she would stand by the stove, brushing her hair. Perhaps daring to hope their years of running were over?

At the snarl of a coyote, Rhett rose. Ellie too heard it. Her fingers paused, head turning toward the sound. He didn't need to tell her what she already knew—scavengers fought over the horse Pete had shot. Several times, Rhett caught the glint of eyes in the deep darkness.

Other predators prowled nearby, drawn to the scent of blood and the hopes of an easy meal. Because of that, he kept the shotgun close, but found himself wishing for a rifle. When he was again certain they were safe, he sank to his haunches.

In the distance, a wolf howled, its call long and mournful. Ellie sucked in a sharp breath, her large eyes fastening on Rhett. In the flickering firelight, her fingers visibly trembled.

"He calls for his mate." Rhett spoke softly to dampen her fears. "You needn't be afraid."

"Isn't that a wolf?" She gulped.

"Yes, but far away. He won't bother us."

"But I've heard stories…"

"Lies abound where ignorance dwells." He waited, but his words didn't appear to soothe her agitation. "You've nothing to fear, Ellie." He pointed to the dancing flames. "The fire'll keep away creatures. And the horses will alert us of any danger." Tied nearby, the two geldings appeared to doze. Even so, their ears flicked back and forth, alert despite their sleepy appearance. He patted the shotgun, hoping he wouldn't need to use it for animals or outlaws.

Her mouth spasmed. "Are you sure?" The tautness in her neck confirmed her fear.

His chest tightened at the urge to gather her in his arms, like she had Nicholas. But that kind of comfort would be inappropriate. Rhett shoved away the impulse.

"I am sure." He directed his thoughts to the countless nights he and Ma had slept under the stars with little more than a single knife and a prayer. God had protected them. However, Rhett sensed this young woman did not have the assurances he had. How had she grown up in a city full of churches and not learned of the Lord's grace and love?

Although Ellie resumed raking her fingers through her hair, her shoulders lost none of their tension. He concluded that this might very well be the first night she spent outdoors. Every sound and movement in the dark must frighten her.

He threw another stick into the fire. "You've nothing to fear, Ellie. I'll watch over you." When her eyes widened, he added, "And the others as well, of course."

Her acute gaze pierced his soul. "You mean, you'd stay awake all night? For me?"

He took his time answering. "Yes."

She too spoke slowly. "I've learned that true loyalty cannot be bought. I thank you."

With a boldness he had never experienced before, he continued to meet her stare. He sensed she needed reassurance. Had she been wounded by those who proved untrustworthy? Perhaps.

In the shimmering light of the fire, he imagined he saw a blush rising to her cheeks. She was the first to look away, but her softening expression told him his offer pleased her.

One sleepless night would be a small price to make certain she felt safe.

His empty stomach grumbled loudly.

Her eyebrows rose. "Hungry?"

He nodded.

"I confess I can't get my last meal out of my mind." She grimaced. "Now I wish I'd eaten every last crumb."

He tamped down the urge to tell her of the many times he'd gone without food. For days. About how grateful he was to have work where he could get a decent meal on a regular basis. And, on occasion, a comfortable bed in which to sleep.

Something about this young woman compelled him to share his life. He wondered at the affinity he felt with her.

"What will happen tomorrow?" Ellie's voice again grew tight. Scared.

"Pete will return with wagons. And more men." When her pinched brow didn't relax, he added, "He'll bring provisions and a way to transport Mrs. Rushton in comfort. He's reliable. And a fine man."

One of the finest Rhett had ever met. In short order, they had become good friends.

With quick fingers, Ellie braided her hair. Then she wrapped her arms about her knees. "Tell me about yourself, Rhett. I never did catch your last name."

He answered slowly. "Callaway. And as far as my life goes, there's not much to tell."

"I'm sure there is." She leaned forward. "You're educated. The way you speak gives that away."

Amused, he puckered his lips as he debated how much to say. "I had a mentor."

"You mean a private tutor?"

"Not exactly. A retired preacher took me under his

wing." Though Russell Callaway proved to be a tough taskmaster, Rhett considered him a father. The man ultimately became the husband Ma said she had never found in Pa. However, her second marriage was short-lived. They were wedded for ten days before tragedy struck that took Mr. Callaway's life.

I miss him. Greatly.

Rhett fell silent, uncomfortable with sharing more.

"If he wasn't your private tutor, then why'd he agree to teach you?" Ellie's innocent question begged to be answered.

"He was a man of discipline, hard work and faith. As a youngster, I was nothing like that. Not that my mother didn't try—but he taught me how to be a man. Without his intervention, my life might've gone a different direction."

Ellie's lips pursed, a bemused expression settling on her face. "He disciplined you with a heavy hand?"

"No." Rhett shook his head for emphasis. "He saturated me—my life—with grace. When I least deserved it."

Her head tilt indicated that she didn't understand his explanation. "What do you…?"

Mrs. Rushton stirred, interrupting her.

Ellie jumped to her feet and rushed to the woman's side.

"Where are we?" Mrs. Rushton's hoarse question wafted to Rhett.

Though Ellie's reply was unintelligible to him, he could hear her soothing tone. The injured woman seemed to ask a dozen questions before drifting back to sleep.

While Ellie returned to the camp's center, Rhett dragged a heavy log closer to the fire. "How is she?"

"I honestly don't know." Ellie again sat. "It's a good sign that she awakens—but this is the fourth time she asked where she was. And she acted as though she didn't recognize Nicholas." Brow pinched with worry, she stared into the fire.

"It's late. You should sleep."

"I—I can't." Ellie shook her head. "Every time I close my eyes, I feel like I'm back inside the stagecoach. Just after…" Her chin quivered.

The accident?

Rhett nearly offered to pray aloud for her. But she might consider that unseemly. Besides, he worked for a company that stressed no familiarity between workers and passengers. Ellie was free to ask her questions, but he should not initiate a conversation.

He raised his eyes.

Lord, please help Ellie. Give her Your peace.

When Rhett again met her gaze, she seemed to understand what he'd done. However, after a few minutes, tension again gripped her.

Chewing her lip, she toyed with her braid. "Tell me more about your mentor."

He took a slow breath, contemplating how much to say.

"Please forgive my intrusive questions," she hastened to add. "Talking helps keep me from thinking about…" She grimaced.

If this was the way the Lord decided Rhett should help, he would be happy to oblige. "My mother became his housekeeper, even though their views about God differed."

Quite drastically—at least at first. But the Lord softened Ma's heart until she embraced the Good News. At the same time, He was also working on Mr. Callaway.

Although he was a decade or more older than Ma, they eventually fell in love.

"Why'd he decide to become your mentor?"

He chuckled at the memory. "Mr. Callaway said he couldn't abide a wild boy, with no manners or education, running around his house."

"Callaway?" Surprise crossed her face. "But didn't you say that's your last name?"

Rhett hissed at his slip.

"How's that…?" Ellie's eyebrows rose. "Did they marry?"

No use hiding the fact. "Yes."

Her smile widened. "How lovely."

He remained silent.

"You don't think so?" she pressed.

"Yes, I do." Forcing a grin, Rhett tossed more sticks into the fire.

Opposite him, her fingers stilled. "Something horrible happened, didn't it?" Her hushed question filled the night. "Tell me."

He was struck by her perception. Over the years, he had learned to mask his emotions, but Ellie had a way of delving into his soul. However, he felt like he could tell his story without recrimination. At least part of it.

"There was an incident. At the settlement. Where Mr. Callaway did what he called the Lord's work." Rhett paused. With painful awareness, he realized he had never spoken of it before.

"Go on."

He swallowed the tightness in his throat that had nothing to do with thirst. "A conflict. In the Dakota Territory. Between the military and the locals. Tempers had been running high for months. Many battles have happened across this land, initiated by both sides."

"And Mr. Callaway died?"

Rhett nodded. "He tried to intervene and was caught in the crossfire."

Afterward, nobody admitted to starting the fire that consumed his house. When the military urged them to leave the area, Rhett and his mother were on the move again.

Ma told him that Mr. Callaway intended to legalize Rhett's adoption, but never made it to a solicitor's office. Regardless, Rhett took his mentor's name.

Ma begged him to never reveal his birth father's identity. Made him promise. Even after every member of the Walker Gang had been arrested or imprisoned, Ma warned him to never share their shameful secret. Folks never forgot—and rarely forgave.

"How sad." Through the smoke of the fire and the sparks that flew into the air, the sorrow on Ellie's face struck him. "How old were you?"

"Sixteen." Yet better prepared to deal with life than when he was eight, when they had fled after Pa's death. With the skills Rhett had picked up from his native friends and the education he'd gotten from Mr. Callaway, he could help provide for his mother. Although they still had their share of hardships, sleepless nights and hungry days were a thing of the past.

Expression troubled, Ellie drew up her legs and wrapped her arms about her skirts. "I'm sure you miss him."

Rhett threw another stick into the fire. "Despite the sorrow, I consider myself blessed. God provided. Again and again."

Mr. Callaway taught him to be grateful for all things, not only through what he preached, but in the way he lived and breathed the gospel. Time and again, he demonstrated the Lord's love and forgiveness for all men.

Except for the popping fire and the distant sounds of animals, silence filled the night. For many minutes, Ellie didn't move beyond her fingers absently twirling her braid. Finally, her gaze met his. "You're quite a man."

He could not suppress his grin. "But apparently my skills are suitable only for stagecoach work."

He meant it as a joke. It had been only four months since their move to Cheyenne. Riding shotgun was the first permanent job he'd found in the area.

Most folks seemed to have forgotten about the Walker Gang, but there were exceptions. Like Mr. Tesley. Ma always said Rhett looked the spitting image of his father. No doubt his eye color provided a clue. The three outlaw brothers were known for their "sky-blue eyes."

The only reason for their return to the area was Ma longed for home. How could Rhett deny her wishes? She worked as a milliner while he supplemented her income so that one day they could buy a small parcel of land with a tidy house.

Ellie leaned toward him. "Perhaps you could use your skills for something different."

He rested his arms on drawn-up knees. "Tell me where to find this work."

"My uncle's ranch." She scooted closer. "He wrote me that he's always looking for good help. And from what I've seen, you have a knack with horses."

He tamped down the impulse to accept her offer. For now he must fulfill his promise to Pete to stay on with the stagecoach company for a year. Rhett owed his friend that much.

"Who is your uncle?" He spoke slowly, buying time for a graceful way to decline.

"William Marshall. His ranch is not too far from Casper." Her voice rose, a smile playing on her lips. "You may think it presumptuous of me to make the offer without asking him first, but he really is looking for help. He told me so. I am traveling there now. Why don't you talk to him?"

With such a welcoming invitation, how could he say no?

Then cold reality stifled the warmth that had begun to blossom in his chest. He had heard of William Marshall, a long-time resident of the area. Heard of his hard-fisted business practices. No doubt he knew about the Walker Gang.

"I appreciate the offer."

"But…?"

"I have an obligation to Pete. And to the stagecoach company."

She rubbed two fingers across her chin, clearly pondering his words. "Very well. But give me your word you'll keep my offer in mind—and that you'll come see me if you ever reconsider."

Heat again suffused him at the thought of seeing her in the future. Warmth that had nothing to do with the bonfire.

As Ellie sat on the other side of the flames, her face and hair glowed. The excitement in her eyes and open expression beckoned to him. Despite her filthy dress, dirt-smudged face and torn sleeve, she appeared the epitome of beauty.

No, her loveliness radiated from within.

Something expanded in his chest—as though a tight

lasso around his heart had unraveled, allowing him to breathe.

"I give you my word. Gladly." He hadn't meant to whisper, but somehow, speaking aloud felt almost sacrilegious.

The sweet smile she bestowed on Rhett completely captivated him.

Ellie awakened, disoriented. Darkness blanketing the campsite, she sat up. The fire had died down to glowing coals. Occasional bright sparks snapped upward before fizzling out. Nearby, Mrs. Rushton's form appeared as an inky hulk with Nicholas snuggled beside her. The faintest glow in the east promised a new day.

But where was Rhett? In the many hours after they had settled, Ellie awakened several times. She had drawn comfort from seeing his watchful form, motionless as he sat by the fire or stood sentry, listening to the night noises. Now, he was nowhere to be seen.

Fighting panic, she rose and peered into the surrounding darkness. Had he abandoned them in the middle of the night? A silly and unwarranted thought. After all, he had promised to watch over them.

A sound reached her ears—the faintest drone. Rhett? Ellie listened, trying to pinpoint his location. As her eyes adjusted, she saw his silhouette in the distance. A nearly full moon hung in the sky while countless stars paid homage to the greater light. Rhett stood with hands clasped to his chest, head raised. In worship? Prayer? He spoke just loudly enough to prove he *was* praying.

Intrigued, she listened. Nobody she knew prayed that way. Back in Chicago, Sunday mornings were filled with silent lips, bowed heads and bended knees.

Drawing nearer, she caught snatches of phrases.

"Thank You…my Father…provision…continued safety…increase my love for You."

Father? Rhett spoke the title as if he meant it—in a familial way. She had never heard anyone address God as Father except in the rote sense. But…love? In her understanding, everyone's primary responsibility was to fear and serve God.

As Rhett's hands lowered, she beheld his expression. Ecstasy etched his features, clearly visible in the brilliant moonlight. Face lowering, he fell silent, as though listening to the God of the heavens.

What Rhett had told her that evening—about his life—hit her so hard she nearly doubled over. How could this man worship a God who would allow such tragedies to happen? And yet she had no doubt Rhett loved Him, evidenced from the rapture on his face. She didn't understand. For her, God reminded her of her father. She'd spent years trying to please them both. No matter what she did for God, no matter how hard she worked to take care of the poor and do Christian acts of service, He was never happy. All she sensed from Him was tolerance at best, contempt at worst.

Rhett appeared to have a different relationship with God, obvious from the joy on his face and his reverent words.

Her confusion transformed into jealousy. She wished she could grasp what Rhett had.

Uncaring whether or not he heard her, Ellie wheeled and dropped onto her blanket. But it was a very long time before she again slept.

Chapter Four

"We'll get you to your uncle in no time." With one arm in a sling, Pete handed Ellie up into the wagon along with Nicholas. "And don't worry about Mrs. Rushton. Doc is seeing to her."

"But…" Having run out of protests and reasons to delay, she pressed her lips together. For the dozenth time her gaze strayed to Rhett. Before they parted ways, would they get to say their goodbyes?

She had no time to find out. In the flurry of the morning's activities, Pete had arrived with several other men and wagons as Rhett had promised. Before she had a chance to talk to him, the men loaded her belongings and she was on her way.

The few times she glanced over her shoulder, he was nowhere to be seen.

Disappointment pierced her. Perhaps the camaraderie she and Rhett had shared over the night's bonfire had dissipated in the stark light of day.

The trip to Casper dragged. Nicholas chattered, asking hundreds of questions as he sat between her and the wagon driver. Since the man didn't answer, Ellie felt obligated to entertain the child. After they reached town, Mr. Rushton met them and took charge of his son. The driver unloaded the Rushtons' possessions. Once freed from the obligation to look after Nicholas, Ellie looked about.

Casper was not the quaint burgh she had imagined. A handful of ramshackle buildings met her gaze appearing as though a strong wind or a single match could obliterate the structures. According to her uncle, the town had not yet been incorporated. He expressed hope about that happening once the railroad reached this part of the territory.

The wagon driver returned to escort her to the hotel. After they arrived, the proprietor offered her a place to freshen up. When she mentioned she wouldn't be spending the night, he seemed to already know that her uncle was on his way.

"I have instructions to provide a meal, miss, if you like."

"Yes, please."

"It being Sunday and all, we don't have many customers at this time o'day."

She didn't mind, not feeling up to visiting with anyone. While the proprietor served her a light dinner, exhaustion hit her in waves. Images of the stagecoach accident continued to flash through her thoughts.

As the man set and removed dishes, she fought to focus on his chitchat. Finally, he left her with a cup of tea. She grew restless as the afternoon's sun crept into the sky. Would Uncle Will never arrive? More than once, her fingers crept up to her sore neck to massage the ache. Her whole body complained of stiffness as she yearned for a decent bed. She brushed at the dust on her skirt, longing to change out of filthy clothing.

As she finished her lukewarm tea, an oily scent assaulted her senses. Staring out the window, she ignored it.

"Miss Elinor?"

Ellie jumped at a man's nearby voice, her teacup rattling in the saucer. When she turned to face him, the rancid scent of old pomade struck her in full force. A rough-looking cowboy stood nearby. A dark-striped shirt, speckled with grease spots, met her gaze first, then the shiny gun that rode low on his hip.

She craned her neck to see his face.

"Guy Bartow. Yer uncle's foreman." He swiped his hat from his head, then performed an awkward half-bow. "Pleased to make your acquaintance."

Nodding in reply, she studied his dark brown hair, slicked back, and a knotted, red kerchief at his throat. A black smudge of dirt behind one ear proved he had been too hasty with his ablutions.

Her neck began to ache from leaning back so far. As her eyes began to water, she resisted the urge to press a handkerchief to her nose. The foreman was so close, she couldn't move.

She attempted to clear the odor of his pomade from herself with a cough. "How'd you do?"

"Er, good as good can be." One finger edged along the inside of his shirt collar.

Peering around him, she looked for her uncle.

Apparently anticipating what she searched for, Mr. Bartow went on. "Will, uh, Mr. Marshall said he were sorry he couldn't come. And that I's to carry you to the ranch."

Her mouth gaped as she tried to process what he meant. Confusion further enveloped her when he yanked back her chair so hard that she nearly fell to the floor. Had he literally meant *carry* her?

She staggered to her feet. The table squawked loudly as it scraped the floor, dishes rattling. Bartow grabbed her arm and hauled her upright.

"Ouch." Ellie couldn't stifle her protest at his tight grasp.

"Thought you was falling."

"I'm not…" But the awkward angle twisted her leg. Her ankle gave way.

He grabbed her other arm, but instead of merely steadying her, he drew her close. Much closer than was polite.

Instinctively, she arched away and out of his hold. Once freed, Ellie straightened her bonnet, debating about how harsh her rebuke should be.

Then she scolded herself for thinking he was taking advantage. After all, she had just met the man. But as she backed away, she caught sight of his crooked grin. Why was the oaf smiling?

He hooked a thumb in his belt. "Ain't the first time I've had that effect on women."

Clamping her jaw, she managed to stifle a caustic retort. He was Uncle Will's foreman. No sense offending him. Still…

She lifted her chin. "Why don't you save *effect*, Mr. Bartow, for cattle wrangling." After grabbing her handbag, she swept past him and out the door.

Struggling to gather calm, she stood outside as she yanked on a glove. The foreman's heavy footsteps followed, then stopped. Aware he stood behind her, she concentrated on buttoning the glove. The stench of his pomade seemed to curl around her as he, no doubt, ogled her.

As she pulled on her other glove, she spoke to him

in a frosty tone. "Would you please see to my trunks and bags?"

"Uh, o'course. Be back right quick."

Mr. Bartow clomped into the hotel.

A sigh of relief escaped her.

As she waited on the stoop, she acknowledged the greetings of those who passed by. Women nodded their hellos while men touched the brims of their hat or half saluted. Their genuine smiles warmed her heart. And with each greeting, Ellie felt her irritation fade.

Wyoming Territory is now my home. I could do some good here.

Despite its small size, Casper simmered with life. In the distance, men constructed a building. The sound of their hammers punctured the air. Wagons, coaches and foot traffic busied the streets. Though everything looked rough compared to back east, she had no doubt the town would grow and prosper. In time, Casper would grow into a thriving city.

Across the road, a familiar figure, riding an unusually colored horse, caught her attention.

"Rhett!" Ellie called. When he didn't respond, she snatched a handkerchief from her pocket and waved as she called his name again. With his bulging saddlebags and a bedroll strapped behind him, he appeared ready to take a long trip.

After glancing her way, he steered his horse across the flow of traffic. He remained seated atop his mount, expression neutral. Without moving his head, his gaze darted to the people nearby before settling on her once more.

"What a uniquely colored horse." Ellie eyed the gelding's dark body and white rump with spots. "Is this an appaloosa?"

"Yes."

"He's beautiful. What's his name?"

"Wash." Rhett's gaze continued to roam.

Although she barely knew him, he seemed unusually subdued.

"Aren't you continuing on to Billings?" Earlier she'd overheard the hotel proprietor speaking to one of his employees about the stagecoach. Why wasn't Rhett with them?

He answered with a mere shake of his head.

His expression appeared as grim as when Mr. Tesley insulted him. A cold premonition washed over her. "Why?"

"The stagecoach company ended my employment." Rhett spoke in a detached manner.

"They…they fired you?"

His mouth tightened. "Apparently I'm responsible for the broken wheel."

"But it wasn't your fault. How can they…?" She trailed off when Mr. Bartow's oily pomade intruded upon her senses.

The foreman positioned himself beside her. With deliberation, he turned his back to Rhett.

"They're bringing the wagon 'round now, Miss Elinor." When he moved closer, standing squarely between her and Rhett, she backed up a step.

"Thank you, Mr. Bartow." She worked to keep her tone polite as she indicated the man still on the horse. "I was about to thank Rhett for his help yesterday."

"Rhett?" He squinted up at the man on horseback.

"Mr. Callaway," she hastened to correct, aware she had addressed the men differently.

The foreman's lip curled. "I know who he is."

"Last night, in the wilds, he protected me. *Us.* Mrs. Rushton and her son."

"Seems we owe him a debt of gratitude." Mr. Bartow jabbed back the brim of his hat with his thumb. "I'll ask Mr. Marshall to speak to the stagecoach company on your behalf."

Rhett finally spoke, face impassive. "That won't be necessary."

"No trouble a'tall. As soon—"

"I no longer work for them."

Ellie again tamped down her outrage as she schooled her tone. "Then let me remind you again, Mr. Callaway, I'm sure my uncle would be pleased to hire you."

A hint of gratefulness softened his expression.

"Dunno as you should speak for Mr. Marshall." The foreman aimed his comment at Ellie as he scratched his cheek. "He don't like hiring men who aren't from 'round here."

"Once I tell him everything this man did, my uncle won't hesitate to employ him." She squared her shoulders when Mr. Bartow's eyes narrowed. "I can assure you, in our numerous correspondences, Uncle Will has mentioned a need for good help."

"Don't matter. All hires go through me."

That seemed to end the conversation. Glancing between the two men, Ellie clasped her hands. If she couldn't assure Rhett of a job with her uncle, she feared he would ride off to destinations unknown. Then she would never see him again.

Bartow stepped closer. "But seein' as how this is so important to you, p'rhaps I could put in a good word with the boss."

She forced herself to smile. "I would really appreciate that."

As the foreman studied her, his tongue poked the inside of his cheek as though in thought. He swiveled. "So, Callaway. Heard you can tame a horse without speaking. And you're a hard worker. That true?"

Rhett's gaze settled on the foreman. "You may see for yourself."

"Then consider yerself hired." Bartow gave one sharp nod. "Subject to Mr. Marshall's approval, o'course."

Joy swept over Ellie at the foreman's pronouncement. When Mr. Bartow turned to meet her gaze, she tempered her expression. The wagon, with a boy driving, rattled around the corner and drew the man's attention. In the back were Ellie's trunks and bags.

"Miss Elinor?" Bartow held out his hand.

As the foreman handed her up into the seat, she risked a glance at Rhett to see what his reaction was. Her heart soared when he mouthed, *Thank you.*

Ellie felt as though the wagon ride to Uncle Will's ranch took as long as the earlier one to Casper. Mr. Bartow tried to engage her in conversation, but he said little that interested her. Not only that, she couldn't seem to concentrate. After a while, the foreman fell silent. When she attempted to talk about the history of the county, he answered in monosyllables.

How different from the natural ease of her exchange with Rhett the night before.

Several times she glanced over her shoulder to locate him as he rode at a respectful distance. She found herself wishing he was the one driving the wagon.

When they crested a hill, Mr. Bartow reined the horse and pointed. "There she is. The purdiest place in the county."

Pretty? Ellie squinted at endless tracks of dirt dotted by a half dozen buildings of various sizes. Nearer to them were the burned-out shells of a couple structures—the ruined remains creating an odd and inexplicable sight. Cattle and horses clustered in groups around the area. Everything seemed to be varying shades of brown.

Is this it? When she rose to get a better look, the foreman urged the wagon horse forward, throwing her off balance. She sat back down with an undignified *oomph*.

When she caught the foreman's smirk, she glared at him. Had he done that on purpose?

As they drew closer to the ranch, she could see men staring in their direction. One ran toward a small cabin that was not far from a large house. Chickens in the yard scattered. A couple dogs slunk along one corral, keeping their distance from the cowboys. From the small cabin strode one man. He positioned himself in the center of the yard, gaze fixed on them.

Uncle Will? The only photo Ellie had of him was several years old. He had visited Chicago several times, but the last was when she was nine. Everything else she knew of him came from the sporadic letters he had written to her after Mama's death. His correspondence with Ellie had increased after her father died.

From the way the crowd hung back, it had to be Uncle Will. Ellie noted his brown hair with a touch of gray at the temples. He still wore a large mustache, which she remembered so well. His broadening smile told her the man who waited to greet her was indeed her uncle.

"Ellie!" Arms spread, her uncle moved toward the wagon as they reached the ranch. He noticeably favored one leg.

"Uncle Will." Without waiting for Bartow's help, she leaped down. In seconds she was in her uncle's embrace, tears blurring her vision. "I'm so happy to see you." She buried her face against his coat.

Memories washed over her at the smell of mint and grassy fields on his clothing. She recalled so clearly leaning against him during his last visit while his calloused hand awkwardly stroked her hair. Mama had looked on with a doting smile as Ellie chattered about her desire to become a doctor, just like her daddy.

"I'm grateful you're all right." Uncle Will's rough voice brought her back to the present. "Glad to hear the stagecoach crash wasn't worse."

Ellie pulled away, but maintained her hold on his arms. "I'm fine. And so very happy I can be here. With you."

His imposing eyebrows were still as dark as coffee. Under his groomed mustache, his mouth moved with suppressed emotion as he squeezed her shoulder. "You must be tired. And hungry."

"Those can wait. But what about you? What happened to your leg?"

"Still trying to be a doctor, eh?" He chuckled. "It's nothing. I jumped off the wagon yesterday and landed wrong, is all."

"But you're limping."

"Twisted my ankle. It's already on the mend." He took her arm. "Come inside. Let's get you settled. I can't wait for you to see your rooms. They're all ready for ya."

He steered her toward the large house. An elderly couple waited on the porch while numerous ranch hands leaned on fences or stood in a semblance of attention. She nodded and smiled to them as her uncle led her up the steps to the open door.

When they reached the top, she remembered Rhett. "Uncle Will, wait a moment, please."

Face still beaming, her uncle leaned attentively toward her. "What is it, Sunshine?"

She smiled at his old nickname for her. "I took the liberty of offering work to a man in Casper." She stammered as she sought words to champion Rhett without betraying that the stagecoach company had fired him. "He—he was in need of a job. And was a great help to me personally. His reputation is exemplary."

Though Ellie borrowed Pete's words, she felt justified using them.

"I could always use another good man around here." He smiled as he looked around. "It okay with Guy?"

"He said yes. As long as you approved."

"Then I don't see it being a problem." Will scanned the group in the yard as though to pick out his new hire. "So where…?" His voice died as his amiable expression blinked out of existence.

If someone had doused Ellie with cold water, she wouldn't have felt the chill as much as she did when her uncle's brow lowered and his mouth hardened. For what felt like several minutes, he stared at Rhett. When Uncle Will finally settled his stony gaze on her, she shivered.

He jabbed a thumb over his shoulder. "You referring to him?"

"Yes. Rhett Callaway."

A muscle in his cheek twitched. "No thanks."

"No…?"

"I'm not hiring him."

"But Rhett's a fine man." She kept her voice low. "He not only saved my life but—"

"We don't hire men like him."

Men like…?

Ellie backed away from the ice in his tone. She gulped air and tried again. "You don't understand, he—"

"No. *You* don't understand." Her uncle spoke through clenched teeth.

She clamped her mouth shut. Where had her beloved uncle disappeared to? She stared at the man who looked like Uncle Will, but sounded nothing like him. He sounded like his brother—her father.

A lifetime of experience in dealing with that tone said to drop the subject. To acquiesce. But the unfathomable injustice toward Rhett—before he'd had a chance to prove himself—rankled. If Uncle Will would let her explain, she would convince him he must hire Rhett.

"Excuse me, Mr. Marshall." The foreman's voice floated up from the bottom step. He pulled off his hat and crimped the brim. "I promised Miss Elinor that I'd put in a good word for him. I've heard Callaway's a hard worker. And since we lost those men last week, we've been shorthanded."

Expression still rigid, Uncle Will turned to gaze at his foreman.

"I'd say give him a couple months." Bartow's fingers tightened and relaxed on his hat brim. "Try him out."

Still her uncle said nothing. Everyone around them seemed to hold their collective breaths, gaze flickering between the two men. Only a few dared to study Rhett, who remained unmoving atop his horse. His face was as expressionless as the cattle that poked their heads through the barbed-wire fencing across the yard.

"Please, Uncle Will." Ellie whispered for his ears only.

He acted like he didn't hear her.

"As a favor to me?" she dared to plead. "Please?"

His gaze flickered to Ellie before his jaw jutted. He thrust a finger at his foreman. "All right. But keep a tight rein on him." His eyes narrowed. "I'll give him a couple months to prove himself. That's it. But he's *your* responsibility, Guy. Hear me?"

The foreman snapped to attention. "Yessir."

Without another word, Will turned and headed into the house.

Lingering on the porch, Ellie risked a look at Rhett. She expected relief on his face. Or at least gratefulness, but no. His mouth had flattened, and his brows squeezed together. Like he was sorry he took the job?

I'll talk to him later. Apologize for my uncle.

How could Uncle Will treat someone that way? Every dreamy castle in the sky she had built of her glorious future in Wyoming Territory threatened to crumble.

However, if no one else remembered their manners, she would. "Thank you, Mr. Bartow."

Ellie turned and followed her uncle into the house. However, the joy of their reunion had soured. Why was he so opposed to Rhett? Did Uncle Will know something she didn't?

Mr. Tesley's words came back to her. *He's got outlaw blood.*

Was Rhett really related to an outlaw—someone Uncle Will had encountered? She waffled between wanting to ask her uncle and explaining that he had to be mistaken about Rhett. However, during their precious moments of camaraderie about the campfire, she had neglected to ask Rhett about Mr. Tesley's remark. Was there more to Rhett's story than what he'd shared?

When the time was right, she would question both Rhett and her uncle.

* * *

Rhett dismounted, aware of the covert glances thrown his way. Most men dispersed to their various tasks, but some acted as though he was invisible. A mere handful gave him a sharp nod before sauntering away. Only the elderly woman on the porch outright stared at him.

"Don'tcha have work to do?" The foreman glared at the lingering men. As soon as they scattered, he bee-lined for Rhett. "Come with me."

After tethering his horse and untying his bedroll, he followed Bartow to a dilapidated building. Not the bunkhouse? Across the yard, the long narrow building looked considerably more inviting.

"This is your spot." Bartow pointed to a dusty corner.

Rhett glanced at the dirt floor, thin walls and gap-ing holes between weatherworn boards. But at least its roof appeared intact. A new barn towered several yards away, proving this shed was no longer used for hay and grain. Instead, miscellaneous tools occupied the space. He said nothing as he slung his bedroll off his shoulder. When he turned, the foreman studied him, eyes mere slits.

"Don't expect any special treatment while you're here." All Bartow's earlier amiability had disappeared. "Rumors about your work don't mean squat. I expect you to pull your own weight."

Rhett kept his face neutral. "That'll not be a prob-lem."

The foreman sneered. "We'll see. Make sure you don't show during meals either. You eat after everyone else. Got it?"

"Yes," he answered slowly. "I do." Bartow wasn't the first tyrant he'd encountered. If Rhett had to guess, he'd say that the foreman disliked Ellie's warmth toward him—and he was punishing Rhett for it now. No matter. In a few days, the foreman would relax after Rhett proved himself.

"Just do your work. And keep your big bazoo shut." He turned, then swiveled back around. "Another thing—don't be gettin' all cozy with the boss or his niece. You mind your place." He emphasized his words with a finger jabbing the air. "Or someday you'll wake up and find your head lying next to you."

Though Rhett remained silent, he made a point to not break eye contact. He kept his shoulders relaxed and arms loose at his side, not giving the foreman a reason to see him as a threat.

Bartow's lip curled as he apparently made up his mind about something. "Humph." He turned and strode away.

After the foreman reached the yard, two men immediately came alongside him—like they were his personal guards. With interest, Rhett studied them.

One had a predominantly crooked nose. The other had a white streak in his hair, visible under a worn hat. From the shady interior of the building, Rhett took note of their features, determined to steer clear of all three of them. However, he reminded himself not to jump to conclusions about the Double M Ranch no matter how he felt, especially about the foreman.

Rhett glanced around at his quarters. The space appeared to have housed hay at one time. Above, some boards rested on beams. Up there, he might find a safer and more comfortable place to sleep. He climbed up and settled his bedroll. Later he would add some straw. This arrangement would suit him just fine.

Sitting in the cramped space with his head brushing the rafters, he contemplated his new life. Suspicion, he was used to. For years, he and his mother had wandered from town to town—always viewed as strangers. He'd grown accustomed to feeling like an outsider. But something about Bartow went beyond that. His earlier display of friendliness had been a show, obviously to impress Ellie.

Instinct told Rhett to leave. However, concern for his new friend gained the upper hand. Guy Bartow's pointed attention toward her seemed almost sinister. The foreman wasn't merely seeking to curry favor.

Raising his face, Rhett crossed his legs. "What would you have me do, Father God?"

He already knew the answer. Stay. If nothing else, he needed to discharge his promise to Ellie.

No, he admitted to himself, this went much further than merely keeping a promise.

He considered. In the rough west, she appeared a rare flower amid a tangle of weeds—one that must be sheltered. Protected. Rhett could not rid himself of the feeling that he needed to watch over her.

For so many years, he'd felt directionless. He took whatever work he could find, but he had no home, no real purpose. Until now. Watching over Ellie felt like what he was meant to do.

In the meantime, he would do nothing to embarrass her. After all, she had put herself out when she vouched for him. Because of that, Rhett vowed to labor harder than any other worker on the ranch to win over William Marshall.

And, perhaps, to win over Ellie?

Chapter Five

Ellie stood in the middle of the bedroom and surveyed her trunks and bags, neatly stacked beside one wall. They would have to wait to be unpacked. She ached to crawl onto the fluffy bed with a colorful patchwork quilt of blues, greens and yellows. However, she didn't want to take time to rest. Not just yet.

Assuming I would *sleep.*

Every time she closed her eyes, images and sounds from the stagecoach accident tormented her. Even now, her heart thumped uncomfortably. She shook off the feeling. Perhaps the horrid memories would fade in time.

When Ellie emerged from her room, she found only the housekeeper inside the great room, setting the long table. More than a dozen tin plates lined the surface while the smell of food permeated the house.

"Mrs. Johnson, is my uncle around?"

"On the porch." Continuing to work, she indicated the door with a tilt of her head. The woman seemed wholly intent on her task.

Ellie watched a moment longer before going outside.

"Ah, there you are." Her uncle arose from the log

bench, arms spread to hug her. Then he peered down at her. "Did you find everything to your liking?"

"Yes. The bedroom is beautiful. And so spacious." She took a seat on the bench.

Her uncle had filled the space with keepsakes from a bygone era. A second, connected room boasted of a bathing area with a potbelly stove. She didn't tell him both the bathtub and washstand were archaic compared to what she was used to. The comparison would merely distress him. Long before she'd traveled to the wilds of Wyoming Territory, Ellie had determined to be content with the lanterns and fireplaces as well as the lack of other modern conveniences she was used to. Those weren't as important as being with her uncle and having the chance to begin a new life.

He patted her hand. "How do you like the bathing room?"

"It's amazing."

"Glad you like it."

"I didn't see another bedroom in the house—just a doorway to the kitchen area. Where do you sleep?"

"That's my place." He pointed to a small cabin a short distance away. "On the other side of the house are cabins for the Johnsons and Guy. The rest of the men sleep in the bunkhouse. We've got barns, stables, outbuildings. We only gather at the main house for meals, otherwise it's all yours."

"Really?" Then a sneaking suspicion came to her. "Did you move out for me?"

"Nah, did that a long time ago." He scratched his chin with his thumbnail. "Guess maybe I've been hoping you'd settle here someday."

Settle? Her heart soared to hear him say that. In their many correspondences over the last five months, Ellie had not been certain if her uncle wanted her to remain on the ranch. But would he change his mind when he learned what she wanted to occupy her time while she lived here? She intended to use her medical skills, to be a help to Uncle Will and neighboring ranchers.

But perhaps that subject was best left for another time. He might need to warm up to the idea.

Turning away, he coughed before again focusing his attention on her. "I'm sorry I couldn't be there for my brother's funeral. How was it?"

"Very beautiful. So many people came to pay their respects." Ellie couldn't help shivering at the memory of the closed casket. "And, I'll say it again, you wouldn't have arrived in time. Father's accident made it imperative we bury him immediately."

Though she'd not seen his mangled corpse, the report alone gave her nightmares. One significant detail had been missing—how intoxicated her father likely had been when he had stepped in front of the heavy-laden wagon.

"And your father's estate?" Uncle Will's gentle voice drew her back. "All settled now?"

Estate? A sound of derision escaped her.

After the creditors had taken their share, not much remained. Although not penniless, she could not have afforded to keep the grand Chicago house, even if she'd wanted to. For several years, Father had managed to hide his true financial condition by closing down part of the house, letting staff go and borrowing money. Upon his death, all had been revealed. Once upon a time, Ellie believed he wanted her to work alongside him in his medical practice because he appreciated her. Eventually she understood he desired her help because he didn't have to pay her a wage.

She managed to speak in an even tone. "It's done. I have nothing—and no one—in Chicago." She squeezed his hand and smiled. "That means you're stuck with me."

His eyes appeared to glitter more brightly. "I'm more than happy to be *stuck* with you."

"We'll see." Ellie straightened. "Because the first thing I need to know is who tended to your ankle."

"Cookie patched me up."

Cookie? Her uncle must be referring to the elderly man who had stood with Mrs. Johnson when she'd arrived. "But he's the cook, isn't he? Not a qualified medical practitioner."

Uncle Will laughed out loud. "I know they use those highfalutin words in Chicago, but you don't need them out here."

"I'd like to take a look."

"Nah." He stretched his leg out before him. "Though I appreciate the offer."

Before she could insist, the sound of a man clearing his throat interrupted. Mr. Bartow stood at the bottom of the porch, sweeping off his hat and nodding at them. "Boss. Miss Elinor."

"Call her Ellie," her uncle said before she could respond. "You don't mind, do you, Sunshine?"

A little. But she gave him a tight smile. "If that's what you want Mr. Bartow to call me."

"And you should definitely call him Guy." Her uncle rose. "If the men heard you say 'Mr. Bartow' they might get ideas about you two."

Flames scorched her cheeks, especially when Guy guffawed.

Her uncle gripped the column of the porch. "Whatcha need, Guy?"

"I jes' came by to tell you the new hire is settled. Got him a nice, cozy place."

"Good. Good." Her uncle gave one stiff jerk of a nod. "You go over the rules with him?"

"Yessir. We'll keep him in line."

Ellie studied the two men, disliking the shift in tone.

When Guy caught her look, he straightened, expression softening. "Have no fear, Ellie. I'll make sure he feels right at home."

She managed a small smile, then jumped when a loud clanging sounded nearby.

Guy laughed. "Jes' the supper bell." He leaped up the stairs and held out his arm. "May I?"

Ellie slipped her hand through her uncle's arm. "I already have an escort, thank you."

Hazel eyes twinkling, Uncle Will beamed at her. "Sorry, Guy. Maybe next time."

She tried not to stiffen at the implication of *next time*. Instead, she squeezed her uncle's arm. "With you as my partner, no other man has a chance."

His eyebrows shot up. "You learn that line from one of those Chicago dandies?"

"Mmm-hmm. From the very best." Ellie didn't add that they were a worthless lot. Many of them seemed more worried about their boots than her. Not like…

She caught her breath at the memory of sky-blue eyes, watching her from across a bonfire. Rhett had known she was afraid—and he forfeited his sleep to watch over her and the Rushtons all night. What kind of person would do that for a friend, much less a stranger? Not only that, but he had endangered himself by securing the gelding because she had asked.

Rhett is like no other man I've ever met.

"Ellie?" Uncle Will ducked his head.

She shook herself. "Yes?"

"I asked if you were ready to go in."

"Of course."

As her uncle led her into the house, her thoughts again strayed to Rhett. She couldn't help but be thrilled that he'd accepted the job offer, despite her uncle's unfriendliness. She hoped Rhett would soon settle in and prove what a fine man he was. In no time, her uncle's attitude toward him would soften.

And with Rhett nearby, she would see him on a regular basis.

Strangely, her heart thumped in anticipation.

"And most important," Uncle Will announced as they finished supper, "this is my niece, Ellie, from Chicago. Treat her with respect. The Marshall blood runs through her veins, so watch out or she'll put you in your place."

Though several men chuckled, Ellie detected the cautious look many threw her direction. She returned their smiles but remained uncertain if her uncle's comment contained more warning than jest.

Uncle Will held up one hand, recapturing everyone's attention as he sat at the head of the table. "And to celebrate her arrival, the Johnsons prepared a special treat."

That announcement elicited applause and whistles as the housekeeper carried in gargantuan servings of cake. Fighting a growing weariness, Ellie merely nibbled at her dessert. The day had been overly long and her body protested many hours of travel—not to mention the bumps and bruises from the stagecoach accident. Her head began to pound at the relentless, raucous laughter and loud voices.

Perhaps the fact that Rhett wasn't there further unsettled her. Since their arrival a couple hours ago, she'd not seen him. He hadn't made an appearance for supper. Where was he?

She pressed her fingers to her uncle's arm. "If you don't mind, I'd like to unpack a little before it gets much later. Please excuse me."

"Of course." He rose when she did, pulling out her chair so she could move away from the table.

All of a sudden, the sound of scraping chairs and benches filled the room as men shot to their feet. Ellie pressed her lips together at the complete bewilderment on some of their faces as they followed their boss's example.

She gave a little nod as she spoke to the assembly. "Thank you for your warm welcome. I look forward to getting to know you better in the future."

"I know I speak for all the men," Guy was quick to reply as he hooked a thumb in his belt, "when I say we're pleased to have ya here. And we look forward to getting to know you too."

His tone seemed to contain only sincerity, so why did her cheeks burn? Perhaps it had something to do with the crook in one eyebrow and smug smile.

Or was it because her uncle's eyes gleamed as he glanced between the two of them?

Stomach cramping with hunger, Rhett peered around the shed's opening as a number of men left the main house. In the distance, he caught the sounds of a harmonica, men talking, the clink of money. Inside the bunkhouse, the lights of lanterns glowed while shadows moved behind curtained windows. He turned his attention back to the house in time to see the ranch owner and foreman. They walked across the yard, Marshall limping as they talked in low voices. An older, wiry man shut a side door to the house. Cookie? He wandered to a small building between the large ranch house and bunkhouse.

Where was Ellie? Earlier Rhett had heard men chatting as they ate their meal. Occasionally the sound of her laughter had caressed his ears. Now the building lay quiet. Lights sprang up inside but after a while, he perceived no noise coming from the interior. He headed to the nearby pump and washed up.

With caution, he mounted the porch steps and peered inside through the open door. Only an elderly woman remained in the room, clearing dishes from a sideboard. Even though he'd made no sound, some instinct caused her to look up.

"There you are." She pointed to a lone dish loaded with food. "Eat."

"Thanks." He grabbed the tin plate and prepared to head back out.

"No, ya don't," she scolded. "Eat in here. I don't wanna hafta chase down that plate."

Grinning, he slid onto the long bench. After a silent prayer of thanks, he dove into the generous portions of meat and beans with a slice of bread. He washed down the food with a cup of lukewarm coffee that was so thick a spoon might stand up in it. Although the woman continued to clean up, he was aware of the several glances she shot his way.

He pushed the empty plate away and stretched his back.

"More?" The woman pointed to a doorway, leading to the lean-to. "We've plenty."

"Please. Everything's delicious."

She dished another plateful of meat and beans. When

she returned with a hunk of bread and then refilled his cup, she added, "Nice to serve someone with manners."

"Thanks" and "please" were all he needed to say to be considered mannerly? Hiding his smile, he ducked his head as he ate.

The woman continued to watch him. "I've heard about you. From some folks 'round here."

Focusing on the food, he grunted in acknowledgment. The less he said, the better.

"Cookie—he's my man—says you go by Rhett?"

He nodded as he kept eating.

"Huh." Her eyes narrowed. "I once knowed a man by the name of Everett. Kinda looked like you. Funny that your names are similar."

Pretending ignorance, he shrugged.

Had she really known his father? The woman's age proved she would have been an adult when the Walker Gang was most active. However, wisdom said to keep his mouth shut.

"Same jawline. Same blue eyes. I never forget a face." She paused before adding, "You related?"

Plate empty, Rhett reached for the piece of bread, willing his hand to remain steady.

"No matter." Leaning a hand on the table, she whispered, "I know who you really are."

Rhett drew in a slow breath. If true, what was she going to do with her knowledge?

Before he could speak, the door across the room swung open. The old woman drew back, then picked up the empty plate.

"Rhett!" Ellie stood in the open doorway.

A frothy white dress, edged with fine lace, had replaced her dark violet traveling attire. Her loose hair flowed over delicate shoulders. Once again, the picture of a rare flower blossomed in his mind.

She drew closer, a smile lighting her face. "I was just unpacking. Where've you been?"

Trying not to stare, he finished his coffee. "Getting settled."

"Oh." Confusion flitted across her features. Doubtless, she was trying to understand how putting away a bedroll and saddle could take so much of his time. "You missed a wonderful supper."

"I ate just now. Thanks."

Her gaze shot to the woman across the room. "Mrs. Johnson, is there any cake left?"

The housekeeper shook her head.

"That's too bad." Ellie slid onto a seat across from him. "I wish I'd saved you my piece."

She rested her forearms on the table, gaze again sidling to the older woman. Was Ellie uncomfortable speaking to him in front of someone else?

"Could I get tea, please?" she asked the woman.

"Sure, miss. I'll have to heat water." The housekeeper moved away.

"Thank you." Ellie directed her smile at him. "I hope your quarters are comfortable."

He thought of the drafty building, but decided the shed was more pleasant than sleeping in the open. "Good enough." His gaze cut across to the gray-haired woman who had finished putting on a kettle and grabbed a broom. Although she seemed intent on her work, he knew she listened to every word. The rough bristles scraped across the floor with a rhythmic *shree-shree* sound.

"I'm glad." Ellie spread her hands to indicate the

well-furnished house. "Do you think this place beautiful? I hope you'll be happy here."

As long as you're here, I will be. The unbidden thought popped into his head. Ever mindful of their audience, Rhett clamped his jaw to keep from speaking the words aloud. His bold pronouncement might unnerve Ellie.

"I'm sure I will be." He spoke slowly, captivated by the way the soft light caressed her milky skin. In the light of the lanterns, her blonde hair gave off a golden glow. When the scent of lavender tickled his senses, he breathed deeply.

The pink on her cheeks deepened as she lowered her gaze.

He cleared his throat. "Thank you for giving me the opportunity to work here."

Ma counted on the money he sent each month. Though she wouldn't be destitute without it, he liked to provide enough so she would never worry about food or shelter again.

He didn't mind repeating his thanks. "I appreciate the job."

"Oh, no trouble." Despite Ellie's smile, a small furrow appeared on her forehead. She shot another glance at the housekeeper. "Although I'm sorry your welcome wasn't, um, warmer."

He shook his head, wanting to tell her that the reception wasn't all that surprising. According to the foreman, Will Marshall preferred to hire locals. A lot of riffraff wandered about the country, especially with the railroad pushing deep into Wyoming Territory. Marshall's response *had* seemed a little more pointed than Rhett expected—but he would adjust.

He could take care of himself, but he worried about

his mother's safety. Perhaps returning to Cheyenne had not been a good idea no matter how much Ma desired it.

"Here ya are, miss." Mrs. Johnson set a steaming cup of tea before Ellie.

"Thank you."

Rhett waited until the woman returned to her task before speaking to Ellie. "How's your neck? I noticed you were rubbing it earlier."

He clamped his mouth shut. Stupid to have said that, proving he'd been watching her.

"When?"

He had no choice but to answer. "In the wagon. On the way here."

"It's better." She spoke slowly as she began to toy with a strand of hair.

She seemed to do that when nervous or anxious, but he found the habit endearing. The way she fluttered her eyelashes when she smiled entranced him.

If he had not been so smitten, he might have paid closer attention to the sounds outside. When footsteps thumped across the porch, Rhett bolted upright. He and Ellie were no longer isolated along a dirt road in the wilderness. He could not afford to stare at her without consequences.

"Ellie, I…" Will Marshall halted on the threshold, gaze darting between the two of them.

She too rose, looking as though she'd been caught doing something inappropriate. After stammering a hello, she fell silent. Mrs. Johnson continued to sweep, moving closer as though not satisfied with her earlier work. Not once did she look up.

Marshall's hard stare fixed on him. With deliberation, Rhett picked up his cup before half-bowing to Ellie. "Thank you for the meal."

Confusion etched her brow, but she didn't contradict him. Rhett intended for the ranch owner to assume she had provided the food—and that was the only reason she was sitting at the table with him.

Keeping his gaze lowered, he set the cup on a sideboard, then headed toward the door. His new employer stepped aside with a jerk. Without looking back, Rhett walked purposefully down the steps and across the yard.

The thought flashed through his mind that he was a fool for displaying his back to his new boss, considering the man's expression. Never had Rhett seen such unveiled suspicion before.

What caused Marshall to harbor such distrust? This seemed to go deeper than disliking outsiders. Perhaps the Double M Ranch and the Walker Gang shared more history than he'd first imagined.

In the morning, Ellie heard men's voices in the next room. From the sounds they made, she determined they were eating breakfast. Too sleepy to arise, she rolled over in bed. Then she groaned at her aching body as the bruises from the stagecoach accident made themselves known.

The faintest light shimmered against the curtains, telling her the day had barely begun. She pulled the blankets over her head and tried to block out the noise from the next room. After sleep continued to elude her, she rose.

By the time she washed and dressed, the house had emptied. A plate of flapjacks sat on the still-warm stove, while a huge pan of bacon rested nearby. Yawning, Ellie helped herself to the food and coffee. She had nearly finished her meal when the door opened and her uncle strode in.

"There you are, Sunshine." He kissed the top of her head. "I was wondering if you'd sleep half the day."

"It's not even eight." She stifled a yawn. "That's hardly half the day."

"Around here it is." He poured himself a steaming cup of coffee and sat nearby.

"I see your ankle has improved." Ellie waved her fork in his direction.

"Told ya it was on the mend."

"Uh-huh." She cradled her coffee. "Next time something like that happens, *I* will tend to you. And if any of the ranch hands have injuries, I plan to see to them, as well."

"Yes, Doc." He chuckled, eyebrows rising. "But I thought my brother didn't send you to medical school."

Her cheeks grew hot. "Not that I didn't want to go. Do you realize I was accepted to the Women's Medical College of Pennsylvania? I could've gone if…" She bit her lip, surprised at how the memory of her father's harsh mockery still hurt.

"No doubt you would've made a wonderful doctor." Uncle Will patted her hand.

Would have? Her fingers curled under the hand he touched.

"If you want to tend to scratches and bruises," he said more softly, "you're welcome to."

Despite the kind words, she could only hear the condescension that laced his tone. She knew she was capable of so much more.

"I must warn you, though," he went on, "the men'll line up to flirt."

She set aside her annoyance. "I'd be glad to see to anyone's injury, if it would help you."

"Huh." Will took a mouthful of coffee, then smoothed his mustache with a knuckle. "Then I'd never get any work done around here."

"If needed, I'll tend to them on their day off."

He frowned at her as though she had just started speaking French.

"Naturally, I meant Sunday," she added. "I'm sure the Lord wouldn't mind my tending wounds since He healed on the Sabbath."

Will's brow cleared. "Yes. Of course."

His reaction and tone fueled her suspicions. "You *do* allow them Sundays off, don't you? Or at least a chance to go to church?"

His thumb rubbed the handle of the tin cup as though to polish off the soot. "They're off on Sundays. What they do with their time off is none of my business."

Something about the way his eyes shifted bothered her. "Don't they follow your example?" When he didn't reply right away, she understood. "Oh, I see. You don't go either."

Will scratched his head. "I'm not much of a church-goer."

"But, when you visited Chicago, you did." She had a clear memory of him sitting in the pew with her and her mother. What had changed?

He looked away. "That was a long time ago."

Before she could ask him if he would reconsider, he added, "You're welcome to if you want. I'm sure Guy would drive you."

"I'd rather go with you." She spoke in a low tone, hoping Uncle Will would agree.

When he said nothing more, she bit her lip to keep

from nagging. Perhaps sometime soon she could convince him.

With a couple gulps, Will finished his coffee. "I'm sorry, but I need to skedaddle. Got work to do."

"Wait." Ellie rose with him. "Isn't that what your men are for?"

He flashed her an indulgent smile. "'Round here we do things a bit different than back east. I work alongside my men."

"Yes, but…" Disappointment washed over her. "I thought we'd spend the day together."

"Not today, I'm afraid. We're shorthanded. That means we're behind work."

"Of course." How selfish of her to want him all to herself. "Will I see you during dinner?"

"Perhaps. We usually eat around one or two. Whenever Cookie sounds the bell." With that, her uncle was out the door.

She stared after him, an odd sensation gripping her stomach. This wasn't going as she'd imagined. The realization struck her that so far, nothing had.

"I need to give him—and me—time." She spoke aloud, not only to convince herself, but as a reminder that she now dwelled in Uncle Will's world. He had a way of doing things and a schedule that she was as yet ignorant of. Though she knew little of ranch operations, she must become a student.

In the meantime, she would get settled. This was now her home.

Back in her bedroom, she set up a photograph of her parents on a small desk. She draped a favorite knitted throw across the foot of the bed and placed her father's clock on the mantel. Next, she tackled sorting through the wreckage in her medical bag, careful to pick out the broken glass. Though some items were spoiled, she was able to salvage much. The thought crossed her mind that she should restock soon. If memory served, Casper boasted of a small drugstore.

As she fingered the tin of astringent powder, memories of two days before rushed back at her. What had happened to the horse she had stitched up? In the bustle of getting to the ranch, she'd forgotten to ask. Did Rhett know? Ellie rose to peer out her bedroom window, but it faced away from the ranch yard. Barren and blistered hills, dotted by scrub brush met her gaze. Not exactly the beautiful view she had envisioned. She missed the lush green grass and bountiful trees of Chicago.

She squeezed her eyes shut. "Irrelevant. This is home."

When she grew weary of the isolation, she grabbed a light shawl and bonnet before heading out the front door. The hot sun now shone high in the sky, so she stayed on the shaded porch to look around the ranch.

In the distance, men repaired barbed-wire fencing that stretched for miles. Another couple of workers were shoeing a horse. A young man worked the bellows while the blacksmith shaped metal on the anvil. His hammer hummed as he beat a rhythmic tattoo. As Ellie peered around, she finally spotted Rhett in a nearby field. He appeared to be digging holes. For fence posts? From where she stood, she counted six mounds of dirt. His buckskin jacket draped a nearby post. His sleeveless shirt revealed muscled arms. The bandage she had bound around his wound was missing.

After draping her shawl over the railing, she wrapped one arm around a porch column and watched. Not once did he pause as he worked, but dug with diligence, intent on his work. If he looked up, Ellie was prepared to wave in encouragement. Her thoughts leaped ahead.

Had any of the ranch hands befriended him? She hoped Rhett was settling into his new job and that Guy had discovered what a fine man his new employee was.

"Miss?"

Ellie jumped as Mrs. Johnson approached.

"Made some fresh sassafras tea." The housekeeper held out a drink. "Well water makes it cold, but we got ice if you want." She pointed to a distant shack, built into the side of a hill.

"Thank you. This'll be perfect." She took the glass from the woman, who disappeared into the house again without saying another word.

Truth was, Ellie wasn't interested in tea. However, as she held the drink, her gaze again strayed to Rhett. Perhaps he would care for some cool refreshment.

Before she changed her mind, she walked with purpose toward him. He must have caught a glimpse of her, because he stopped working as she crossed the yard. As he waited, he flexed his shoulders as though to relieve the tension in his muscles. A small smile danced across his lips. Was he more delighted to see her or the drink she carried? Warmth crept over her as she imagined his blue eyes glittering in anticipation.

The sound of horse hooves, rapidly approaching, stopped her in the middle of the yard. She swiveled as Guy and two men thundered toward her. When they were within ten feet, they pulled up.

"Whoa." The foreman held up one hand as though a military commander in a campaign. "How do, Miss Ellie." With a flourish, he swept his hat off and gave a partial bow. "Dee-lighted to see you on this fair day." The other two men nodded in greeting.

"Hello." She clamped her mouth shut, at a loss of what else to say. In her peripheral vision, she could see Rhett, watching. Condensation from the glass dripped over her fingers.

"Boys, where're yer manners?" The foreman knocked the younger man's hat off. His companion swept off his before Guy could reach him, revealing a streak of white hair. "We've a lady present."

As the foreman dismounted, she squelched a sound of impatience.

Guy fixed his gaze on the glass of sassafras tea as he settled his hat back on his head. "Now that looks right inviting. Tasted it yet?"

"No." She chewed on the inside of her lip. Too late she realized what her intended actions might mean to the other ranch hands. After all, Rhett had just begun working there. How unwise for her to single him out and treat him with special favor.

She held the glass toward Guy. "Mrs. Johnson said she just made this."

"Real sweet of you to bring it to me." He winked.

"It's all yours."

Guy snatched it out of her hand and took a gulp. "Not bad. O'course, not as good at painting my tonsils as some other drinks, but—"

A sharp shriek interrupted, followed by a drawn-out cry.

Ellie swiveled toward the sound. The young man who'd been helping the blacksmith gripped his wrist. His face twisted in pain.

Without hesitation, she rushed toward him.

Guy's footsteps followed, but with his longer strides, he reached the man ahead of her. "What happened?"

"I…" The young man groaned.

"Burned hisself." An older man stared at the angry red welt that rose on the meaty part of the thumb. "I told Matt not to take his eyes off the hot metal."

A crowd began to gather.

"Get Cookie." Still holding his sassafras tea, Guy barked at a loiterer. "And tell him to bring butter."

"No. Not butter." Ellie stepped forward while the man froze and gawked at her. Without explaining, she grabbed the glass of partially finished tea from Guy's hand. "Here. Hold this against your burn. *Now.*"

When Matt merely stared at her, she seized his forearm and pressed the cold glass on his thumb. He yelped, but she hung on. After several seconds he no longer resisted her hold.

Ellie stared into the young man's face. "Keep the wound cool as long as you can. After it stops burning, you can put butter on it. But not now. That would be the worst thing to do."

Gulping, the youngster's gaze shifted to those who stood around. Ellie too caught the looks of the men, catching expressions of doubt, surprise and grudging admiration.

"What happened?" Cookie shuffled their way.

"Matt burned himself," a man volunteered.

"Get me some butter," the elderly man ordered the speaker.

"Ellie says no," Guy volunteered. Crossing his arms, he leaned back as though waiting for how she would respond.

Before Cookie could fuss, she spoke. "Butter is a wonderful ointment for burns. But later. After the burn has cooled." Back in Chicago, that treatment had worked on a kitchen girl who had scalded her foot, but the scowl on Cookie's face discouraged offering an explanation. Ellie looked around. More of the men's expressions seemed to mimic Cookie's now as they sided with him.

She'd seen those looks before on the faces of her father's colleagues.

Practice medicine? You? Their sneers echoed in her memories.

Ellie took a deep breath. Soon enough, the young man would learn which treatment would be most effective. No use forcing a showdown with Cookie.

"I'm not the one who's hurting. So it makes no difference to me." She spun to face Matt. "The cold of the glass or the butter—*you* decide what feels best." Without another word, she turned on her heel and stalked back to the house.

"Hey." Guy called after her, but she pretended not to hear.

After she reached her room, she realized she should have stayed and fought for what was best for the young man. Sighing, she paced across her room for several minutes.

Practicing medicine was her dream—a dream she would fulfill regardless of who stood in her way.

Next time, Ellie promised herself. Next time she would not give up so soon. Even if it meant challenging the foreman, the cook…and even her own uncle.

Muscles burning, Rhett dug one final hole before he allowed himself to rest. Swiping his forearm across his brow, he hissed when salty sweat bit into the not-quite-healed wound on his forearm. Though the supper bell had rung almost an hour ago, he had continued to work because he wanted to finish his task. Already the sun shimmered as it perched on the hilly horizon. Orange streaks cut across the sky, bringing a cool breeze.

He spread his jacket on the ground, then sat on it as he reflected on the day. The incident with Ellie in the ranch yard came back to him. What had transpired with the blacksmith? Rhett had heard the yell and had started across the yard when he saw Bartow. Since the foreman had gathered with the men, Rhett decided to steer clear of the crowd. They seemed to have matters well in hand without him.

As he rested, he heard the buckskin mare he'd seen off and on during the day in the adjoining field. Her rounded belly indicated that she would foal in a few weeks. She must be something special, he reasoned, since she shared the pasture with no other horses. Her wide shoulders gave her an aura of power when compared to her sleek neck and small head. And her coloring was beautiful—the black mane, tail and hooves contrasted with her tan body.

After rising, Rhett climbed between the barbed wire to get a closer look.

The moment he stepped into the pasture, her head shot up. He stopped, merely watching her. Several times, she snorted at him and pawed the ground in warning. Stifling a smile, he copied her movements, which caused her to stiffen in surprise. He grinned.

You're not intimidating me.

Tossing her head, she chuffed. He mirrored her motions and stepped closer. Each time she challenged him, he mimicked her and moved nearer until he was within two arm's lengths. Then he waited.

She was both curious and cautious. Several times, she stretched her head toward him. Rhett maintained his relaxed, confident stance. Slowly, he raised his hand.

Would she allow his touch? One minute, she stood rigid, ears and eyes fixed on him, the next she wheeled away from him with an indignant squeal. He chuckled as she bucked as though reveling in rebellion and freedom.

"This won't be the last you see of me." He spoke more to himself than the mare. In truth, the challenge of taming her thrilled him. She had spirit, but was not mean. The look in her eyes proved she was intelligent. As he watched her prance around the pasture—showing off—he grinned. Horses were sociable creatures. Intelligent ones craved friends.

Me.

This mare needed gentling. Perhaps—the thought ran through his head—Ellie would someday ride the horse. What a sight the pair would be with her fair hair and the mare's dark mane. No doubt Marshall intended to train the horse, so Rhett wouldn't interfere with that. He would merely befriend her.

After pushing himself between the barbed-wire fencing, he picked up his shovel. For the first time in years he felt like whistling. No doubt his friend Pete would chide him for his efforts, but Rhett indulged himself with a few bars of "Billy Boy."

"Where'd that chucklehead get to?" An irritated voice rose to the rafters, rousing Rhett from a doze.

He took care to make no noise as he rolled over and confirmed that Bartow was the speaker. A few seconds later, footsteps tromped out of the shed.

"I thought you said he was in there." The foreman's voice rose from outside.

"Guess he left," answered another man. "But I didn't see where he went. Maybe he…"

The voices faded along with the men's footsteps.

Rhett considered his options. Reveal his location and he might incur less wrath. But instinct told him to keep his sleeping spot secret for now. Even if it annoyed the foreman.

What did Bartow want? Rhett had finished the day's work, so why the exasperation?

When he'd finished his task, the men had still been eating, and Rhett had decided it best to lay low for a while. Get his meal later. But while he'd waited, he had fallen asleep. From the pooling shadows, he determined his nap had lasted no more than a half hour.

In seconds, Rhett shimmied down to the ground and peered between the slatted boards. The two men were no longer visible. He ducked out the back, then made his way to the house, keeping out of sight as much as possible. His stomach grumbled while his stiff muscles howled in protest. As he'd done the night before, he approached the door with caution. This time, no one was inside the main room and the door to Ellie's room remained closed. He dared not creep closer to find out if she was inside. A generous plate of food sat on the sideboard. His? Ignoring the old woman's instructions from the night before, he grabbed the tin and headed outside.

He stood at the side of the building, wolfing down the meal. Only the dogs seemed to notice him. Postures wary, they came within a couple yards. Keeping his body relaxed, Rhett tossed the two a few morsels. They pounced on the food, then waited for more, still maintaining their distance. When he ignored them, they sat on their haunches and watched his every move. Tongues lolling, they salivated as he finished his meal.

Smart dogs, smart horses.

They weren't quick to give their trust, proving that they'd endured a fair share of neglect. The challenge of befriending not only them, but the mare, piqued his interest. Someday their friendship might prove beneficial.

Rhett wiped his hands on the grass then dumped scraps off the tin plate and onto the ground. As he walked back toward the porch, he glanced over his shoulder. The dogs pounced on the leftovers, but they ignored him. Good. Already they'd lost some of their wariness. After washing the plate at the pump, he replaced it, then went back out.

As soon as he emerged from the main house, Bartow and another man stalked in his direction. Obviously heading for him.

Rhett descended the steps and waited.

The foreman jabbed his finger at Rhett. "Where've you been?"

A rhetorical question? Bartow must have seen him go into the house. When the foreman's glower deepened, he answered, "Eating supper."

"I know *that*. I meant before now."

Rhett waved to the fence posts behind him. "Digging holes." He pointed to the man beside the foreman. McCoy? "Like this man instructed."

"Boss, I told him to do at least ten holes," the speaker interjected. "He did eighteen."

Bartow turned on him. "I don't care how many." He swiveled back to Rhett. "When you finish one task, don't assume you're done for the day."

"Very well." Rhett spread his hands. "What do you wish me to do now?"

The foreman straightened his shoulders with a jerk. "Nothing. I…" His jaws moved like he had put something bad-tasting in his mouth. "Don't do it again." Without another word, he stomped off.

McCoy remained behind, face twisted with indecision. "The boss likes to…" He jammed one hand in his pocket, but apparently decided not to finish his thought. "We need new fence posts to replace the old ones in that pasture, but first on the south side." He pointed to where Rhett had already started. "Just keep working on it until I say otherwise."

"Be glad to. How soon would you like the whole job finished?"

"Uh…" The man shrugged. "Say by Tuesday."

"Very well." That would be plenty of time for Rhett to not only place the posts, but work with the mare and dogs.

"Okay, then." McCoy turned on his heel.

Rhett stared after him before walking in the opposite direction. More than ever, he planned to keep out of the men's sight when he wasn't working. Whatever McCoy planned to say obviously had something to do with Bartow keeping tabs on everyone at all times.

Somehow, Rhett suspected it had to do with more than his being a foreman.

Chapter Six

"Washday, miss." Mrs. Johnson tapped on the open bedroom door as Ellie sat at her desk.

She had been up earlier than usual that morning, knowing that the housekeeper planned to do laundry that day. However, she wanted to finish writing a list of needed medical supplies while it was fresh in her mind. "Thank you. I'll be done momentarily."

Mrs. Johnson rested a hand on the doorjamb. "Could I ask you to bring your things outside? My sister's wanting my help."

"I'd be glad to."

The housekeeper set an empty basket at the foot of the bed before bustling away.

After a few minutes, Ellie rose. As she gathered her linens, her mind kept returning to the sheet of paper on her desk. She jotted down a few more items. Cookie planned to take a trip to Casper soon and promised to pick up anything she requested. She needed to replace the items that had been lost or ruined on the trip out west.

When ready, she carried the basket through the great room, but paused at the window to view the scene outside.

A woman, who was presumably Mrs. Johnson's sister, appeared to be deep in conversation with Rhett.

Several things struck Ellie. The woman, who was much younger than Mrs. Johnson, seemed to know Rhett. The woman's hair was a burnished brown, pinned into a thick bun. Eyes alight, she kept touching Rhett's arm in a familiar way. What were they talking about?

From where Ellie stood, she couldn't see his face. He nodded a few times as the woman spoke. Mrs. Johnson hurried past them but paused and turned when her sister called out to her. Several minutes passed as the three conversed, then Mrs. Johnson went on her way.

Ellie knew she should carry the basket outside, but she hesitated to intrude upon their conversation.

Finally, Rhett walked back across the yard while the woman continued to watch him.

An odd feeling rose in Ellie. She realized that she did not like the idea of another woman enjoying what appeared to be the same camaraderie she and Rhett had shared. Was this envy?

A slightly out-of-breath Mrs. Johnson entered the house, startling her.

"Ah, there ya are, miss. I thought you'd forgotten."

"Oh, I'm sorry."

"I could see you were busy with your writing." Mrs. Johnson reached for the basket. "I'll take it."

"Tell me, is that your sister?" With a tilt of her head, Ellie indicated the woman outside.

"Yes. Although really a half sister. I was nearly all growed when Alice was born." The housekeeper moved to go outside, but Ellie held up a hand to stop her.

"It seems she knows Rhett. I saw them speaking."

The woman's expression changed ever so slightly

and her shoulders squared. "They do, miss." Her lips pursed as she studied Ellie.

The seconds ticked by as the woman did nothing but scrutinize her.

Ellie's face felt singed like she'd been out in the sun too long. "I—I was just curious."

She expected the housekeeper to hurry out the door, but the woman continued to remain silent. Making up her mind about something, she set the basket of laundry on the floor.

"Pert near three years ago, Rhett came across Alice's husband. He was in a bad way. Mauled by a bear. Would've died if Rhett hadn't gotten him back home safe. From all accounts, the soldiers Rhett was working for as a scout were pretty mad. Felt like he was wasting their time. But my Alice will never forget his kindness."

And neither will you. That seemed obvious from the intensity with which Mrs. Johnson spoke. And that would explain the young woman's kindly expression as she'd talked to Rhett. Naturally, she would be grateful.

Ellie spoke slowly. "Thank you for telling me."

"One more thing, miss. If'n you ever hear trash talk about Rhett, don't believe it." Mrs. Johnson picked up the linen basket, then slowly straightened. "He's a rare man, that one."

After a single nod, she headed out the door.

Pondering the housekeeper's words, she slowly exhaled. That was the most Mrs. Johnson had said since her arrival. Ellie returned to her room and the list on her desk, but her thoughts kept returning to their conversation.

What little she knew about Rhett intrigued her, but she sensed there was more to him than she imagined. A rare man? She was beginning to believe that.

But what surprised her the most was her strong re-action when she'd seen Alice and Rhett talking. Had Ellie really been jealous?

If I don't do something soon, I'm going to scream.

Tired of her afternoon nap, Ellie thumped her pillow. She felt all she'd done was rearrange her possessions, then wander about the house and the yard. Mrs. Johnson and her sister had been busy with the wash, and they'd made it clear she was in their way when she had tried to help. In the middle of that hubbub, Uncle Will had rushed off once more to take care of some business.

That meant she was again on her own.

Her eyes lit on the small carved figurine of a horse her uncle had given to her when she was a child, and then her mother's Bible. Now that she had been at the ranch nearly a week, she was ready to get on with her life. Apparently her uncle wasn't going to help. His rid-ing off to take care of who-knew-what seemed to indi-cate that he had an inflexible schedule and a plan that didn't include her.

"So what does he expect me to do all day?" She glared at the rough wood ceiling. "Sit around and cro-chet?"

She wanted to tend to the cowboys' wounds, but all of them seemed to prefer Cookie. No one would tell her how Matt's burn was healing. The three men that she had spoken to about the cuts on their hands avoided her questions. Cookie finally pulled her aside and told her in no uncertain terms that he would ask for her help if he needed it.

That seemed to end that—at least until Ellie could make her case to her uncle. But that could not happen until he stayed around the ranch long enough for them to talk.

After rising, she smoothed the blankets on the bed. For the third time that day, she rearranged the pillows.

Apparently it was up to her to find her own place and purpose on the ranch.

Ellie studied the Bible on the desk. The first challenge would be church. If Uncle Will refused to accompany her, then she would go without him. Unfortunately, taking the wagon and driving it herself would be impossible. Her father had taught her many things, but hitching up horses and driving them wasn't one of them. Servants had always taken care of that.

But the idea of *not* going to church appalled her. It was her Christian duty to be a good example not only to her uncle, but to all the ranch hands. A week ago, she had not been able to attend, but that was because she was still on the road. Now that she was settled, she had no excuses not to.

Should she ask Guy to drive her as Uncle Will had suggested? She didn't relish the idea of spending hours alone with the foreman to and from town. As she fingered the Bible's embossed leather cover, she determined to put aside personal preferences.

As soon as Ellie heard the noise of supper being prepared, she flung open her bedroom door and stalked out. Mrs. Johnson glanced up before continuing with her task of arranging tin plates and cups on the table.

Ellie watched for a moment. "Can I do that?"

The frown the woman cast her way broadcasted a definitive "Stay out of my way." But her words were kinder. "No thanks, miss."

She stepped to one side as Mrs. Johnson made her way around the table. When Cookie hustled in from the side door with a steaming kettle, Ellie moved to help him.

"I got this." He bent from the weight of the cauldron-sized pot, struggling to place it on the sideboard. "Ya don't wanna get burned."

True. He had wrapped a thick cloth around the pot's handle and clutched it with gnarly fingers. Still, Ellie clenched her hands to keep herself from jumping in to help.

When he began to dish the stew into a bowl, she reached for the spoon. "I can do that. If you like." Without pausing, Cookie shook his head.

"Oh, miss, you don't want to spoil your dress." Mrs. Johnson spoke from behind her. Before Ellie could answer, the woman grabbed the filled bowl.

Making a small sound of frustration, Ellie backed away. In no time, the gray-haired couple had everything ready. Two large tureens of stew, along with several loaves of bread, sat on the table. An assortment of condiments also waited. Ellie studied the Johnsons as they glanced back at her. Clearly they were uncomfortable with her desire to pitch in.

Obviously no helping with food preparation and service.

"If ya like, miss, you can call the men to supper." Cookie held out a clean ladle.

Well, that was something.

Squelching a sigh, she took it and walked out to the porch where the large triangle hung. With more confidence than she felt, she used the utensil as she had seen him, clattering it around the inside of the heavy metal. The clanging was loud enough to alert anyone in the immediate vicinity that food was ready. Within minutes, men appeared from all over the yard, responding to the call.

Fixing a smile on her face, Ellie nodded as they streamed by. As Guy came up the steps, she held up her palm. "A moment, please."

He didn't bother to hide his smirk. "Sure thing, Ellie."

As the men passed, several grinned. One snickered.

She waited until all of them entered the house before she spoke. Drawing in a slow breath, she drew herself up. "I was wondering…" She chewed the inside of her lower lip, trying to force herself to ask him to drive her to church. Surely she could tolerate a few hours of Guy's company.

A ranch hand, trotting across the yard, distracted her. At first, she thought it was Rhett, but she was wrong.

"You was wondering…?" Guy prodded. Resting a hand on the porch column, he leaned closer.

She opened her mouth, but the words stuck in her throat.

The latecomer leaped up the stairs, two at a time, but came to an abrupt halt when he caught sight of them. Confusion transformed into a knowing grin.

With one jerk of his head, Guy indicated he should go inside.

The man complied, a stupid grin plastering his lips.

Guy turned back to her, eyes widening. "Yes?"

"I…" Ellie cleared her throat. Impossible to ask him! She could not abide the idea of riding alone with him all the way to Casper. "I was wondering. Since you're the foreman, you would know—why don't *all* the workers come when the dinner bell rings?"

"Huh?" He straightened, pushing the brim of his hat back.

She stared down at her hands, clenched against her

abdomen. "I noticed Mr. Callaway has not been present for any of the meals. Do you know why?" She again looked up at Guy.

His lips pursed and eyebrows clashed together. "I…" He shrugged. "I guess he don't care to join us."

"Is that normal? I mean, Cookie and Mrs. Johnson obviously are busy with preparation and serving, but do any of the other men eat at different times?"

He shrugged again.

Unwilling to single Rhett out as the sole purpose of their conversation, Ellie pressed on. "Which leads me to my next question. Do you know how Matt is doing?"

"Matt…?"

"The young man. With the blacksmith."

"Think he's doing okay." Guy scratched his neck. "He don't live here. He's just an apprentice."

Ellie inserted a level of sternness into her tone. "Please find out. And let me know."

The foreman continued to squint at her. "Yes, ma'am."

As he remained unmoving before her, she held out her hand to indicate the open doorway. "Go eat. Before your food gets cold."

"Sure." He nodded. "Uh, thanks." Without another word, he wandered into the house.

Ellie remained outside, blowing out a breath of relief. And a small sense of victory. She strolled along the porch to the other side of the house and perched on the bench. There. She'd let Guy know she would follow up on any injuries that happened on the ranch. However, she had not yet settled how she was going to get to town. Or church.

Somehow she knew that if she let this matter slide tomorrow, the situation would only grow more difficult to resolve the next time.

* * *

Muscles aching, Rhett reclined on his sleeping spot in the rafters. His stomach complained about his missing supper. Dusk had fallen, but he didn't feel like climbing down for food. Perhaps he had pushed himself too hard in his zeal to prove what a fine worker he was. Now he was paying for it. Not only was his body sore, but his hands were blistered and his feet ached from all the shoveling.

At least he could rest on the morrow. As the men had quit the house after supper, they chatted about their plans for the evening as well as their excitement about sleeping in. Some had ridden off already, no doubt on their way to Casper to spend their hard-earned money.

Rhett closed his eyes. What would he do on his day off? He pictured the nearby mountains. Perhaps there would be an appropriate place to worship. His horse needed a good stretch of the legs, and he wouldn't mind getting back into the saddle. Yes, that's what he would do.

As he dozed, the squeaking shed door startled him into wakefulness. Stealthy footsteps entered below. Rhett froze, listening.

"I know you're somewhere around and you can hear me." The housekeeper's voice pierced the shadowy shed. "Guy Bartow is a sneaky varmint. And I know he told you not to come up to the house during meals. So here's what me and Cookie decided. You can go into the kitchen lean-to anytime you want. Use the back door an' help yourself to anything in there or the root cellar."

Material rustled as though she was preparing to leave.

Without moving, Rhett spoke. "Thank you."

The footsteps paused, then the door creaked shut.

He waited a little while, then clambered down. Mrs.

Johnson's permission would simplify his life considerably. At the mention of food, his stomach began to leap in anticipation. He made his way across the yard in the dark, then through the door leading into the lean-to. As promised, a bounty awaited. Careful not to make a mess, Rhett helped himself to beans, ham, bread and an opened jar of canned peaches. After he finished, he found a bucket of water and washed the plate and utensils he'd used. He was about to depart when the sound of horse hooves caught his ear.

Hand on the latch, he waited for the rider to depart. After listening more closely, he realized that someone was coming into the ranch yard, not leaving. Several horses nickered. He detected Marshall's and Bartow's voices. As they were talking, a third speaker joined them. Ellie.

Trapped, he hunkered down to wait. With them in the yard, they would see him if he exited the lean-to. He didn't want to jeopardize the Johnsons' generosity or cause any trouble. An interminable amount of time passed until footsteps moved inside the house. He was about to escape when he heard Ellie.

"What do you have against church?" Her voice drifted from the next room. "Or is it God you have a problem with?"

Unable to leave, Rhett flattened himself against one wall.

"My beliefs are mine," her uncle answered. "You don't need to try'n fix 'em."

"I'm not." She sighed. "I thought we were family. And families go to church together."

Marshall snorted.

"Would you at least consider it?" Ellie's wistful tone tugged at Rhett's heart. "Especially since this is my first Sunday here and—"

"There's nothing more to talk about," her uncle interrupted in a hard voice. "Got it?"

Again she sighed, the sound full of more sorrow than exasperation.

"Remember Chicago?" She paused, seeming to wait for a response. "When you came to visit, you always went with Mama and me."

"That was then, this is now."

"But…" Again, she paused, her voice quavering. "Going to church is—"

"This discussion is over. And my answer is still no." Silence filled the house. "I don't want to hear about it again."

Heavy boots stomped across the room. Marshall's steps faded down the stairs.

Time to leave.

Rhett waited a moment longer, then reached for the exterior door. An odd sound made him freeze. Was Ellie crying? He remained listening, undecided. To go into the next room would be to betray that he had overheard their conversation. Besides, she might not want his advice or comfort. After slipping out the door, he latched it as quietly as possible.

Evening enveloped the ranch, yet enough light remained to expose Rhett. Across the yard, Bartow and another man stood, deep in conversation. Going back to the shed that way would be impossible. Rhett edged along the side of house, careful to not draw attention as he moved away from the men. Not until he reached the back of the house did he draw a breath of relief. Here he could wait until night fully fell. In the cover of dark he could slip past the men.

He tensed at a sound—a stealthy step on the porch

that encircled the house on three sides. He crouched by the raised porch, listening.

"I don't see why…"

A whisper reached his ears. Who was that? And who were they talking to? He heard only one set of footsteps.

"Stupid, stubborn." A sharp sniff followed the words. "Why am I even here if…?"

Understanding dawned. Ellie was talking to herself.

With care, he rose to peer through the porch railing.

The frill of her skirt was about eye level. Head lowered, she paced back and forth as she muttered. Her fists clenched, one thumping against her skirt as she walked.

Mild amusement turned to concern. She obviously was in distress. About her uncle? She sounded like she wanted to talk to someone. Why not God?

Ellie stopped, looking toward the distant mountain range. "If he won't, then what?" With her silhouette outlined against the dusky sky, she swiped fingers across her eyes.

"Forgive the intrusion," he said softly before he had the sense to remain quiet.

With a gasp, she whirled.

"It's me. Rhett." Spreading his hands in what he hoped was a disarming gesture, he moved closer. "I'm sorry if I startled you."

Clasped together, her fists pressed against her heart. She merely gaped at him.

Several feet from the porch, he paused. "I couldn't help but hear. Is something wrong?"

"Where did you come from?"

He hesitated to tell her but needed to explain his presence somehow. "I was getting supper. When I heard you talking, I…"

Her hands slowly relaxed to her sides. Enough light

from the rising moon showed her mouth open, then close. Like she wanted to ask him a question?

"What is it?" Keeping his voice soft, he stepped closer. "What has so distressed you?"

She stared at him another few seconds before her head suddenly ducked. "Everything." A sniff followed. She dabbed at tears on her cheeks.

He knew what he should say—what his mother taught him. He should apologize for intruding on her privacy and excuse himself. However, his feet felt weighted, as though caked with mud. If Ellie had been praying, that would be one thing. But she sounded so forlorn, like she could confide in no one—not even God. Rhett couldn't abandon her when she needed someone to talk to.

Moving slowly, he gripped the railing's vertical slats and looked up at her. "Anything in particular?"

Tears darkened her lashes while a shiny streak marred one delicate cheek. She studied him as though assessing his trustworthiness.

He remained unmoving, praying she would see that he would never betray her confidence. "Tell me."

She looked at her hands that twisted together. "Nothing's as I expected." Though she spoke in a soft voice, he detected her dejection. "Not the ranch. Not my life. Not—not my uncle." She gestured toward the house.

He waited for her to go on. When she didn't, he prodded, "How so?"

"It's silly, I know, but I thought things with Uncle Will would be like they were in Chicago, when he visited. He was so loving. And kind. He promised so much in his letters."

Gripping the railing, Rhett pulled himself up and

balanced opposite Ellie. "And he's not keeping those promises?"

"No." She shook her head. "He's different. He used to be so easy to talk to. But now, he won't even listen to me."

Several reasons why popped into Rhett's head, but he kept his mouth shut. He'd heard the rumors about Will Marshall, about the coldhearted businessman who let nothing stand in his way. His name was known from Casper to Denver and beyond. But such information wouldn't comfort Ellie, only distress her.

"I'm sorry." What else could he say?

The floodgates seemed to open as her shoulders suddenly relaxed. "I don't know why he…well, for instance, his attitude about you. I don't understand why he is so irrational. If I told him how kind and helpful you were after the accident, I'm not sure he would believe me."

"You've no need to correct his thinking." Rhett straddled the railing, then swung his leg over to her side. "I don't want to be the reason you two argue."

"But, don't you see, that's the trouble." She stepped closer. "There shouldn't be any arguments. When I asked him to hire you, he shouldn't require reasons. My word should be enough. But it wasn't. And that's what hurts." Her voice cracked.

Having no thought but to comfort her, he dared to take her slim hand between his. Ellie's breath caught, but she didn't pull away. Remaining mute, he allowed her to cry. Silent, painful tears slipped down her cheeks. While he waited, an answer came to him.

She needs a friend.

She needed someone who didn't take from her but gave. Considering his parentage, the difference in their social standing and their present circumstances, he had nothing to offer but friendship.

"I cannot change your situation," he said simply. "But I know One who can."

A small hiccup escaped her. "Who?"

"Our Father God."

She jerked her hand away. Of all possible reactions, he hadn't expected that.

"Don't you believe He can?" Rhett questioned.

"I…" She shrugged. "Why would He? Besides, my feelings aren't important."

"They are to Him because *you* are. He cares for you, therefore He cares for what concerns you."

Ellie rubbed her upper arms as though struggling to believe his words.

"If you won't pray," he said as he stepped closer to emphasize his words, "then allow me the privilege."

Her head moved slowly back and forth as though in disbelief. "You've been nothing but mistreated since your arrival. Why would you concern yourself with me and my uncle?"

Because I care for you.

The answer hit him so hard that he nearly confessed it aloud. He opened his mouth to tell her, but clamped it shut.

They stood a mere foot from each other. The soft light of the moon caressed her face as a light breeze stirred her hair. He watched as realization dawned in her widening eyes. Everything in him wanted to kneel before her, take her delicate hand and pledge loyalty.

He couldn't. Not yet. He must prove himself a faithful friend first.

Steeling himself, he stepped back. "I promise you, Ellie, I'll pray for you and your uncle. That he will cherish you. That he will see—and value—all that you are."

With a small nod, he turned and leaped over the railing and onto the ground.

"Wait."

Her soft cry stopped him. He looked up to see her leaning over the railing, her golden hair spilling over her shoulders.

"Thank you." A tremulous smile rested on her lips.

He bowed as his mentor had once demonstrated, with a grand flourish.

Her smile broadened.

He took another step back and prepared to wish her good-night when she said, "I need a favor."

"Anything."

"I want to go to church tomorrow. But I have no one to take me—no one I'm comfortable asking, anyway." She made a small sound of impatience. "Could you drive me? We'll need to leave before anyone else is up."

He didn't understand her desire for secrecy but agreed anyway. "I'll be ready before dawn."

"I suppose that's early enough. I don't know when the service starts."

"Then we'll certainly arrive on time." He knew the schedules of many Cheyenne churches, but not of those in Casper. His stagecoach job had always managed to interfere with Sunday worship when he passed through this part of the territory. "May I borrow your uncle's wagon? I don't want there to be any misunderstanding."

She straightened. "*I'm* borrowing it. That will not be an issue."

"Then I'll see you in the morning." He managed to speak softly though his heart hammered in anticipation. Before he said something stupid, he slipped away into the night.

Chapter Seven

In the morning, Ellie felt like a fugitive as she slipped from the house. Rhett was already waiting in the yard. Without a word, he handed her up into the wagon. Fingers on the harness, he led his appaloosa so that the wagon wouldn't make any undue noise. Once they cleared the yard, Rhett climbed beside her and clicked for his horse to go.

Dawn was just breaking. After they were well away from the ranch and into the hills, Ellie peered over her shoulder at the scene behind them. Smoke began to rise from the chimney of the cooking lean-to, proving that Cookie and Mrs. Johnson were now up. Early-morning birds chirped in glee over the new day while the rustling in the nearby brush proved that creatures were hunting for their breakfast. The *clop-clop* of the horse's hooves was the only other sound she heard. The crisp smell of pine warmed the air as streaks of light streamed through the trees.

Embarrassed about her behavior the night before, Ellie kept turning her gaze everywhere but to the silent man beside her. Most times, her eyes rested on her gloved hands, clenched in her lap. She smoothed her gown and shifted in the seat, but couldn't find any words. What could she say? She cast a sideways look at Rhett, but he seemed content with the quiet. With his gaze fixed on the road ahead, he acted like nothing unusual had happened between them.

In truth, she didn't understand last night's exchange. One moment she'd been crying, then Rhett appeared out of the darkness. Before she knew what was what, he was holding her hand. However, he had treated her with concern and respect. Some men, including her own father, were kind to her only when they wanted something. Not Rhett.

Ellie cast a glance at him again. What sort of man was he?

A better man than any I've met. Or known.

Mrs. Johnson had called Rhett a rare man. More and more often, he proved this to be true.

When one corner of his lips curled upward, she realized she'd been staring at him. Turning away, she hid her heated cheeks by pretending to study the scenery. She tucked her hair into her bonnet to shield her face with one hand.

Why was she always gaping at him?

True, he was handsome. Despite his rough life, he always appeared well-groomed. He needed no padding under his jacket to build up his shoulders like the dandies who had primped and pranced about her in Chicago. Her father had encouraged their attentions, but only because he seemed to view the number of suitors as a reflection of his own importance. Now Ellie understood he never intended to marry her off because he needed her to help with his failing medical practice.

After Father died and creditors revealed the depth of his debts, all her admirers melted away. She sighed, pitying her father for throwing away his giftedness as a doctor. His skill was unparalleled.

Ellie's gaze strayed to Rhett's muscled hands as he guided his horse. She recalled the feel of his strong fingers, the skin roughened by work. Father's delicate hands were as soft as hers, yet his heart was hard as flint. Rhett's character seemed to be reflected by his hands—strength tempered by gentleness.

As she studied them, she caught a glimpse of his raw palms.

"Your hands." She straightened with a jerk. "What happened?"

He glanced at her then his blistered skin. "Too many fence posts."

"Don't you own any gloves?"

His grin grew bemused. "I've never needed any before now."

"But…" She tapped his wrist. "Let me see."

He clutched the reins with one hand, then showed her his other.

Taking care not to open his hand too far, she turned it palm up and examined the skin. "If you don't care for these sores, they'll fester. I can't imagine what pain you'd be in then." She gingerly fingered the hard edge of a blister that had broken open and dried. "You can't dig any more holes until these heal."

He pulled away to grasp the reins with both hands. "They must heal by tomorrow."

Making a sound of frustration, she glared at him. Then she considered. Of course he was right. Minor injuries like blisters were no excuse not to work. If she said anything to Uncle Will or Guy, it would only make matters worse. "When we get back to the ranch, I need to put some salve on them."

He appeared as though he would refuse, but finally answered with, "As you wish."

Lifting her chin, she determined to see her plan through. "All right then."

She would provide medical care to Rhett. Perhaps the others would see what she was capable of and give her a chance.

As they traveled, she reflected that this trip to town was pleasant compared to the one with Guy. Several times, Rhett pointed out features of the landscape or the hiding spots of various creatures. The wagon climbed in elevation as they wended their way through rocky foothills. Beyond them lay the town of Casper.

As they crested the hill and headed down the other side, they again met towering pines. For some reason, Rhett slowed the wagon, then stopped.

Ellie studied him. "What are—?"

"Shh." He held up his hand, staring hard toward the trees.

Several seconds ticked by as she watched him. Had he seen a bear? Or a wolf? After putting a finger to his lips, Rhett slowly pointed. Scarcely daring to breathe, Ellie turned in her seat.

He leaned closer to whisper, "Be patient."

Squinting into the dusky tree line, she saw nothing at first. Finally, the movement of a deer's twitching ear caught her attention. Ellie spotted the doe's form and large eyes staring their direction. Seconds later, a spindle-legged fawn appeared from between the trees to stand beside its mother. Ellie must have squeaked in pleasure because they suddenly bounded off.

"How did you know?" She turned to Rhett.

He grinned. "If you know where to look, you can see much."

Perhaps it was his nearness or the way his blue eyes gleamed, but Ellie felt an unexplainable rush of heat to her cheeks.

"Thank you." She looked back at where the deer and fawn had been, but they were long gone.

After Rhett clicked to his horse, they continued on their journey.

One question begged to be answered—why did this man constantly unsettle her? But the answer to that question puzzled her more. If he perplexed her, why did she feel more comfortable with him than with any man she'd ever met?

Rhett stood in the back of the church, ready to slip out the door at a moment's notice. Quite a number of folks filled the tiny, makeshift building, ranging from farmers to ranchers. Some appeared to be railroad workers. From the number of buggies and wagons outside, people had gathered from all over the area. Wouldn't be long before the burgeoning population built a real church building. The region promised to explode in growth, especially when the railroad reached Casper. Some estimated that would happen in the next couple months.

"Pardon." A man squeezed by Rhett as he remained by the door. Many more filed past him to stand by the back wall.

He was glad Ellie hadn't insisted he join her up front. Several young women had greeted her, squealing with excitement after she introduced herself and told them she was settling in the area. A few gushed over her elegant bonnet and her gray gown with its fine lace. Only the repeated clearing of throats from the more mature in nearby seats calmed the commotion.

Finally everyone settled and the singing began. Rhett found his throat tightening at the words of the cherished hymns. But when the congregation starting singing "And Can It Be?" his eyes filled with tears.

Several beloved lines resounded in his spirit—"My chains fell off, my heart was free, I rose, went forth, and followed Thee."

This song had been Mr. Callaway's favorite. But more importantly, these were the words that had released Rhett himself from the shackles of hate and anger after years of hiding from outlaw relatives.

As the congregation sang all the stanzas, Rhett's chest burned until he felt like he couldn't breathe. Once again he was humbled by the change God had wrought in his heart. What might his life have been like if his mother hadn't smuggled him away?

The answer was simple. By now, he'd be in prison or hanged like the other members of the Walker Gang.

Emotion overwhelmed Rhett. He stumbled out the door and sought a quiet spot to fall to his knees. After a time, he gained control of himself. As promised, he prayed for Ellie and her uncle. Hatred from some unknown source shackled Will Marshall's heart. What it could be, Rhett didn't know.

When he finished his prayers, he debated going back inside but disliked the idea of disturbing the parishioners. Instead, he made his way down the quiet street. It didn't take long to reach the livery. He had another promise to fulfill—find out what had happened to the stagecoach horse Ellie had stitched up.

The lone stable lad welcomed him. Rhett recognized him as the one who worked only Sundays.

"Ira." He greeted him with a nod.

The boy stopped brushing a mare and stepped from the stall. "What can I do for ya, Mr. Rhett?"

He grinned at the "mister" part. This lad was the only one who referred to him that way. "A few days back, did Pete bring a horse here?"

"Stagecoach Pete?"

"The same."

"Yeah, he's out back. The horse, I mean." The boy grinned. "I ain't seen him yet. Got some fancy gentleman's horses to care for first. You're welcome to go look, if'n ya want."

"Obliged." Rhett went out to the back pen.

When he saw the gelding, his heart sank. Neglect marked the animal, not only in his unkempt coat, but in his listless look. No doubt the stagecoach company hadn't bothered to decide the horse's fate—they were just waiting for nature to take its course.

"Hey." Rhett spoke softly as he entered the pen.

The gelding didn't bother to raise his head.

He swiveled toward Ira, who stood in the doorway. "Get me a brush and a rope." If Ellie saw the horse in this condition, her heart would break.

The gelding didn't move as Rhett removed the clods of mud from his belly, then worked on his shoulder and back. As the day warmed, he shrugged out of his jacket. He kept brushing, losing track of time as he sought to make the horse as presentable as possible. When he was done, he examined the wound on the leg. It didn't look good, the flesh around the oozing cut appearing inflamed. Someone had already removed the stitches.

If anyone could help this horse, it would be Ellie.

When Rhett led the horse from the pen, the stable boy protested. "I don't think you're allowed to take 'im."

"Pete'll arrange the details to buy him. Can you leave

a message at the hotel? They'll contact him next time he comes through town."

The lad made a face. "Y'sure he'll want *that* horse?"

"It's not for Pete, but Miss Ellie Marshall." Rhett pulled a small coin out of his pocket. "Can you relay the message?"

"Yessir." Ira caught the coin midair. As he returned to his grooming job, he whistled.

Rhett grinned. Amazing what kindness could do when greased with a little money.

As he led the horse through town, he grew aware of the curious stares of the townsfolk. Several were coming from the direction of the church. Was the service over? By the time he reached the building, he saw his guess was correct. A handful of people stood outside, visiting with Ellie, who stood in the center of a group.

As he made his way to the wagon with the gelding, he glanced her direction several times. Her face alit, she chatted with none other than Mrs. Rushton and Pastor Charles. Nicholas played nearby with a couple boys about his age. From the looks of the woman, Mrs. Rushton seemed to have recovered from the bump on her head. The only sign that remained of the accident was a slight discoloration of her forehead and around one eye.

"Thank You, Lord." Rhett breathed a prayer of gratefulness as he tied the gelding to the back of the wagon and tossed his jacket in the back. While he waited for Ellie, he busied himself with the harness. After a few minutes, the sound of swishing silk and the pleasant scent of lavender alerted him that she approached.

"There you are." Her breathless voice greeted him.

He turned, noting the pretty flush on her cheeks and her wide smile.

"I was beginning to wonder if you left me."

"No chance of that." He nodded toward the green-garbed woman who called to her son. "How is Mrs. Rushton?"

"Very well." Ellie pressed one gloved hand to her chest. "I was so worried—" She broke off with a gasp as she caught sight of the gelding. Wide eyes met Rhett's. "You found him. The chestnut."

He merely nodded as he followed her to the back of the wagon.

"There's a good boy." Ellie removed her gloves to stroke the gelding's nose. Her brows pinched together. "What's wrong with him? He's..." She paused as though unable to find the words to describe the horse's apathy.

"Nothing your care won't fix."

Her frown deepened as she tucked her gloves into a pocket. "We should get him back to the ranch."

"I'm ready to leave."

In no time, they were both back in the wagon. Ellie waved to those who called their farewells.

When they were well out of town, Rhett cleared his throat. "You were planning to buy the gelding, right?"

"Yes. I told you I was."

"I wanted to make certain. I told the livery boy that you would see to payment."

"Oh, so you didn't..." Her face colored. "I'm sorry. Had I known, I would've given you money."

"That isn't a problem. Pete will take care of the details and get the gelding for the best price."

"Thank you." She briefly rested her hand on Rhett's forearm. "The horse's in bad shape, isn't he?"

Distracted by the touch of her warm hand, he took a moment to answer. "Yes."

She turned to look behind. "I hope we got to him in time."

As did Rhett. With all his heart, he hoped Ellie's medical knowledge would be enough to save the horse. But the longer her soft hand rested on his forearm, the greater the realization that she would give the horse everything needed—safety, good care and, most important, affection. Her gentle spirit overflowed with love.

He pondered that as they rode while she chatted about the wonderful sermon Pastor Charles had preached. Nodding, Rhett didn't correct her misconception that he had been present for the whole service.

After a few miles, he announced they needed to stop because the gelding had begun to limp. When Ellie insisted on checking the horse, he helped her down from the wagon.

A small furrow appeared between her brows as she patted the horse's neck. Worry billowed around her.

Seeking to distract her, he asked, "What do you plan to call him?"

Ellie's fingers rested on the gelding's shoulder. "I was thinking Tripper. Since he seems to be doing that a lot."

"A good name." He smiled, wishing he could comfort her. "I'm glad…" He paused, mindful of what he was about to say. "I'm glad you'll care for him." He refrained from adding *for the remainder of his life*, knowing that the horse might not live much longer.

"He *will* get better." The determination in Ellie's tight jaw left no doubt that she intended to do all she could to save Tripper.

Rhett gritted his teeth, keeping his pessimism to himself. "And I'll help in any way I can."

Her smile was worth a whole herd of horses.

Later, they again stopped for a rest. Before Rhett could help her, she leaped down. Ellie was glad to escape the wagon and walk around for several minutes. Pausing, she turned toward the sun. She lifted her face, the heat tingling against her skin.

Breathing deeply, she let the peace of the scenery flow through her. This truly was a day of rest, so unlike her Sundays in Chicago where she worried about wearing just the right clothing with just the right accoutrements to impress...

Who were they again? She chuckled to herself when she realized she'd already started to forget their names.

In this so-called uncivilized part of the country, people had greeted her with genuine joy. They seemed less impressed with her frilly gray gown and matching bonnet than with who she was. Some had gushed over all she'd done for Mrs. Rushton, showing admiration for the care she'd provided.

The creak of the wagon distracted Ellie from her thoughts. Rhett retrieved something wrapped in a towel. Bread and cheese? He also pulled out a canteen of water.

She spread her hands. "Where did you get this?"

"I picked it up from the house this morning."

"It must have been early. I didn't hear you."

He smiled with some secret knowledge.

"How'd you know I was hungry?" She laughed as she accepted the food.

"I knew *I* was."

She looked around for somewhere to sit, but the wagon seat didn't look appealing. Neither did the nearby rocks and dirt.

Rhett solved the problem by letting down the wagon's gate. But that presented a new problem—she had no way to climb up.

"Allow me." He had apparently guessed her dilemma.

A moment later, he lifted her and set her on the sturdy backboard.

Ellie gasped, but managed a "Thank you."

Eyes lowered, he released her and stepped back. Everything had happened so quickly that she didn't have time to protest. The thoughts still rumbled—he had no trouble lifting her, yet he had not used the opportunity to become inappropriately suggestive.

Like Guy might have.

As she nibbled on the bread, Rhett stood nearby, viewing the panorama while enjoying his own portion of the meal. As magnificent as the scenery was, her gaze kept returning to him as he ate. When he turned and caught her, she frowned at her piece of cheese.

He stepped closer. "Not to your liking?"

"Oh, no. I was just wondering…" She cast about for something—anything—to say.

"You were wondering…?"

"About…" She pointed to his clothing, stumbling over her words. "Why you dress. Like that." When he didn't answer right away, she added, "If you don't mind my asking."

A small smile pulled one corner of his mouth as he stepped closer. "But if I *did* mind—"

"You don't have to answer."

His grin broadened. "But there's the hitch. It's in the asking, not the answer."

Heat rose to her face at his cryptic reply. Or was it because she was captivated by his brilliant blue eyes? As her pulse began to pound against her throat, she feared he would detect it.

"Because you've asked," he said softly, his face growing solemn, "I'll gladly answer."

But he didn't immediately. Instead, he stared at the sky, then the hazy purple mountain range in the distance.

"A couple years ago, I did some scouting for the military, south of here." He waved his hand in the ranch's direction. "The various peoples we encountered were often put off by uniforms. I found buckskins smoothed down some of the suspicions we aroused by our travels."

"That makes sense."

Scouting? Ellie imagined that was likely in connection with the incident Mrs. Johnson had mentioned concerning her sister's injured husband. However, she didn't want to delve into that subject now.

"Besides, they're comfortable and durable." He grinned as he spoke.

She took a sip of water from the canteen. "I must admit, when I first saw you, I thought you were part of Buffalo Bill's Wild West show."

He chuckled. "My mother once accused me of the same."

"Your mother?" Ellie brushed off her hands. "Does she live around here?"

"No."

When he said nothing more, she pressed. "Where then?"

"Cheyenne."

His clipped answer was followed by a subtle shift in his expression before he turned away. Ellie got the distinct impression that he didn't want to talk about her. That had also happened when she had asked about his family when they were sitting at the campfire. He had been open about his mentor, but not about his mother. Ellie also realized that he never spoke of his father. Why?

Rhett turned back to her. "Did you want more to eat?"

"No, I'm done."

As he packed up the remainder of their food, she studied him. Why was he so reticent? The more he resisted, the more curious she became. She tried a different tack. "I never asked where you grew up."

He kept his eyes averted as he continued to work. "Are you asking now?"

"Yes." As he cast a glance her direction, she managed to keep her expression innocent and open.

"We lived around Cheyenne until I was eight. Then we moved southeast."

"To Colorado? Or Kansas?"

"Both. For a time." Hands at rest, he finally met her gaze.

"Where Mr. Callaway died?"

"That was more Dakota Territory."

She wanted to ask him about his first father, but Rhett's whole demeanor seemed to say, "That is off-limits." Why? What made him so nervous?

Backing away, Rhett peered at the sky. "It's late. I need to return you to the ranch before your uncle worries."

He *needed* to? His choice of words struck her, reminding her that she now lived in a different place where people took the law into their own hands. If her uncle believed for one moment that Rhett had insulted her, he wouldn't hesitate to string up his newest worker on the closest tree.

"Let's hurry then." Without waiting for his help, Ellie leaped down from the back of the wagon. Soon, they were on their way.

But for the remainder of the drive, she couldn't help

but think she knew so little about the man seated next to her. Yes, he was courageous, strong and a hard worker, but what did she really know about him?

What secrets did he carry that he was unwilling—or unable—to share?

Chapter Eight

Rhett proved correct about Uncle Will. Although Ellie had left a note about where she'd gone, her uncle came down the porch steps to meet the wagon with a glower that made her gulp. A half-dozen men followed. From all appearances, her return interrupted a late Sunday dinner.

Yanking a tucked napkin from his shirt, Uncle Will tromped toward them.

She had just begun to speak when his gaze widened.

"What is *that*?" He pointed to the gelding.

"A horse. That I bought." Without Rhett's assistance, Ellie climbed down from the wagon. "He was one of the stagecoach horses that was injured in the—"

"You *paid* for that hack?" Uncle Will's derision appeared to override his earlier irritation.

The crowd in the yard grew.

"Yes." Ellie lifted her chin.

"I hope you gave no more'n two bits. Doubtful he's worth even that."

Out of the corner of her eye, she saw the ranch hands sniggering or elbowing each other. She cleared her throat. "I haven't yet settled on a price."

Uncle Will made a sound of contempt. "Regardless, you've wasted good money."

"Irrelevant." She squared her shoulders. "Besides, it's done. The gelding's mine now."

"I suppose *he* had a hand in this?" Her uncle's head jerked in Rhett's direction.

"No. It was my doing. He followed my orders."

The look her uncle shot at Rhett was pure disgust. "Then he's a bigger fool than I thought."

Something snapped in her. "Rhett can't do anything right in your eyes, can he?"

As soon as she spoke, she regretted her words. How foolish to not only draw attention to him, but stir her uncle's wrath. Especially in front of his men. But she plowed on. "Is this the way you treat all newcomers? Because I haven't been exempt either. Ever since my arrival, you've kept me from doing what I love most— tending to people's needs. And going to church. Or helping in any way. Do you expect me to sit around like a—like a trinket?"

Silence met her rant. But strangely, she felt like a weight had lifted. She had grown weary of being ignored. It felt like a replay of what she'd experienced with her father after Mama passed. He paid attention to her only when he needed her—to help with patients or to pick up after him. Later in his life, she was his living crutch as she put him to bed when he was too drunk.

However, Ellie realized that she should have chosen a better time for this conversation with her uncle. A dozen men crowded around them, eyes fixed on their boss, apparently waiting for his reaction. And from their faces, they expected an explosion of anger.

"I'm sorry." She stepped closer and spoke in a lowered voice. "Please forgive my sharp tongue. I should not have spoken out of turn."

Risking a glance at Uncle Will, she expected any expression but the one she saw. The harsh lines of his face relaxed while a bemused grin twitched under his mustache.

"You sound just like your mother, Adeline." A soft gleam settled in his eyes. "She put me in my place a time or two. And I deserved it."

Ellie snapped her mouth closed, not only to keep herself from speaking, but to hide her shock.

"Well, it's your money. I have no say." Her uncle ran a thumbnail across his jaw. Minutes seemed to tick by while he seemed to ponder what to do. "All right. You want to do some doctoring? Here's your chance. Prove you can keep that horse alive and you'll have my support to treat anyone on the ranch."

Of its own accord, her mouth dropped open again. She hurried to draw herself up and press her case. "I'll need Rhett's help. He's familiar with Tripper. And the horse trusts him." Ellie risked a glance in Rhett's direction to see his reaction. Still seated on the wagon, he stared ahead without moving, like he had turned to stone.

"Tripper, eh?" A snicker escaped Uncle Will. "Apt name. Fine. Put the gelding in the barn. Then you can do what's necessary to nurse him back to health."

She dared to clarify one point, especially in front of Guy and the other ranch hands. "And Rhett can tend to my horse? Anytime necessary?"

Rhett wouldn't abuse the privilege. She was sure of it.

"Let it be so." With a wave, her uncle dismissed

that small point. "Now come inside before dinner gets any colder."

Uncle Will swiveled on his heel and tromped up the steps to the house. Gathering her skirts, Ellie hastened after him. However, when she reached the porch, she stopped to look back at Rhett.

The sun, high in the sky, illuminated his face. He remained unmoving as the men in the yard dispersed. Only when most had disappeared did he click to his horse to head toward the barn. Before he moved past the house, though, he threw a glance her direction.

His wink was all the approval she needed.

"There's a boy. Good boy." Keeping his voice low, Rhett ran his hands over the gelding's neck and shoulder. Tripper was in bad shape, evidenced from his lackluster coat and weight loss. Most alarming was his dull eyes. Like life was not worth living.

"Don't give up." Rhett gently scratched the horse's head. "Your life promises to improve immensely."

The horse appeared not to care.

The barn door, creaking open, warned Rhett that they were no longer alone. Already a few of the ranch hands had come in for a look, as though to gauge the horse's survival chances. However, from the swish of skirts, Rhett ascertained that Ellie was the visitor this time.

"Hello?" Her gentle voice called in the gloom of the building.

Rhett kept his voice low to not spook Tripper. "Here. In the corner stall."

The rustling drew closer. Ellie's lovely brown eyes met his before turning to her horse. Worry wrinkled her brow as she studied him. "I came as quickly as I could."

She took a deep breath, gaze still fixed on the gelding. "Is he really as bad as my uncle paints?"

"Maybe." Rhett clamped his mouth shut, not wanting to promise more than was wise.

"What did they do to you?" she whispered as she stroked the horse's cheek.

"It's what they *didn't* do." When Ellie tilted her head, Rhett went on. "They isolated him, then fed him too little."

Horses needed companionship. Neglect could kill faster than anything else he knew.

For the first time since they'd returned from town, the horse gave a tentative nicker and nosed Ellie. Again, Rhett was struck by God's gift to her. Tripper instinctively knew she was a friend.

"Your touch is medicinal." Rhett hadn't meant to speak aloud, but he wasn't sorry he had. Perhaps in bringing healing to this horse, she would find it for herself. He sensed her deep sorrow, evidenced by her distrust of God's love. Who had wounded her?

Ellie's eyes widened. "I didn't do anything yet."

"Yes, you have." Rhett merely smiled. When her mouth puckered, he added, "You took him from a bad situation and brought him to a place where he knows he's loved."

"Oh, that."

"Don't discount the value of your kindness. It can have an enormous impact on a horse. Or a person."

He had no doubt she knew he referenced himself. As he met and held eye contact with her, a pretty blush rose to her cheeks.

She was the first to look away. "I brought—brought the salve I was talking about earlier. On our ride. To town." She removed the lid from a tin.

A strong scent tickled his nose, overpowering other barn odors. "Smells powerful."

Even Tripper's eyes widened and his nostrils flared.

"Rub the salve into his wound." Ellie nodded toward the horse. "It'll help your hands at the same time."

"Now?"

"Please." Her eyelashes fluttered.

"If you would be so kind as to hold Tripper's head…"

They traded places. As he moved toward the horse's rump, her grip tightened on the halter. Rhett ran his hand along the gelding's ribcage, taking care to move slowly. Just because Ellie was there didn't guarantee the horse would remain calm, especially with the wound appearing so inflamed.

"Easy, boy." With caution, Rhett inched his hand closer. The flesh felt hot.

The gelding visibly shuddered.

"It's okay, Tripper." In a noticeably lowered pitch, Ellie's sweet voice soothed. "We are only trying to help. That salve will feel so good."

As Rhett scooped out a handful, he watched the horse's ears. They would tell him when to proceed.

As expected, Tripper's ears only flicked back for a moment before pointing ahead. His attention seemed riveted on the blonde beauty before him, who stroked his face and murmured soft words. Rhett rubbed the salve on the wound, smiling to himself as he worked. If Ellie did that to him, he would forget everything but her too.

In no time, he finished.

"Put some salve on your other hand," she instructed without looking away from Tripper.

Grinning, Rhett did as she commanded.

"Good boy."

He nearly laughed aloud when he assumed she was talking to him, but no, she appeared to be still talking to Tripper.

She finally turned. "Is there anything else we can do for him?"

"I provided hay and water. But he should have grain to help him recover quicker."

"A regular supply won't be a problem."

He grinned, not doubting it for a minute. Ellie Marshall was a strong-willed and resourceful young woman.

"Isn't that better?" she asked Tripper as she resumed stroking his neck.

Rhett studied his tingling hands. Whatever was in the salve felt good.

"I, uh…" Ellie drew his attention back to her. "I wanted to apologize. For what I said earlier."

He spread his hands. "What do you mean?"

"I shouldn't have pried into your family." She spoke slowly. "I could see that you didn't want to talk. It's a very great fault of mine. Being curious. Sticking my nose where it doesn't belong."

"Friends get to do that."

She blinked. "Friends?"

"Yeah." He screwed the lid back on the tin. "Leastways, I consider you my friend."

Her lips still formed a little O. Then a shy grin softened her mouth. "Thank you."

He studied the metal container, wanting to share more of his life with her. But would she think him impertinent? "I made a promise. To my mother. She asked that I never mention the man who fathered me."

"Then I'm more than sorry for prying."

"I would tell you more. If I could." But even as he spoke, he wondered at his boast.

When will I be able to speak my true name without shame?

But would he want to? The moment he accepted Mr. Callaway's message and felt God's work inside him, Rhett felt as though he passed from death to life. A new life replaced his old.

Much like his name change from Walker to Callaway. He was less the son of Everett Walker and more the adopted child of God.

"It's late." Ellie's soft voice interrupted his thoughts. "Have you eaten yet?"

"No."

She squared her shoulders. "From now on I want to see you at the table. Along with everyone else."

"Not yet."

"Why not? You need sustenance, like everyone else."

He cast about for the right words. "First, let me prove myself. To the men. To your uncle."

"But…" One hand clenched. "It's not right."

"No, but it is wise."

Her chest heaved as though she wanted to continue arguing. But his mind was made up.

Perhaps she saw that. She sighed into the silence.

"Someday," she finally spoke, her voice low and determined, "I promise, you will take a meal in the house. Without fear. Head held high."

Something tightened in the pit of his stomach at the sight of her, eyes blazing, cheeks darkened and mouth set. How he wished her statement would come true.

With that came a desire for her to be seated beside him. He gloried in that beautiful possibility.

Chapter Nine

In the morning, Ellie slept until her usual time. The house sounded empty—the men must have already breakfasted and started the day's work.

Yawning, she considered that she rather liked the quiet, so unlike her mornings in Chicago. Here, no one would be ringing the front bell. No servant would peek in to see if she were awake or enter to rouse her. Someone wouldn't be lurking in the hallway to pounce on her to tell her that her father was already waiting. Or remind her she was already late for breakfast or a dozen appointments.

After stretching, Ellie finally rose for the day.

Her uncle surprised her when she emerged from the room, sitting at the table and frowning over a ledger.

He looked up when she stopped on the threshold. "G'morning."

"Good morning." After shutting her door, she sauntered closer.

As if on cue, Mrs. Johnson appeared with a plate of flapjacks and ham, with a steaming cup of tea.

"Thank you."

The woman merely nodded before disappearing into the kitchen.

Ellie sat where her breakfast waited, uncertain about her uncle's presence. After their showdown the day before, she felt a little hesitant to speak to him. Would he be the amiable man she saw last night at supper? Or the taciturn taskmaster she was more used to?

After bowing her head to pray, she began to eat. He ignored her. As his pencil scratched the paper, she risked a few glances at what he worked on. It appeared to be an accounting. Of the ranch? A few more peeks let her know that he had experienced some losses over the last few years. The recent harsh winter had taken its toll on him like everyone else.

She was just finishing her breakfast when a violent cough took hold of him. Uncle Will retrieved a dark kerchief and covered his mouth until the fit passed. After pocketing the material, he went back to his ledger.

Feigning disinterest, Ellie took a sip of tea. "Does that often happen?"

"My figuring?" He frowned as he bent over the paper, but she wasn't fooled. He only pretended to misunderstand her.

"Your cough."

He scratched some figures before answering. "Comes and goes."

"Hmm." She let it pass, tamping down a growing worry. Would he let her examine him? No. She needed to prove herself with Tripper first. And Ellie would. Then she would attend to her uncle.

"I was wondering." He set down his pencil. "Would you be interested in seeing the ranch? Been meaning to take you."

She sucked in a quick breath. "Today?"

"Yes."

"I'd like that." Ellie smiled. "Very much."

"Good. Got different clothes? Or do ladies back east wear fancy dresses like yours to go riding?"

"I'll change." She rose and smoothed down her skirt. The silk morning gown she wore was utterly unsuitable for horseback.

When she reached her bedroom door, he called, "I'll be in the yard, saddling up a couple horses."

She hurried to change into her riding pants, blouse and jacket. As she studied her boots, hat and gloves, she couldn't help but think how out of place they were compared to western wear. She shrugged. They were all she had. However, she did forego the riding crop.

As she walked across the yard, she couldn't help but notice how the nearby men stopped working to stare. One man called to his companion who nearly toppled a wheelbarrow he was pushing. The tittering got louder by the time she reached her uncle.

When he turned, he nearly leaped back. His gaze rose to the elaborate feathers on her hat, eyes widening like he'd never seen fine-crafted bonnets before. His whistle—somewhere between admiration and derision—went on and on until she felt like her face was on fire.

She planted one fist against her hip. "Okay, say it. The hat's absurd." In Chicago, her bonnet had been quite fashionable seven months before. But here, elaborate accoutrements must appear ridiculous.

His gaze strayed upward again. "We'll stay out of the woods. Don't want you to get caught in the tree branches."

Laughing, she pulled on her gloves.

He stared downward now, frowning over her outfit. "But I'm afraid we don't have a sidesaddle."

"Even though this looks like a skirt, it's not. I can sit astride."

"Good." He turned to adjust the height of the stirrups. "You take this gelding. He's gentle."

She couldn't help but smile at his assumption that because she was dressed in fancy clothing, she couldn't ride. Perhaps she'd get a chance to show off her skills.

They headed out of the yard, men opening the gates for them so they could pass into the fields. Every time they came across the ranch hands, the men would stop their work to gawk. In a scarlet gown, Ellie felt like a cardinal among ravens. Finally she and her uncle reached a vast open range. Following his lead, she pushed her mount into a canter. They paused atop a rise.

The view took her breath away. Waves of grass blew gently in the morning breeze while in the distance, towering mountains appeared hazy gray next to the brilliant blue of the sky. The vast openness of the landscape squeezed down on her, making her feel extremely small. And yet, she felt she could really breathe for the first time ever.

Did you make all this, God? For mankind to enjoy? Including me?

The questions that rose unbidden made her feel as though her soul somehow expanded. This land was so vast and beautiful. Perhaps Rhett was right about God. Did He care for her too?

"I see it affects you like me." Her uncle's quiet voice punctuated the hushed quiet.

"I—I'm..." She couldn't find the words. Her doubts about relocating to the West vanished. This was where she belonged. This was where new life awaited, far from the filth, noise and crowds of a big city. After many minutes, she said, "I understand now why you settled here."

"Yep." His soft smile tugged at her heart.

She stared again at the open range. "Only a crazy person would miss its beauty."

"Ellie," he said after a few moments, "I'm happy you joined me. I wanted so long…" He stopped as though unable to verbalize his thought. "I'm glad you're here."

He looked at her with such tenderness that her eyes stung. A thought struck her she'd never seen that expression on her own father's face. As a matter of fact, for as long as she could remember, he had never really looked at her like she was a person. Even when she cared for him during his drunken stupors. Always derision or—at best—tolerance met her attentions. No matter what she did, she could never win his love.

Something must have changed on her face because her uncle reached across the gap between their horses to touch her arm. "What is it, Sunshine?"

She swallowed the bitter memories and managed to smile. "I'm glad you invited me." She turned her face away to press one gloved fingertip to the corner of her eye.

Uncle Will said nothing in response.

Tightening her grip on the reins, she nodded. "I'm ready to go on if you are."

"Then follow me."

They rode for what felt like hours, but Ellie had already determined she would never tire of the scenery. Every time they crested another hill, the panorama would again render her speechless. She stared in wonder at a herd of deer bounding across the fields as well as the numerous birds they flushed in their passage, squawking in protest. Once they happened upon a bear and her cub to which they gave a wide berth.

"If you ever come riding alone," her uncle cautioned, "make certain you carry a rifle. A knife would be a good idea too."

Though she agreed, she didn't have the heart to tell him she knew far less about weaponry than horses. Perhaps he would consent to teach her?

Finally they came across a vast number of cattle. In the distance, a few men were moving through the herd.

Uncle Will reined in his horse and squinted below. "I wonder why they're out here. I thought they were working the west range today." He leaned one elbow on the saddle horn as they watched. "Looks like Guy and a couple of men...but what are they doing?"

Though Ellie peered below, she knew nothing about cattle operations. From the direction of the ranch, a rider came into view, heading toward Guy. When he reached the foreman, Ellie could see the men stare in their direction after the man pointed at them.

She tightened the tie on her bonnet. "Looks like we've been spotted." Small wonder considering her red garments.

A few minutes later, the rider headed back toward the ranch, but Guy apparently decided to meet them on the hill. While they waited, their horses grazed under the shade of a tree.

When he reached them, Guy squeezed the brim of his hat. "Howdy."

Uncle Will nodded. "What're you doing out here?"

"Checking for unbranded cattle." The foreman shifted in his saddle. "But the reason I rode up here was to tell you that Sugar's not acting right."

"What's wrong?" Her uncle's voice grew tight.

"Not sure. Heard Mack was looking for you. I sent a rider just now to tell him I'd pass on the message."

Uncle Will turned to her. "I'm sorry, Ellie. I need to head back. Guy, could you see her safely to the ranch?"

"Sure thing." One corner of the foreman's mouth twitched.

Without another word, her uncle kicked his horse into a trot, then gallop. Within minutes, his form melded into the landscape.

Ellie stared after him, then fixed her gaze on Guy. "What was that all about?"

"Sugar's his favorite horse. 'Bout due to foal." He thumbed back the brim of his hat.

"Something wrong with her?"

He sat back in his saddle. "Oh, I wouldn't fret."

If the news worried her uncle, then Guy was taking it a little too nonchalantly. "I'd better get back too." She reined her horse to follow her uncle.

Nudging his mount, Guy blocked her. "What's the rush? Ain't it a beautiful day?"

"It is, but I'd like to go with my uncle."

"Why hurry? The ranch ain't going nowhere." His smirk grated on her. "You don't have to either."

She glared at him. "Let me by." Again, she pressed her heels into the horse's side, but Guy blocked her again.

"C'mon, Ellie. You can get off your high horse, so to speak. We're alone. No need for them fancy airs."

"I beg your pardon?"

"Like that." He grinned. "Showin' off with them snazzy words. Cain't say I don't like 'em. But they do give a feller ideas."

She spoke through gritted teeth. "Whatever ideas you may have, Mr. Bartow, are the result of your imagination. Nothing more." Wheeling her horse, she pushed by him before he could block her way again.

Guy yelled, but she kicked her horse into a gallop, heading the direction her uncle had gone. Without checking, she knew the foreman followed. Hunkering down, she pushed her mount harder. On she rode, ignoring his calls.

After a half hour, she slowed and dared to peer over her shoulder. Guy was nowhere in sight.

However, she wasn't certain she was still going in the correct direction. Since the gelding was sweat-soaked, she reined him to a trot, then a walk.

Attempting to cheer herself, she spoke aloud. "I hope I'm not halfway to Cheyenne."

She continued moving ahead, but the ride grew more rough. Grassy plains became rolling hills, which grew rockier. As she paused at the top of a small rugged crest, she untied her bonnet to swipe perspiration from her brow. A gust of wind snatched it from her hand. Yelping, she watched her bonnet roll down a hill and bound away.

"It was worthless anyway," she muttered, justifying her disinclination not to chase after it. Besides, she felt safer atop her horse. A chill—which had nothing to do with the weather—gripped her all of a sudden. The land, which appeared so beautiful while she rode with her uncle, had taken on an ominous air.

Back east, she knew Chicago backward and forward. Wherever she went, buildings and signs could inform her of her location. But out here, only grassy hills and distant mountains met her gaze. She saw no landmarks, nothing familiar.

On she rode, then changed directions when she thought she recognized the landscape. Again Ellie stopped. This couldn't be the right way. Heart hammering, she drew the unmistakable and frightening conclusion.

She was lost.

Rhett straightened to swipe his forehead with his arm. Truth be told, he needed a break from the hard labor of placing posts for the new fencing. As he tamped down dirt, he thanked the Lord that this was the last one. All that remained of this job was to put away tools. For today, anyway.

A commotion in the yard drew his attention. Will Marshall rode in at high speed, then reined sharply. One of the ranch hands came running.

"Take care of my horse." Marshall leaped off, then yelped as he grabbed his leg.

The one he had hurt several days ago.

No doubt, the jump from his horse had not been a good idea. The boss paused to mutter under his breath before limping toward the pasture, the one where the pregnant mare was kept.

Rhett carried the tools back to the shed. Though the afternoon was still young, he was glad he'd finished this task. Shovel there. Pickaxe there. With care, he laid down a pair of worn gloves that had mysteriously appeared in the shed only that morning. Who was his secretive benefactor? Thinking it might be Ellie, he smiled.

He was still inside the shed when raised voices from outside reached him.

"Where's Mack?" Marshall's tone rippled with annoyance.

A low voice replied, words unintelligible.

"Who told him Sugar was about ready to foal?"

Again an indiscernible answer.

Sugar? So that was the name of the beautiful buckskin Rhett had visited several times. Only last night, she had allowed him to approach her and even touch her. With care, he had run his hands across her back and down her legs while she quivered with nervousness. The mare was as high-strung as they came. Because of mishandling? He had no doubt she had learned to mistrust humans.

From the shed's open door, Rhett saw the boss limp into the yard. "I want to know who's been messing with my mare."

Rhett's ears pricked up. Earlier, he had seen some idiot on a horse chase Sugar around the pasture. Rhett did not understand why the man drove her, but it wasn't his place to ask questions. Besides, after a few minutes, the ranch hand left, riding hard to the southeast.

Remaining inside the shed, Rhett continued to listen.

"She's all lathered up." In the yard, Marshall's voice echoed with irritation. "But it's not because she's about to foal."

"Dunno, boss," a ranch hand answered before calling to another man. "Whitey, you seen anyone mess with the mare?"

"Just the new hand." Whitey turned and pointed at the shed. "An' he's in there."

Three pairs of eyes turned in his direction. No use laying low. Rhett walked into the yard, gaze fixed on Will Marshall.

"This true?" His boss scowled at him.

Rhett hesitated to answer, uncertain what part of true he wanted to know about.

"You been messing with my mare?"

He took care to frame his answer. "I attempted to

gentle her." When that response didn't seem sufficient, he added, "Since this is her first foal, it will be easier if—"

"Who gave you permission to even get near her?" The ranch owner took a step in his direction. "I oughta clean your plow."

Rhett drew himself up. "I've done nothing wrong."

"That's my call, not yours."

As his boss drew closer, Rhett maintained eye contact.

"That's it. Pack your gear and…" Marshall's words died at the sound of thundering hooves. They all watched as Bartow rode hard in their direction.

Rhett noted the man's pale face and his lathered horse. As Bartow drew closer, Rhett realized that Ellie was missing. Hadn't she ridden out earlier with her uncle? If so, where was she now?

The foreman reined in.

"What's up, Guy?"

Bartow's face appeared pinched with worry. "Did your niece make it back?"

"No." Marshall's brows clashed above his nose. "Why? Where is she?"

"I—I don't know. We was riding, then she took off. I thought maybe she returned here ahead of me."

Marshall's face turned white. "You *left* her out there?"

"No, boss. I…" Bartow shook his head. "We were out by the herd. Kinda south. She wanted to race. And I let her get a head start. But I lost sight of her. I thought she'd be here by now."

For several seconds, the boss remained silent. "Get a few men and head east. I'll ride southeast with a couple more. If you find her, fire off a couple rounds and send a man back here to report in. Every hour."

"Yes, boss."

Rhett had heard enough. From the position of the sun, he determined it was midafternoon, hours since Ellie and her uncle had ridden out. Likely she was tired and hungry. But more important, she had no means to protect herself. Time was of the essence.

As Marshall and his men scattered in different directions, he hastened to saddle Wash. He slipped out of the yard mere minutes after Bartow. No one seemed to notice.

For what felt like the hundredth time, Ellie rode to the top of another small knoll and peered around. The same unhelpful scene met her gaze—endless grass, rocks and jagged mountains in the distance. Where was a town? Or any homes? She had heard about "soddies," but had seen nothing that indicated ownership beyond roaming cattle and some sheep that looked like tiny white dots. She had steered clear of a herd of bison, their hulking forms filling her with fear as she imagined them stampeding. Back east, she had heard of their unpredictability.

She swallowed the dustbowl in her throat as tears stung her eyes. "God? Do you see what's happening? Do You care?"

The desperate prayer—if it could be called that—escaped her lips. She unbuttoned her constricting collar. Perspiration trickled down her spine. As she paused to consider which direction to go, her horse chuffed and chomped at the bit. She pushed on, longing to rest. Again, she stopped when she second-guessed herself.

The sun, once so high in the sky, now blazed in her

eyes. What would happen when it slid below the horizon? The thought of spending a night alone in the wilds of Wyoming Territory terrified her. All too well she recalled the sounds of snarling beasts as they tore the flesh of the dead horse the night of the stagecoach accident. Panic threatened as she imagined them hunting her.

A tear splashed down her cheek.

She curled over the pommel of the saddle. "Please help. Please."

For many minutes, she waited in silence for an answer. Any answer. But no rainbow appeared in the sky, pointing the way to Uncle Will's ranch. She stifled a sob when her horse lowered his head and began grazing.

Rhett was wrong. God didn't love her or care what happened to her. It was just as she'd always believed— He was too busy running the universe to bother with her insignificant request.

Gathering the reins, she searched the horizon, then chose a direction. With more bravery than she felt, she announced, "We'll go that way."

On she rode, aiming for a large rock. If nothing else, she would rest in the shade. A headache began to pound. She could think of nothing but water as her throat grew more parched. With stiff joints, she dismounted, taking care to keep a tight hold on the reins as her horse grazed on nearby grass.

Ellie didn't know how much time passed as she dozed before her gelding jerked on the reins. Head high, ears pricked forward, he seemed to be aware of something unusual.

Muscles protesting, she scrambled to her feet.

In the distance, a horse and rider appeared.

"I'm found," she whispered, yet at the same time fretted about the man being an outlaw. She remained hidden behind the rock as she watched. Several times, the rider stopped to study the ground. Looking for something?

With bated breath, she watched the rider draw closer. After another few minutes, she recognized the spots of an appaloosa. "Rhett!"

He must have heard her because he reined in and looked around. At the same time, her horse whinnied a long welcome.

As Rhett kicked his horse to meet her, Ellie moved from the shadow of the rock.

Sobs of relief kept her from calling to him again as he rode hard to meet her. But as he drew closer, she forgot her fears at the sight of his horse. Something out-of-place perched on his gelding's head. A hat?

Hysteria gripped her when she realized Rhett's horse wore her lost bonnet.

When he drew closer, she tried to stifle her laughter. But she could not control the dueling emotions of relief and astonishment. Tears again choked her. She leaned an arm against her horse's saddle and pressed her face against it.

God heard my prayer. The truth overwhelmed her.

After several minutes, Ellie gained control of herself. She felt wrung out, yet filled with an amazement that she could not even begin to understand. Later, when she was alone in her room, she would examine this foreign, yet astounding awareness of God.

All the while, Rhett said nothing as he remained seated on his mount.

Ellie pressed her gloved fingers over her lips, again fighting the urge to cry. "You—you found me," she finally managed to say. Tears continued to slip down her cheeks.

"Are you all right?" Rhett's soft voice pierced through her embarrassment and relief.

She managed a nod.

"Thirsty?"

Again, she could only dip her head. He dismounted before untying her bonnet from his horse's bridle. After dropping his reins, he brought it to her.

She quickly secured her bonnet on her head.

"I know of a stream, not far from here." His gaze never left her. "When you're ready."

"I—I am." But when she tried to mount, she was too stiff to get her foot into the stirrup. The muscles of her back and legs screamed in protest.

"Allow me." Rhett knelt with cupped hands.

After she stepped on them, he lifted her with ease.

He mounted. "Follow me."

Taking a deep breath, Ellie nudged her gelding forward.

She didn't know how long they rode, but it no longer mattered. Rhett was here. He would protect her. Time and again she swiped tears from her cheeks.

After he led her to a stream, they watered the horses. Ellie dismounted and drank deeply, as well. Water never tasted so good. When she rose, she saw that Rhett waited. He too had dismounted, but appeared to stand sentry over her.

"Do you need to rest?" His quiet question wrapped her in feelings of protection. "Or should we get back to your uncle's ranch?"

"I want to go home." Although she spoke calmly, the words choked her. She pressed her hand to her chest.

"Home it is."

"Wait." Her one word checked him. She fought for

her voice. "Thank you, Rhett. For finding me. Rescuing me."

A smile softened his face. As he helped her mount, he said, "Thank me later. After we reach the ranch."

"Don't you know the way?"

"Yes. I did some scouting out here for the military years ago." He swung himself into his saddle. "But we should hurry."

She glanced around, noting they had plenty of daylight hours. "How far away is it?"

"Not far. But the longer we're out here, the bigger the problem." Her confusion must have been evident because he added, "We're alone. On the prairie. Your uncle may draw a wrong conclusion."

Her cheeks burned at the insinuation. "Once I explain—"

"Preferably before my lynching."

His words alarmed her. They both knew of Will Marshall's temper.

"We need to get back." She stifled her emotions. "Now."

Rhett gave one curt nod as he pointed. "That way."

They set off at a trot, then canter.

Anxiety for her friend caused her to push her mount to a gallop. A quick glance behind showed he kept up. But it also revealed a group of riders, riding hard to intersect them.

The person at the head of the group was none other than Guy Bartow.

Chapter Ten

As Rhett rode in the middle of the group, he assessed the men's mood. Their faces were grim, gaze continually shifting. Ahead, the foreman led the way back to the ranch with Ellie close behind. No one spoke.

Four of the five men who flanked Rhett were ones he recognized as the foreman's closest friends. All were armed. Even if Rhett considered an escape attempt, he wouldn't get far. He made certain to appear relaxed, giving no one a reason to draw their six-shooter and end his life.

After they arrived at the ranch, one man ran up to grab Ellie's bridle. "Y'uncle is expecting you, miss. In the house."

After throwing Rhett a worried look, she dismounted and went inside.

His escort closed ranks. Apparently they were to wait.

After slipping off his horse, Bartow tossed his reins over a hitching post. He gave his men a look that spoke volumes. "Keep an eye on him." He too headed inside.

Yawning loudly, Rhett rested his elbow on his saddle horn as he pretended boredom. He assessed how many hours remained of the day. With this much light, he had no chance of high-tailing it out of there with his skin intact. Time crawled. Rhett wasn't too worried. Yet. Will Marshall must be interviewing his niece. Still, Rhett prayed that the ranch owner would accept the truth.

After a quarter of an hour or so, the foreman walked onto the porch. His head jerk seemed to indicate the boss was ready to see Rhett. Without waiting for the others, he dismounted and tied his horse before heading inside.

"Here he is, boss." Bartow crimped his hat as Rhett joined the few inside.

He remained by the door, aware of the two men who positioned themselves behind him. The meaning seemed clear. Marshall wanted to ensure that Rhett not leave without permission.

His gaze settled on the ranch owner as he sat in a lone chair. Like a judge and jury?

Ellie stood beside her uncle, hands twisting together. Wholly focused on the foreman, Marshall appeared to purposefully ignore her.

She yanked off her bonnet. "I'm telling you, regardless of what Guy insinuated, we were not lost."

Bartow drew himself up. "And I say you was the lostest looking thing I ever seen."

She rounded on him. "We were heading in the correct direction, were we not?"

"After wandering around for hours."

"That was when I was alone." Ellie's chin puckered. "*Before* Rhett found me."

"Then why was you riding away from him?" He threw a thumb in Rhett's direction. "Me and my men saw you, galloping as hard as you could."

Cold reality hit Rhett. They thought he was chasing Ellie? To do her harm?

Ellie planted a fist at her hips. "I was in a hurry to get back."

Silence met her pronouncement, but it was obvious from the expressions of the men—Marshall in particular—they didn't believe her.

"Besides," she said through gritted teeth as she turned back to her uncle, "if he accosted me, do you really think I would defend him now?"

Accosted her? Rhett's mouth grew dry. If that's what they thought, his comment about lynching would become a reality.

He kept his hands relaxed at his side, but his mind raced. If he acted quickly, he could catch the man on the left with an elbow to the throat. One hard shove to the man on his right would knock him into Bartow. That would give Rhett precious seconds to reach the open door, leap on his horse and take off. In short order he would reach the mountains where he could lay low until it was safe to head to the next county. Of course, someone might get a shot off that would kill him, but that would be better than getting lynched.

Bartow threw up his hands, drawing attention to himself as he spoke to Ellie. "We found you. More important, we saved you."

"That's a lie." Her voice rose. "The only person I needed saving from was—"

"Enough." With difficulty, Marshall rose and limped toward his niece. "You're here now. That's all that matters."

"No, it's not. The truth matters." She pressed clenched fists to her side.

"Ellie…" He lowered his voice. "Just drop it."

Her chest heaved, lips pressing together. The meaning seemed clear. She would drop the subject if matters went her way.

The ranch owner now turned to Rhett. "However this played out, I'm grateful you located Ellie."

A relieved breath escaped him. Perhaps he didn't need to run for the hills.

Marshall took another step toward him. "But I do seem to recall ordering you to pack up your gear and skedaddle."

He had? A replay of the day rushed through Rhett's mind. He remembered the boss berating him about the mare, but not issuing any actual orders. Before reaching that point, they had been interrupted by the foreman.

Regardless, it seemed his employment had come to an end.

So be it. Rhett squared his shoulders. At least he wouldn't have to run for his life. With deliberation, he met Marshall's gaze but avoided Ellie's. He took a step back. "Very well."

She thrust herself between him and her uncle. Crossing her arms, she glared at Marshall. "He leaves, I leave."

If she had announced she descended from the moon, it would not have had a bigger effect. The ranch owner staggered back.

"You heard me." Every word from Ellie sounded like a rifle report. "And you know I mean what I say."

Marshall blinked, but his shoulders slumped as though he couldn't believe it.

"I was lost, but Rhett found me. *He* rescued me." Ellie stepped closer to her uncle. "He told me exactly which direction to go. I was so anxious to get back—

to you—that I pushed my horse to a gallop. *That's* the truth."

Despite Bartow's snort, Ellie didn't break eye contact with her uncle.

Watching the man's face, Rhett prepared to bolt. Just because Ellie would leave—and he had no doubts she would do as threatened—didn't mean Will Marshall wouldn't take his fury out on him. No telling what ran through the ranch owner's mind.

Out of the corner of his eye, he caught the sneer on Bartow's face. The same look marked the two men who flanked Rhett. They weren't watching the ranch owner, but the foreman. Like he was the real boss.

With care, Rhett pulled back an inch, ready to run.

"Fine." Marshall's limp hands fell to his sides. "Let him go."

Bartow jerked like he'd been stung by a wasp. "But, boss—"

"I said, let him go." With a jerk of his head, Marshall dismissed the two men by Rhett. Their gaze cut to Bartow before they slunk out.

Again, their reaction struck Rhett as odd. And worrisome.

"And you—" Marshall got right up in Rhett's face "—stay away from my mare."

He made certain to meet this man's gaze. Though Marshall didn't say it, the meaning seemed clear. *Stay away from my niece.*

Rhett spoke with care. "Yessir."

But even as he turned and walked out of the house, he knew staying away from Ellie would never be possible. As long as she lived, he would never be free of her. Rhett would forever carry her in his heart.

* * *

"Easy, boy." Rhett ran his hands over Tripper.

Although the gelding's ears flicked with nervousness, his flesh no longer quivered. With care, Rhett felt along the horse's back leg. It felt less inflamed. More importantly, Tripper no longer held his leg as though it pained him to put weight on it.

Even so, Rhett located the tin of salve that Ellie provided and smeared some of the grassy-smelling contents over the wound. As he worked, he flexed his own hands. Between using the medicine and wearing gloves, his palms had also healed well.

He had just put the tin aside when a creak of the barn door alerted him that someone else entered the building. Enemy or friend?

In seconds, he climbed up into the rafters.

Flickering light from a lantern danced along the dark walls as the person approached the stall. Long before Rhett could see her, he knew Ellie was the visitor from the sounds of her swishing skirts.

Taking care to make no sound, he peered below. Her golden hair came into view, then her creamy gown. A dark shawl wrapped her torso.

"Hello, Tripper." Before entering the stall, she hung the lantern on a nail.

Tripper nickered to her, his welcome far different from the one he'd given to Rhett. His first inclination was to call to Ellie and let her know he was there. But he decided to enjoy watching her interact with the gelding.

You have gifted her greatly, Lord.

The truth of it affirmed itself in Rhett's mind.

"I'm sorry I've been ignoring you." Ellie rubbed her palm over Tripper's neck. "I was gone far too long today, but I came as soon as I could. And I brought you a present."

She drew something from her pocket that Tripper took eagerly. From the crunching sound, Rhett guessed it was sugar cubes.

"No, I don't have any more." She giggled as he nosed her. For several moments, she merely stroked his neck. "Mind if I look at your leg? You're not going to kick me, are you?"

As Ellie continued to chat with the horse, she smoothed her hands over his back and sides, working her way behind him. She made some sound of satisfaction as she examined the wound before moving back to his head.

For several minutes, she stood back, merely watching Tripper.

"I know you're in here."

Rhett puzzled at her quiet words, apparently spoken to the horse.

Ellie swiveled around in a half circle, glancing about the stall, then looking over the half gate. "I can't see you. Where're you hiding?"

Understanding dawned when Rhett realized she was talking about him. He chuckled quietly.

Without descending from his hiding place, he poked his head out. "How'd you know?"

She peered up at him. "Tripper. He kept looking away. Obviously seeking you."

"Ah." Foolish of him to forget the horse. However, Ellie had been far more captivating.

"And I could tell someone just put salve on his wound." She pursed her lips. "I figured it was you."

"True." The smell alone would've been enough. Ellie truly did addle his head if he ignored the clues he had left.

"Do you think he's looking better, Rhett?"

"Much better. I'm confident he'll make a full recovery."

"Really?" Ellie's smile dazzled.

"Yes, really." Rhett positioned himself to climb down when a sound from outside caught his ear. "Someone's coming."

She whirled.

The creak of the barn door echoed through the building.

Ellie glanced up at him as she whispered, "Stay hidden."

Did she sense the unease that infected the ranch? Rhett feared he was the cause.

The heavy footsteps that marched toward the stall told him all he needed to know. Bartow was the visitor.

Ellie continued to pet her horse as the foreman stepped into Rhett's view. Stopping outside the gate, Bartow peered in. He watched for a minute, then looked around, like he expected someone else to be there.

"Ev'ning, Ellie." His deep voice contained a level of caution.

"Oh, hello." She sounded surprised, like she didn't know he stood at the gate.

"I, uh…" He swept his hat off and scratched his head before putting it back on. "I saw you heading in this way."

"So did my uncle. I waved to him as he sat on his front porch."

Clever. Rhett admired the way she warned Bartow not to try anything. The way the foreman had treated Ellie earlier made Rhett feel like he'd tried to swallow an apple, whole.

"That so?" Bartow rested an elbow on a wooden

rung. Silence fell on them both as Ellie continued to pet the gelding. He cleared his throat. "Y'horse ain't looking too bad."

"I'll take that as a compliment." Tone cool, Ellie spoke without facing him.

Bartow ran a hand over his neck, then jammed a fist into his pants pocket. "Listen, I wanted to apologize for earlier. What I said. Out in the field. I's only flirting. Didn't mean to offend."

"You didn't." She lifted one shoulder, as though in dismissal.

"Good." The foreman grabbed the lantern off the nail. "Found out about Matt. Like ya asked. The blacksmith's apprentice. He's doing fine."

She peered into his face. "Thank you."

"How about I walk ya back to the house?"

She let out a little sigh, filled with what sounded like frustration. Because she wasn't finished with tending to Tripper? Or because she wanted to talk to Rhett?

He must've made some sound when he shifted his weight because Bartow's head jerked around.

"Certainly." Ellie spoke more loudly as she hastened out of the stall. "I was done here, anyway."

The foreman lifted the lantern, but turned back to Ellie. The light fell full on her face.

When he offered his arm, she frowned. Her gaze flickered to Rhett's hiding place before she rested light fingers on Bartow's forearm, not tucking her arm around his as he likely expected.

Rhett couldn't see the man's face, but Ellie's expression remained neutral. He got the impression she was attempting to discourage the foreman from getting ideas. As the seconds ticked by, her shoulders grew tight, spine more rigid.

What was Bartow relaying by his silence? Rhett wished he could see the man's expression.

"Shall we?" Ellie prompted, tone frigid.

"This way." Bartow's head bobbed toward the entrance.

Only after they exited the building did the tension ebb from Rhett's body. When his hand began to ache, he realized he was gripping his hunting knife. He forced his fingers to release the polished wooden handle before shimmying down from his hiding spot.

A check out the door assured him that the foreman was leading Ellie to the house. In the growing darkness, he could make out their forms, pausing in the yard while Bartow seemed to share some tidbit of information. From Rhett's vantage point, he could see Marshall. As per his habit most evenings, he sat on a rocking chair on his own porch. He too seemed to take great interest in the couple as they lingered.

Worry for Ellie ate at Rhett.

"Bartow won't try anything," he reminded himself as he continued to watch. Not as long as she was under the protection of her uncle.

But despite his own words, Rhett's reassurance rang hollow. He didn't trust the foreman one bit.

In the morning, Ellie turned her attentions to her uncle. With Tripper well on his way to health, she felt confident about leaving him in Rhett's care. Now she could concentrate on Uncle Will.

"How does that feel?" Ellie plumped the pillow under his calf as he sat in a cozy chair. His foot rested on another chair while a stool provided comfort and support. She smiled at her sneaky way to keep him immobile so that his sore ankle, wrapped in a poultice with her own blend of oils and herbs, would lose some swelling.

"Don't know why you're fussing so much over me." Though Uncle Will growled, she detected the teasing edge in his voice.

She crossed her arms and tilted her head. "Because you like it."

When he turned his head, she knew he hid his smile.

Their showdown about Rhett now seemed like a faded memory. Life had gotten back to normal. Whatever that was. Since her arrival at the ranch, Ellie felt like she and her uncle had been locked in a battle of wills. Today, a truce had been called. The men had eaten breakfast and departed to places unknown. That was probably the only reason her uncle remained at the house and allowed her to fuss over him.

He gave a gruff *humph* before reaching for his book.

Content that he would continue to tolerate her ministrations, Ellie returned the bottles to her medical bag and then wandered to the window.

Rain streaked the windows and turned the ranch yard into a mud vat. That didn't seem to bother the chickens. Some of the braver ones were out, scratching for bugs and worms.

Ellie sighed, reminiscing over how much it resembled Fort Laramie and her first real look at Wyoming Territory. Hard to believe that had been almost two weeks ago. Despite her uncle's gruffness and stubbornness, the ranch felt more and more like home. Besides, he was the only family she had left. Her mother's nearest relative had passed away about the time Grandmother Tess had. The only one left on her father's side was his brother, Uncle Will.

Thank You, God. This seemed a good time to silently express her humble gratitude.

"You're sorry you came." Her uncle's voice broke into her thoughts. "Aren't you, Sunshine?"

Ellie turned. "No. Not at all."

"Your expression." He paused, frown deepening. "It was sad."

She moved closer. "I was thinking about how grateful I am that I still have family. You."

His jaw jutted as he stared into the fire.

She thought that was the end of the conversation, but he surprised her by saying, "You think I'm harsh. Maybe even cruel."

She pulled up a chair, taking care how to answer. "Sometimes."

"In this part of the country, a man's gotta be tough. Decisive. I wouldn't have survived if I hadn't." His mouth spasmed. "Wish I had been years ago."

Ellie had no idea what he meant. However, she sensed she should merely listen.

"Like a buncha folks, I took advantage of the Homestead Act and got my hundred-and-sixty acres. Didn't want to be a farmer, but I knew I could ranch. Those first years were rough, but this place was thriving. I bought more land. I was all ready to..." He paused, something changing in his face.

Ellie rested her fingers on his forearm. "What happened?"

"Outlaws." Mouth hardening, Uncle Will stared into the past.

"They attacked the ranch?"

"A group of men—the Walker Gang—sought shelter here after a robbery. Apparently other ranchers had protected them in the past and they figured we would too." Sighing, he shook his head. "I wasn't here, but the Johnsons were. When they refused to provide accommodations, the gang torched the place. You've seen the burned-out hulk up the road a little ways, haven't you?"

"Yes. I wondered about it."

"The gang killed some of my best horses. Ran off cattle. Hurt some folks."

Ellie took in a slow breath, afraid to even imagine the scene. "Where were you?"

"In Cheyenne. Getting ready to travel east, as a matter of fact. As soon as I heard what happened, I turned around." The downturn of his mouth seemed to indicate there was more to the story than he was sharing.

"Were the men ever caught?"

Uncle Will shifted in his chair. "Yeah. The leader was hanged, although I wasn't part of the posse. Heard two others eventually met their end. Don't know about the rest."

That should have been the end of the story, but Ellie sensed he was holding something back. "At least justice was done."

"Justice?" He snorted with derision. "Justice should've included my getting to Chicago. Before it was too late."

"Too late? For...?"

"For everything." He turned to her, face twisted with long-buried pain. "So pardon me if I'm not all that interested in going to church."

Ellie drew back. Where had that come from? She waited, but he said nothing more.

Had Uncle Will a wife or child who had died in the attack? As far as she knew, he had never married—but she sensed there was a deeply personal pain tied into the experience. Did he hold God responsible?

As she remained dumbstruck, Uncle Will's and Rhett's similar stories struck her. Except Rhett didn't seem to blame God for the evil that had come upon him. From what she'd observed, his faith in and love for the Lord had grown stronger despite all his trials.

Expression softening, her uncle covered her hand with his. "I hope you don't mind the comparison, but just now you look like your mother. With that sad look on your brow. Like your heart is breaking for me. And I appreciate it."

One of the reasons Ellie had come to Wyoming Territory rushed back at her—the letters from Uncle Will to her mother.

"Were you in love with Mama?"

If she had smacked her uncle with the pillow, he could not have looked more stunned.

He finally answered. "Yes." His mouth twitched. "How'd you guess?"

"I found some letters. That you wrote. To her." She rushed to explain as her uncle's face grew pale. "I discovered them when I was emptying my mother's secretary. Before I sold everything." When he didn't respond, she added, "I'm sure my father never saw them."

His Adam's apple bobbed several times. "Did you read them?"

"Part of one. Then I…" She bit her lip. "I felt like I was intruding on your privacy. So I stopped."

"They're destroyed?"

"No. I—I brought them with me." She met his gaze. "In case you wanted them back."

He pondered her words but shook his head.

"I'll give them to you," she hurried to say. "Right now. You can keep them. Or throw them into the fire, if you like."

When she rose, he grabbed her hand. "No. Don't."

Slowly, she regained her seat. "What would you like me to do with them?"

For the longest time, he didn't speak. Ellie watched him struggle with his answer. Finally, he said, "I want you to read them. And then we'll talk." He nodded as though to emphasize the rightness of the request. His fingers, still clutching hers, relaxed as he caressed the back of her hand. "I'd like that. Very much. Would you do that for me?"

Inexplicably, tears rose to her eyes. "Of course."

He sandwiched her hand between both his. His fingers caressed her knuckles several times before he spoke. "I want you to, Sunshine." He repeated himself, a faraway look in his eyes.

For the first time since her arrival, Ellie felt like she was truly seeing her uncle.

After supper that evening, she retrieved the four letters and laid them out on her desk. Taking a deep breath, she opened the one with the earliest postmark and sat on her bed to read.

"My darling Adel," the letter began. *"I know of your engagement to my brother. I beg you not to think me presumptuous for writing to you."*

Uncle Will went on to describe his first meeting with Adeline and how he could never forget one detail of that evening. Did she not feel the same? The missive ended with him imploring her to end his agony by agreeing to see him again. He would watch for her at her box at the theater. One nod and he would know how to proceed.

Gulping, Ellie picked up the next letter. This one sounded very different.

Will urged Adel to proceed with caution and hide her feelings. They were being watched. Frank was becoming suspicious. Tess, Adeline's mother, would certainly oppose the breaking of the engagement. More than once, Tess had let it be known that she favored the soon-to-be rich doctor, not the rough rancher.

The third and fourth letters were very short.

"Yes or no?" was all one said.

And the fourth one had one line. *"Coast clear? Candle."*

Heart hammering, Ellie sat back against her pillows. *Yes or no* for what? And what did Uncle Will mean by *Coast clear*?

The late hour kept her from asking him about that now. And because she couldn't, she dug out her mother's diary.

Ellie needed answers. Now.

Hands trembling, she opened the book to page one.

Chapter Eleven

Rhett trailed the wagon that carried Ellie and the foreman to town. Because two of Bartow's men accompanied them, Rhett made certain to maintain a fair distance between himself and the group.

They were all going to church. Or so the foreman said. Somehow Rhett got the feeling that only he and Ellie were really interested in their destination. However, the boss insisted that Bartow drive her. Rhett had overheard the last of their conversation as Marshall escorted his niece from the house.

And she had agreed—though none too happily.

On the way, the foreman worked hard to chat with Ellie, but she seemed disinclined to talk. In less than thirty minutes, he gave up. By the time they reached Casper, Bartow seemed more than happy to drop her off at church.

"I'm leaving the wagon here since I got my horse." Bartow's voice rang loudly enough for Rhett to hear.

Pretending not to listen, he moved to tether Wash behind the church.

Ellie spoke to the foreman. "You're not coming inside?"

"Nah. Got somethin' more important to do."

Her expression said it all. What was more important than worshipping God? However, relief seemed to take the upper hand, evident in her face.

Bartow tugged on his hat brim in a farewell. "I'll be back around four to drive ya home."

Four? Rhett's ears pricked up. Ellie must have something planned after the service if she intended to stay in town that long.

Staying in the shade of the church building, he watched the foreman unhitch his horse, then grab his gear from the back of the wagon. In minutes, he saddled his mare, then he and his two buddies disappeared down the street.

Ellie turned when some women greeted her. Together they went inside the church.

Rhett waited as congregants flocked through the open door. After the service began, he slipped in the back. Most folks paid him and the riffraff that lingered by the door no mind. The service began with congregants singing.

Tension slowly ebbed from him as the words to beloved hymns echoed through him. Spafford's "It Is Well With My Soul" soothed the familiar ache of missing Mr. Callaway and his childhood friends, all who had died in the same incident. Again, Rhett was grateful that his ma and the elderly preacher had married despite the difference in their ages. During the years his mother had been the man's housekeeper, her attitude had transformed from bitterness to love.

She often said that though they were married ten short days, the joy they shared had been enough for a lifetime.

As Rhett sang, his gaze focused on Ellie, sitting close

to the front. Several young women of the area sat near her. He liked watching how they flocked around her. Last week, her face shone as she chatted with them.

Today, however, Ellie seemed more pensive. He noted how her bonnet often tilted back, as though she fixed her gaze on something above the preacher. Was she considering the hand-hewn cross in the front? Her head would often bow as she seemed to reflect on a thought. From his vantage point, he couldn't see her face. All during Pastor Charles's message, Rhett watched her, praying for a way to comfort her troubled soul.

After the sermon, he slipped out the back when the congregation began to sing. He made his way to the livery where he had to take care of some unfinished business.

"Howdy, Mr. Rhett." Ira appeared from around a horse.

"Hey." Rhett nodded a greeting. "I was wondering if you'd seen Pete recently." The stagecoach driver sometimes attended church but was absent that morning.

"Nope. Think he headed up to Billings yesterday. Want me to keep a lookout?"

"Sure. Let him know I need to speak with him about the horse I took."

The young man bobbed his head. "Oh. He said he settled with the stagecoach company."

"Good."

"Still want me to give him a message?" Ira's eyes gleamed.

Knowing the young man hoped to get paid for his help, Rhett grinned. "Sure. Tell him to find me at the Double M Ranch." He turned and pretended he was about to leave, but swiveled back and flipped a coin at the lad.

Laughing, he caught it. "Thank you, sir."

"No. Thank you."

After Rhett exited the building, he pondered where to go. Church had not yet let out. While he considered his options, he noticed Bartow and his two buddies down the street. They were speaking to none other than Mr. Tesley, the businessman from Fort Laramie.

The four of them appeared deep in conversation. About what? Doubtful Will Marshall instructed his foreman to do business on a Sunday. The only other option was that the meeting was personal. But from what Rhett knew of Tesley, it seemed unlikely these cowboys had anything the businessman would want.

A glance at the sun's position showed that a couple hours yet remained before the foreman would drive Ellie home. Curiosity getting the better of him, Rhett moved toward them. When Whitey, Bartow's closest friend, looked over his shoulder, Rhett cut down an alley to avoid being seen. He inched closer, flattening his back against one building.

"I've handled that amount before," Tesley boasted. "No problem."

Bartow responded. "Then it's a deal?"

"You just let me know when and how many. I'll tell you where."

The sound of a match striking indicated that someone was smoking.

Rhett edged closer, catching sight of Bartow's large hat as he faced Tesley.

"And, naturally—" the foreman lowered his voice "—this remains between you and us, right?"

"That's right. Nobody else needs to know."

Bartow stuck out his hand, which the businessman shook. "I'll drink to that."

Chuckling, the men headed down the boardwalk toward the saloon, away from Rhett's location.

He eased back from the meeting spot before circling back toward the church. The rise of voices indicated that the service was over.

He had almost reached the building when rough hands grabbed him and shoved him against a building. A bony forearm pinned him against the wood planking.

"Where you been sneaking off to?" Whitey shoved his face into Rhett's.

Before answering, he considered. With one quick twist, he could slip out of Whitey's hold. An easy enough move. Rhett stared into narrowed eyes. "Nowhere."

However, he felt obligated to warn Whitey—in a subtle way—that this would be the only time he would lay hands on him. Maintaining a relaxed stance, Rhett moved slowly until his hand rested on the handle of his hunting knife. "I noticed you weren't in church either."

Whitey snorted. "Bartow said we didn't have to go."

Bartow? Not the boss?

The man's choice of words confirmed Rhett's suspicions. Whitey—and likely several other men—considered Bartow the true boss of the ranch. Not Will Marshall. A dangerous situation for the owner and his niece.

From his peripheral vision, he could see church folks gather at the mouth of the alley, watching the confrontation. However, none intervened. And Whitey seemed not to notice the onlookers. Or care.

The pressure against Rhett's chest grew. "I ain't gonna ask you again. Where ya been?"

I should not answer a fool according to his folly, or I will be like him.

The proverb popped into his mind. Rhett raised his voice so that those who gawked might hear. "I was reflecting on Proverbs 26:4."

"Huh?" The ranch hand's confusion quickly transformed into irritation. "Speak plainly, dunderhead."

"You should read the Good Book. It might make you wise if you heed it."

"Why you mealymouthed…" The ranch hand drew his gun and jabbed the tip under Rhett's chin. "It's high time someone taught you to speak respectfully to your betters."

"And how do you intend to do that?" As Rhett spoke, he scratched his ear as a distraction. With his other hand, he carefully drew his knife.

"Thinking of rearranging your brain." Whitey jabbed the gun upward. "I just saw a wanted poster, with your face on it. Why don'tcha explain how that's possible?"

What? Confusion gripped Rhett. *Impossible.* Surely any ancient posters of his father would be long gone. Where'd one come from?

"Let's you and me head around the side of the building." Whitey's voice grew silky. "There we can have a nice chat without upsetting the womenfolk."

The man had to be bluffing. Or spreading rumors to justify his actions.

Rhett considered. One swift move and he could draw blood before Whitey got off a shot. But that one move would very likely kill. There'd be no coming back from that. Not to the ranch—and not to Ellie.

"No, I'm sorry." Ellie paused at the back of the church. For the third time she explained, "I need to get back to the ranch. But thank you."

Last Sunday, Mrs. Rushton had invited her to join the

family for dinner, and she'd accepted. But that morning those plans had changed when several congregants announced they were hosting an all-church feast. A small family meal, Ellie could have handled, but a banquet would be beyond her. Ellie didn't feel very festive—not after reading Uncle Will's letters. Those, combined with Mama's diary, weighted her heart. All she wanted was to go home and weep for her mother's lost love.

"You're staying, aren't you?" One elderly woman smiled as she grasped Ellie's arm.

"Not this time."

"What a shame. We're having such beautiful weather."

Ellie mumbled an excuse and managed to extricate herself. Outside the church, she paused, trying to figure out how to find Guy so they could leave early. A nearby crowd drew her attention. At first, she planned to skirt it, but then she realized Whitey seemed to be the focus of the group.

And with him was Rhett, held hostage at gunpoint.

She pushed her way forward. "Whitey? What're you doing?"

After a glance her way, he straightened. Sunlight flashed off his gun as he holstered it. "Just seeing what this varmint was up to. I think he was thieving."

Doubtful. Not only because she knew Rhett's character, but because he carried nothing. He held one hand up, fingers spread. The other was hidden, but obviously empty. Whitey had fabricated the tale because he was a thug. She'd seen the way he threw rocks at the dogs when he thought no one was looking.

She drew herself up. "That is not your concern, but the law's."

His lip curled, but he had not yet released Rhett.

"Sometimes folks gotta take the law into their own hands."

"What's going on here?" Pastor Charles pushed his way through the group.

"I caught him skulking around." Whitey answered before Ellie could. "Up to no good."

Charles glanced back at the crowd, then again faced Whitey. "Impossible. He was in church this morning. Can't say the same about you, though."

Although Ellie couldn't see the pastor's face, she could see Whitey's. His eyes narrowed as he gauged the minister. Though Charles was a man of cloth, he was by no means small of stature. And half the congregation stood at his back. Whitey was a bully, but he wasn't a fool.

Contempt twisting his face, Whitey spread his hands as he backed away. Without another word, he turned on his heel and stalked down the road.

Pastor Charles turned to the group, his brow lowered. "We're a law-abiding town. If you see this sort of tyranny again, I expect you will do the right thing. Or get the sheriff."

Several people muttered their apologies before scattering.

When Charles met Ellie's gaze, she sighed in relief. "Thank you."

He drew closer. "Are you staying for dinner?"

"Not today." Her gaze flickered to Rhett.

The preacher seemed about to insist, then changed his mind. "You know, I'd really like to see your uncle in church sometime."

Her eyes stung. It took a moment for her to find her voice. "So would I."

"That is my fervent prayer."

She held up her hand to keep the pastor from walking away. "My uncle's foreman, Guy Bartow, will be looking for me later. Could you let him I know I had to leave?"

"Consider it done." Charles gave her arm a comforting squeeze before walking away.

Once she and Rhett were alone, she spoke to him. He had not moved throughout the interchange. "Please hitch your horse to the wagon."

Though his eyebrows shot up, he said nothing. After he moved toward her, she saw his fingers curled around the handle of his knife. She sucked in a slow breath. Had he planned to draw Whitey's blood?

Perhaps she had not saved Rhett's life, but Whitey's. Then the harsh reality struck her—Guy's friend wouldn't let this affront go. What if she had inadvertently put Rhett in greater danger by interfering?

In no time, he pulled his gear off his horse and hitched the gelding to the wagon. Amid the stares of the church folks, they headed out of town. A jumble of emotions battered Ellie as she sat ramrod stiff. Rhett remained silent, his expression serene. Like he hadn't a care in the world. After what he had been through? Ever since their arrival at the ranch, he had experienced ill treatment.

Reaching for a tendril of her hair, she wound it around her finger until it tightened into a painful corkscrew.

Emotions in chaos, the one that dominated was guilt. She was the one who had talked Rhett into working for her uncle. All it had brought him was trouble.

"I'm sorry." Ellie tried to speak the words, but they came out as only a whisper.

Rhett glanced her way, but she couldn't meet his

gaze. With a gentle click to his horse, he urged the gelding up an incline.

They had been traveling about a half hour, traversing the mountainous road. As the heat of the sun beat down upon them, Rhett peeled off his jacket, revealing a worn cotton shirt. He rolled up the sleeves, drawing her attention to the scar on his forearm and hands roughened by hard labor. The difference in their social standing ground in the heaviness of her responsibility all the more.

She had choices. He had little. She had money. Had he any at all?

In her stubbornness, she had convinced him to take a job that he might not have accepted otherwise. The result was more hardship and exposure to cruelty from men like Whitey.

Remorse grew. Air seemed too heavy to draw in. She must say the words and release Rhett from any obligation he felt about staying on with the Double M Ranch. God would want her to.

"I—I'm so sorry." Ellie rested her hand on his bare forearm.

In that instant, she forgot everything except the feeling of Rhett's arm. Warm. Muscular. Very much alive. This was the second time they had touched. Or was it the third? One time had been particularly startling.

We were standing on the porch. And he took my hand.

She recalled the strength of his fingers. Despite the callouses, she sensed his gentleness. Had seen it when he caressed the salve into Tripper's wound.

The breeze that had been blowing moments before dropped to a whisper. Rhett's horse slowed and then stopped. As did Ellie's heart. Time expanded as she luxuriated in the feeling of his sleek forearm under her hand.

Rhett said nothing. Did nothing, except raise his eyes to hers.

She sucked in a quick, perturbed breath. His blue eyes widened as he pinned her with his gaze. She considered his sculped cheeks and strong jaw, always clean-shaven. However, his lips invited. And she felt their call. Oh, how she wanted to answer.

Suddenly aware that she leaned toward him, she pulled back.

And then she could breathe.

A small smile passed over his lips, one that was free of disappointment. Only a tender empathy lingered there.

"You have nothing for which to be sorry." Rhett's deep voice contained a level of huskiness that sent her heart racing anew.

What were we talking about?

Frantic to remember, she looked toward the rocky hills and dry shrubs, searching for her voice. Slowly, she recalled why she had apologized. Still, words had difficulty forming. "I—you—the way everyone has behaved toward you on the ranch. I would never have encouraged you to work for my uncle. If I'd known how he—everyone would treat you."

"I regret not one minute of my time there."

At his quiet assertion, she swiveled back. "How can you not?" She wasn't naive. Rhett must have endured much more than she'd witnessed. What had men like Whitey done already? She couldn't even imagine.

Mrs. Johnson told her that Rhett didn't sleep in the bunkhouse with the rest of the men. Where he'd ended up, she couldn't say. That meant Rhett slept in the barn or one of the drafty, burnt-out buildings on the outskirts. Maybe outside. Yet he never complained.

"Ellie." His quiet voice riveted her attention. He tilted his head. "Don't you realize why I agreed to work for your uncle?"

A storm raged in her heart and filled her ears. Everything in her said to tell him she didn't want to hear. Didn't want to know. Didn't want to believe what the wistful expression on his face proclaimed.

Wasn't he like all the other men in her life? Men who wanted something from her?

No. Rhett is different.

That he had proven many times. He had never asked for anything except to merely offer a pure, yet exhilarating friendship. No strings attached.

"Wh-why?" She swallowed the dust that lined her mouth. "Why did you say yes?"

A slow smile settled on his lips, lighting his face, making him the most beautiful man she had ever beheld. "To be near you. Even if that means I can never be more than your friend."

Friend?

There was that word again. However, this time, it seemed different. She knew—without a doubt—that he wished for more. But he would never take advantage of their relationship. Hadn't he already proved, time and again, that he was trustworthy?

"Are you really my friend?" she dared ask, wanting desperately to hear it again.

His slow nod followed. "From the moment you spoke to me at Fort Laramie. When you asked if you had offended me." A small grin played on his lips.

"I didn't…" She sat back, utterly confounded. She

had? Yes, of course—she remembered now. She had apologized for staring.

"You won my utter devotion that day." He spoke in a whisper as though sharing a secret.

Ellie gaped, mind racing with how to answer such a devastating confession. But she had no need to reply. After a shake of the harness and a click of his tongue, the wagon jerked forward.

His devotion.

Rhett offered that priceless gift, asking for nothing in return. Besides, what could she give? He was a man who owned little, yet lacked nothing. She, by far, was more impoverished.

As she reflected on that devastating fact, he said in a low voice, "Bartow and his men are coming."

Ellie turned in her seat. In the distance, dust rose in the air.

Rhett was right. Guy and his men were riding their way. Fast.

"Why?" Uncle Will stomped across the floorboards with heavy boots. "Why'd you leave town without Guy?"

Ellie opened her mouth to answer, but her uncle swiveled and marched across the room, not giving her a chance.

"We discussed why I wanted him to drive you. Just this morning." Uncle Will threw up his hands. "And you agreed."

Folding her hands, she merely listened. Clearly her uncle wasn't yet ready to hear her reasons. Pride wounded, he needed to rant. And pride truly did seem to be the real issue. She had disobeyed his wishes, and he had no idea how to deal with that.

Sensing the impending storm, the ranch hands had vanished. Even Mr. and Mrs. Johnson had disappeared into their cabin, leaving only Ellie and her uncle in the big house.

Rhett...

She took a shaky breath as she thought of him and what had transpired between them before Guy and his men had interrupted their ride home. If she had any doubts about Rhett's feelings for her, his words had wiped them out. She couldn't escape one soul-shaking thought.

He wants to be near me.

Besides Mama, no one ever desired to be with her. Grandmother never had patience. Father never seemed interested. And God...?

Only recently had Ellie become aware of His love for her. The realization flooded her with an astonishing humility. Did God truly care for her as Rhett said?

When she raised her eyes, she caught her uncle's glare from across the room. Silence reverberated through the room. He apparently had run out of things to say.

"Why did you abandon Mama?" Ellie had not planned to voice the question, but it escaped without forethought. That had been uppermost in her mind from the moment she'd read it in her mother's diary.

If she had thrown her cup and hit Uncle Will squarely in the forehead, he wouldn't have looked more startled. Color drained from his face as he wilted into the nearest chair.

"She was waiting for you." The words of her mother's diary bubbled up. "Night after night, she put a candle in the window. But you never—"

"How'd you know about that?" Uncle Will's hoarse

rasp interrupted. "I never put the details in my letters in case…well, we feared Tess would intercept one."

That very well could have happened. Ellie remembered Grandmother Tess all too well—she was rigid, disapproving and exceedingly proud. The memory of her sharp tongue and stinging slap still hurt. Only Mama's loving arms soothed Ellie after a visit to Grandmother's. But when they returned home, Father was the next torture for them to endure. He often reminded his wife that he had only married her for her money.

Mama had deserved better. How might her life been different if she had married her beloved William?

"Why'd you stay away?" Though Ellie tempered her voice, she felt as though she shrieked.

Her uncle's face grew haggard. Red-rimmed eyes stared into the past, then met hers. "Remember that attack on my ranch I told you about? Instead of traveling on to Chicago, I returned here. Tess made sure Adel heard the news. She told her my whole operation was wiped out and I'd been killed. By the time I finally reached Chicago, Adel was already married. To my brother. They were on their honeymoon in New York." Will covered his face before running his hands across his head. "I should've…" He took a deep breath as his shoulders slumped. "Doesn't matter now."

For many minutes, silence filled the room.

"I'm sorry." Ellie determined to say nothing more about her mother's life—and her own—with Father. The news would only distress her uncle.

His chair creaked as he shifted.

Ellie stared at her hands, clenched in her lap. "Mama kept a diary. Just last night I read about her sorrow. When she thought you'd died." She took a shaky breath. "That's why I didn't stay after church today. They played some of her favorite hymns. And I—I had to get away."

Ellie didn't add that she was in a hurry to get back to Uncle Will. She so wanted to hear that he loved her mother. That Mama had some happiness in a life that had been full of anger, accusations, yelling.

You still love him. *Admit it.* Frank Marshall's voice rang in her mind. But not until last night did Ellie understand what her father meant. He had raged about his own brother.

Uncle Will's jaw tightened, then relaxed.

She rose to rest a hand on his shoulder. "Mama never stopped loving you. Never doubt that."

A deep shudder ran through her uncle. A groan, from deep inside him, escaped. The next moment, he began to cough. He couldn't seem to catch his breath as he struggled to retrieve his handkerchief. For what felt like hours, he hacked into the fabric. When he pulled it away from his lips, he hastened to fold the material.

But Ellie already saw the bright splotch of blood. Her heart froze at the confirmation of her suspicions. Her uncle had consumption.

Chapter Twelve

From the barn's upper beams, Rhett watched with interest as a small group of ranch hands clustered near the bunkhouse. They appeared agitated by the recent events—Will Marshall's announcement of his illness at supper the night before and now the seeming lack of direction for the ranch. Rhett kept his distance from it all. What could he do except continue working and doing what he was hired to do? Besides caring for livestock and fixing fences, Rhett tended to Ellie's horse, Tripper.

Two days had passed since his confession to her. And in that time period, he had barely seen her. She appeared wholly occupied with caring for her uncle. As it should be. But as the hours passed, Rhett grew keen to discover what her reaction to him would be now that she'd had time to think about their conversation.

"Be not of a doubtful mind." He spoke aloud a command he'd told himself often when he had been hungry or afraid. But this anxiety was new to him.

Was she avoiding him on purpose? Did his confession repulse her?

Shaking his head, he sought to rid himself of speculations. His best course of action was prayer. God would reveal His will in good time.

Rhett again lay in the small spot he'd made for a bed. The shed was no longer a safe place. Ever since he discovered his bedroll and some personal items lying in a mud puddle, he had begun changing his nightly location. Sometimes he slept under the stars while other times he chose the barn. But always he was careful to hide his belongings so that no one would find them.

When voices rose in the yard, Rhett again peered through the slats of wood. Bartow strode toward the group, two of his cronies in tow. His raised tone and waving hand let the loitering men know he wasn't pleased.

"Mack," he called to one man while the rest scattered.

Their heads came together. Bartow gestured as he spoke. Mack merely listened. After a few minutes, Rhett determined the foreman and two of his men planned to go somewhere. One of them headed to the corral to get the horses, the other retrieved their gear while Bartow stood waiting, arms crossed as he looked around, like he owned the place. The noon sun spotlighted his self-satisfied smirk.

Rhett had only one possible course of action—follow them.

Until he could slip away undetected, he had to wait. The foreman and his cronies had a head start, but their trail wasn't hard to follow. Riding at a good clip, they were apparently anxious to get to their destination and back before dark.

Rhett came upon them as they were cutting a few dozen head of cattle from the rest. Remaining out of sight, he watched. Soon they were on their way, driving the cattle before them.

More slowly now, Rhett followed. After a time, they came across a way station. The men herded the cattle into the waiting pens.

It didn't take a genius to figure out what was happening. Now Rhett understood Mr. Tesley's comment about being able to handle the amount Bartow provided.

"They're rustling cattle," Rhett muttered to himself. "Stealing from Marshall."

When he had seen enough, he headed back to the ranch. Caution told him to take a circuitous route, so that when he rode back into the yard, it would appear like he'd come from a different direction. Someone was bound to tell Bartow he'd been missing all day.

No doubt Rhett would get a verbal dressing-down as a lazy, no-account bum for shirking work. But he preferred that to getting shot if the foreman even suspected his secret was known.

Rhett rode hard to the north, heading toward Casper before turning southwest. Some folks waved in acknowledgment as he passed through town. The route he took was slower, harder, but no problem for his gelding, chosen for strength and stamina. They stopped to take a long drink at a stream before Rhett pushed on, more slowly this time.

The afternoon's shadows lengthened. He would, no doubt, return later than Bartow and his men. No matter. It was safer that way.

But a few miles from the ranch, Rhett grew increasingly uneasy. Several times he got the feeling that someone was trailing him. Although caution further delayed his return, he made certain to stay out of plain sight. He hugged the tree-lined stream, weaving in and out of the shrubbery as he slowed Wash to a walk.

Whoever was behind him also slowed and stayed out of sight. Dusk had fallen. He pulled his jacket out of his pouch and put it over his cream-colored shirt. Urging his horse to continue toward the ranch, Rhett slipped off the saddle and ducked behind a tree. He had trained Wash to stop after a few yards, within whistling distance. Something told Rhett to wait.

Breath held, he clutched his knife handle.

But whoever followed him seemed to have disappeared.

Then he heard the faintest rustle of movement. A horse, chomping at his bit, drew closer.

"I see you've grown more wary." A voice came from the duskiness. Pete?

Rhett sucked in a slow breath, hoping to confirm what his ears told him.

"You waiting to stick me with that toothpick of yours?" His friend's saddle creaked as he stood up in his stirrups.

Chuckling, Rhett stepped out of his hiding place. "I wanted to make certain you weren't going to stick me first."

Pete patted his scabbard. "I prefer a rifle. Better distance." His grin slowly faded. "But from the rumors I've been hearing in town, you're courting to get shot. Likely in the back."

Although Rhett grinned, he knew his friend could very well be right.

"Got your message. From Ira." Pete dismounted. "But I'm guessing you have more to discuss than an injured horse."

Rhett nodded. But where to start?

* * *

"Rhett?" Ellie stood in the middle of the drafty barn, hoping her whisper was loud enough for his hearing only. "You there?"

No answer.

Where was he?

Under the cover of darkness, she had crept from the back of the house to the shed, which was empty. Finally, Ellie ended up in the barn.

The blackness closed around her as she listened for a sound—any sound—that would alert her to his presence. Since nothing happened, she found herself wishing for a lantern. Then she could check on Tripper. She had not brought one because she didn't want anyone to see or follow her.

Hand extended so as not to run into anything, she crept forward. Her horse chuffed, obviously knowing she was in the barn.

"Hey, boy." She kept her voice low.

Despite the absence of light, she found the gate and stepped into the stall.

Tripper nickered a welcome as she smoothed her hand over his soft, warm neck.

"How're you doing?" After his welcome, she was sorry she hadn't brought him a sugar cube or two.

Standing at attention, her horse allowed her to feel along his back until she got to his leg. From touch only she was able to determine that his wound was nearly healed. It felt cool. However, she noted that he seemed a little thin. "Isn't Rhett feeding you enough?"

She reached inside his feed box, but he had plenty of hay. Not only that, but over the last few days Ellie had noticed the gelding in a small pasture. Rhett's work, presumably.

She patted Tripper's neck. "Next time, I'll bring a treat."

With care, she moved back toward the barn door. She was nearly there when it swung open. Instinctively, she froze. Guy's silhouette filled the doorway.

"Ellie?" Guy's voice echoed in the space. "You in here?"

She stepped forward.

"Yes. I'm coming out." She refused to be alone in a dark building with him.

The minute she walked outside, he remarked, "Thought I saw you go in there." His eyes narrowed. "You alone?"

Her first instinct was to retort that this was none of his business. Instead, she managed a small shrug. "Just me and Tripper."

"Without a lantern?"

She crossed her arms. "Did you need something?"

"No. Well, just wondering how Will is."

"Better." When Ellie had left him in his cabin earlier, he was resting peacefully.

Thank You, Lord, that his awful coughing stopped.

"I don't want to be indelicate, but have you thought about what'll happen after he passes?"

She tamped down the impulse to retort that *indelicate* could be Guy's middle name. "No. I don't want to think about it."

And she didn't really want to continue talking to the foreman. But he seemed to have something on his mind. As she moved toward the house, he followed.

"We should at least talk about your intentions." He matched her pace. "For the ranch."

She stopped. "What exactly are you asking?"

"Ya gonna keep this place? Work it?"

The question floored her. She couldn't imaging running a ranch by herself. "I have no idea." She knew nothing of operating a ranch and had no desire to learn. Not without Uncle Will.

"But you're Will's heir, right? Unless there's someone else out there I don't know about."

She made a sound of impatience. "I don't believe any of this is your concern. If you have questions, you should talk to my uncle." She gathered her skirts and swept away from him.

"What good would that be?" Guy raised his voice. "If he's dead?"

Ellie stopped and turned around.

The foreman marched toward her. "I ain't just asking for myself, but all the men. They're nervous. It'd be nice to reassure them of some plan."

She stepped back when the odors of grease, onions and smoke from a fire overpowered her. "After I talk to my uncle, I'll let you— "

"No, now." Guy's voice grew brittle. "If you do wanna keep it, the first thing you gotta do is grow a little backbone. Stand up for yourself. Otherwise, no man in his right mind will work for you. And you'll end up losing the ranch."

He wanted backbone? By the time she was done talking to him, he'd agree she had plenty.

"To be honest, I miss the comforts of a big city." She drew in a quick breath, determined to explain even if none of this was Guy's business. "I don't want to learn how to round up cattle. Or brand them. If I inherited the ranch, I'd probably sell it and move to Casper or Cheyenne."

Wherever Rhett would prefer.

The unbidden thought came to her mind. And the

realization that she wanted him in her future, however that might look.

"Thank you. That's all I was asking." With a tip of his hat, Guy strode away.

But the moment he left, her rash words filled her with regret.

Uncle Will had paid in sweat—and blood—to build this place into a fine ranch. Would she throw it away so casually?

As she climbed the porch steps, her original plans crystalized in her mind. She had wanted to reacquaint herself with her uncle and practice medicine. Nothing had changed those desires.

Uncle Will needed her. With proper care, he could live for many years. She could learn about the ranch as they worked side by side. In the coming months, Uncle Will could see the truth about Rhett—his character, loyalty and love for the Lord. And as her uncle's attitude changed, so would that of the other ranch hands.

What if they don't?

The unbidden question sprung to her mind. Ellie expelled a pent-up breath.

If not, they could go their way. After she entered her bedroom, names came to mind—Whitey, Hoskins, Blade, Dietmeyer. They all had made it plain, in one way or the other, that they considered Rhett beneath them.

Those four appeared to be Guy's closest friends. Wherever he went, one or more always accompanied him. And although the foreman never openly treated Rhett ill, his four buddies did. How would Guy respond if she fired them?

After retrieving her mother's diary, Ellie prepared to read from it as she had done several nights. She had a quarter of the way to go before she finished it. But when her thoughts kept returning to the foreman and his friends, she laid the diary aside.

If Guy complained about them getting fired, he could leave too.

She gave a mirthless chuckle. "He'd have no doubts about my backbone then."

From a grassy hill, Rhett stood with his friend Pete. As the sun set, they viewed the ranch. Various lights sprung up as daylight waned. He and his friend had been chatting about the stagecoach runs, but mindful of the hour and the need to return to the ranch, Rhett had to ask, "How much do I owe you for the horse?"

Pete held up his palm. "Don't worry about it. The company was happy to get rid of the gelding once I told them he would be no good to them."

"You certain?" He doubted the company would just give away a valuable animal.

His friend grinned. "They owed me."

That meant Pete had likely traded the horse for work. Rhett pressed. "Money is no object."

Pete's eyebrows shot up. "Your ranch job pays that well? Maybe I should work for Marshall. My wife wouldn't mind us settling somewhere."

"The horse wasn't for me."

In the growing dusk, Pete's eyes narrowed. "Ah. Miss Elinor wanted him, eh?"

Something about the way his friend stared at him made Rhett grow cautious about a quick reply. "I told her I'd arrange the purchase."

Eyes narrowing, Pete took his time answering. "Be careful, my friend. You trod on dangerous ground."

Since silence seemed to be the best answer, Rhett crossed his arms.

Pete put his hand on his shoulder. "William Marshall ain't someone you want to tangle with. And he has a particular hatred of anyone named Walker."

Rhett jerked out of his hold.

"Yeah. I know you're a Walker. Have known for a while." Each of Pete's words seemed to strike at his heart. "I recall my pa telling me the gang hit this area pretty hard. Though it was more'n a decade ago, some folks haven't forgotten. Will Marshall could've been part of the posse that hunted them down."

A chill gripped Rhett. Was the ranch owner responsible for his father's hanging? Not that it would change anything. From all accounts, his pa had deserved the penalty.

"I don't exactly know how you're related to the gang," Pete went on. "And I don't care. Just watch your back."

"Regardless, come to the ranch to get paid for the horse." Rhett considered what might be the best time. "How about tomorrow afternoon?"

"Can't tomorrow. I'm making a run to Cheyenne."

"Then the day after."

"I'll be there. One question, though." His friend's mouth pursed. "Why're you making a mountain outa a molehill?"

"Truthfully?"

"Yeah." Pete gave a bark of a laugh. "Truth works for me."

"I'd like another set of eyes at the ranch. See the lay of the land. Then we'll talk. Something's going on there that I…"

He fell silent when Pete held up his palm. Frown gathering, his friend tapped his own lips.

For several minutes, Rhett heard nothing. But he noticed that both their horses had stopped grazing, ears pricked forward. Was a rider approaching?

"Hear that?" Pete whispered.

A low moan and squeal betrayed what was happening.

"A mare," his friend continued. "Trying to foal?"

Rhett nodded. The next thoughts flashed—it had to be Marshall's horse. And she was in trouble.

Chapter Thirteen

"Miss Ellie." Mrs. Johnson's raised voice and persistent knocking roused her from sleep.

Rolling over, Ellie blinked at the light behind her curtains. Was it morning already? She had stayed up too late reading her mother's diary. "Just a…just a minute."

"Hurry." Fading footsteps revealed Mrs. Johnson was retreating.

Still groggy, Ellie sat up. Had something happened to Uncle Will? Shaking sleep from herself, she grabbed the knitted throw from the foot of her bed. Uncaring that her feet were bare, she rushed from her bedroom.

The front door was open. As she stepped onto the porch, the sun's rays blinded her. Mrs. Johnson stood at one corner, leaning over the railing. Squinting from the bright light, Ellie drew closer.

Her uncle's voice finally drew her attention toward his cabin. In the yard stood the beautiful buckskin Ellie had seen only from afar. A gangly foal hugged its mother's side.

Rhett held the halter's rope, his hand on the mare's nose as he spoke low words to her.

"What's going on?" Ellie breathed.

"Dunno, miss." Mrs. Johnson threw her a look. "Heard the ruckus. Saw Rhett walking into the yard with the boss's horse, carrying her foal."

Hadn't her uncle warned Rhett to stay away from the mare? Ellie ran fingers over her forehead to rid the cobwebs from her mind.

The housekeeper nodded her head in Uncle Will's direction. "Guessing Rhett helped her."

A couple men were running from the bunkhouse toward the crowd. However, they drew up short when the mare laid back her ears and shrilled in warning.

"Stay back, fools." Uncle Will's commanding voice filled the yard.

Rhett spoke low words to the mare, calming her. Only when she settled down did Will speak to him.

"Tell me what happened."

Though Rhett didn't raise his voice, Ellie could understand what he was saying. "I came across the mare in the field. The foal was breech."

"Why didn't you run for help?"

Rhett shrugged. "No time. I couldn't leave her to the wolves."

Despite herself, Ellie shivered at the idea.

His explanation didn't seem to soften her uncle, who continued to glower.

"I know you ordered me to stay away from her." Rhett's hand stroked the mare's nose. "But would you prefer I let her die?"

Ellie held her breath, waiting for her uncle's response. From the looks on the faces of the other ranch hands, they did too.

This was the wild mare that ran loose in the nearby pasture. Ellie had never attempted to get near her. Apparently no one could except Uncle Will.

And Rhett. The realization dawned that the mare wasn't skittish about him. Had Rhett tamed the mare?

He disobeyed my uncle.

Yet, if he hadn't…

Any moment, Ellie expected him to fire Rhett. She, along with everyone else it seemed, waited with bated breath.

"Then I guess I owe you my thanks." Will stuck out his hand.

After a second, Rhett stepped forward and shook it. Then he held out the lead rope, but her uncle declined to take it with a shake of his head. "I'll incur the wrath of my niece if I even walk across the yard. I'd be much obliged if you would stable Sugar."

"Yessir."

"You men." Will again raised his voice. "I don't pay you to stand around and gawk. Get back to work."

They hurried to their various tasks. Only then did Ellie realize that Guy wasn't among them. Where was he? She caught sight of Whitey, leaning against the bunkhouse. Even from a distance she could see his curling lip.

Rhett waited until the yard was nearly empty before turning the mare around. As his gaze met Ellie's, he paused.

She could tell he'd had a rough night, from his redrimmed eyes to the scruff on his chin. But though sleepdeprived, he managed a small smile and a nod in her direction.

Her breath caught, but ever mindful of watching eyes, she stifled her own smile. Instead, she inclined her head.

Not only was Mrs. Johnson studying her, but Uncle Will.

* * *

Rhett stretched and yawned, getting his bearings as he blinked awake.

Right. He'd helped with the mare last night.

Rubbing his face, he sat up. Had to be past noon. Though he'd slept several hours, he still felt groggy. No time to lie around any longer, though. Although Marshall had given him the day off, Rhett had work to do.

He stashed his bedroll and other possessions, then swung down from the rafters of the shed. Almost noiselessly, he dropped to the dirt floor before squatting and listening. Wisdom told him he needed to determine where everyone was before sauntering out of the building.

He detected someone in the corral with the horses. Roping them for the blacksmith? Seemed so. In the distance, Rhett caught the sound of a hammer striking metal. He heard the familiar hack of Marshall's cough. Sounded as though he was on his cabin's porch. Likely Ellie was nearby so she could fuss over him. The sound of sloshing water told him that today was washday. Mrs. Johnson was scrubbing clothes while her husband hauled buckets of water to the cauldron. The fire beneath it crackled and popped. Another woman spoke— Alice, Mrs. Johnson's sister.

Rhett rose to his feet and brushed the lingering straw from his clothing. His grumbling stomach told him to get something to eat. Far too many hours had passed since he'd had food.

After he emerged from the shed, he noted Ellie exiting the house. She immediately waved. Aware that Marshall also saw him, Rhett merely nodded in return as he beelined for the back of the house.

But Ellie would have none of that. She gestured him over.

With slowing footsteps, he approached the steps.

"Where're you going?" Her eyes seemed to dance as she asked the question. She was a picture of loveliness, her hair pinned into a loose bun—unlike how it had been that morning, flowing over her shoulders. Instead of a dark green wrap over her nightgown, she wore a gown of dazzling blue, fringed with delicate lace and dark piping. The colors complimented her creamy complexion and golden hair. But it was her smile that dazzled.

Knowing his face would give him away, he kept his head lowered. "I'm hungry."

Rhett knew he sounded like an oaf, but he couldn't help it. Not while under Marshall's watchful gaze. The man might be grateful for his mare's rescue, but that didn't mean he would wholeheartedly approve of his niece getting friendly with a nearly penniless saddle bum.

"Come in, then." Ellie looked worried at the thought of him not eating. "I know Mrs. Johnson always has food in the kitchen. No need to go around back."

"I can find it." He spoke quickly before she offered to serve him. "Thank you."

He hurried up the steps and through the house. Gratefulness and disappointment hit him simultaneously when Ellie didn't follow. From the sound of Marshall's voice, Rhett determined she went to his cabin.

In minutes, he found a bounty—ranging from cold pancakes to slabs of ham. He carried a laden plate into the great room. The first sips of steaming coffee caused him to sigh in pleasure. Mrs. Johnson always had a ready pot, likely because her husband seemed to drink a gallon himself every day.

After sitting, Rhett dug into the pancakes. He was

nearly through when a form filled the open doorway. Marshall. Ellie scooted past him, heading for her bedroom. However, she left her door open.

The ranch owner studied Rhett before taking a seat across from him. "Ellie tells me you're educated."

As he sipped his coffee, he considered how to answer. And wondered why his boss wanted to know. "My mentor was strict about lessons."

"Mentor?" Marshall's eyebrows shot up. "You didn't attend school?"

"Correct, sir."

"Hmm." His boss looked away as though considering. "I suppose you learned the basics? Reading, writing and arithmetic?"

Rhett nodded, hesitating to say more so as not to brag. From the next room, the swish of material told him Ellie was listening.

"And? What else?" the ranch owner prodded.

"Music. French. History."

Marshall's eyes widened. "You good with numbers?"

With caution, he answered. "Fair."

"Huh. I might have you help with the books. I hate all that figuring." Marshall rose and headed to the door. "I was going to ask Ellie, but she's too busy fussing over me."

"Am not." Her protest came from the other room.

Rhett hid his smile behind his coffee cup. Truth be told, his head spun at the thought of helping with the books. No more ditch digging? Fence fixing? The possibility pleased him.

And the prospect of being closer to Ellie. Seeing her more.

Eyes narrowed, his boss studied him from the doorway. Rhett set his cup down and met the man's gaze, aware that he must take care with his answer. "I'm your employee, sir. If I can best help that way, then I'm happy to be at your service."

A cautious grin tugged at one corner of Marshall's mouth. "Dunno if you can do more'n add two and two, but sounds like you've more education than all the cowboys here combined."

Rhett kept his expression neutral, not knowing if that was a good or bad thing. But after his boss headed back outside, Ellie peered around the corner. Her pink cheeks and sparkling eyes told him she was pleased by her uncle's remark.

Perhaps admitting being educated would prove to be a very, very good thing.

Later that day, Ellie sat by the large window, sunlight streaming over her, as she fought to line up two seams. Despite her care, the fabric slipped and pulled out the stitches she had painstakingly put in. Why had her mother not taught her to sew? Embroidery, yes. Sewing, no. Of course, they had servants for tailoring, but they only adjusted the store-bought clothing that she owned.

Growling, she lined up the fabric and tried again. If this tiny little placemat gave her this much trouble, how much more difficult would a dress be? Even stitching up people's wounds was less trouble.

After stabbing herself a couple more times, she rolled up the material and shoved it back into her trunk. Perhaps Mrs. Johnson could give her a pointer or two. That is, if the older woman stopped working long enough.

Wandering back to the window, Ellie looked out. Her uncle and Rhett had left soon after they had talked, but she found herself wishing they would come back.

Mrs. Johnson claimed not to know their destination, so couldn't estimate how long they would be gone. She did volunteer that a few other men had gone with them.

Ellie was about to head to her bedroom when she saw her medical bag sitting in one corner of the great room. Stopping, she stared. Hadn't she put it away the other day? After Mrs. Johnson had scraped her elbow, Ellie had applied some ointment. Shaking her head, she returned the bag to her room and then retrieved her bonnet.

After slipping it on, she headed for the barn. The beautiful day begged for her to be outside, so why not Tripper, as well? Surely she could get a halter on the gelding and lead him to the small pasture by herself.

Rays of sunlight streamed through the wood slats as she paused inside the barn, allowing her eyes to adjust. Motes of dust hung midair, floating on an undetectable updraft. Enthralled by the sight, she watched.

A strange sensation, of a scintillating joy she had never before felt, rose inside. She lifted her eyes heavenward, aware for the first time that God was the reason for her happiness. The overhead beams seemed to part, revealing the heavens above.

Neck tingling, Ellie sucked in a slow breath. Time and space seemed to burgeon, imbedding her soul with the weight of eternity.

"Father?" After speaking in a whisper, she fell silent. She heard no audible voice, saw no flash of lightning, but she knew—without a doubt—that the Lord inclined His ear to her.

The flapping of a bird, somewhere in the shadows, brought her back to earth. But Ellie hugged herself, overwhelmed by the lingering sweet sensation.

The low groan of an animal startled her. She strained to listen. Again, she heard the sound. Tripper?

She hurried toward his stall, confounded by what could ail him. As she opened the gate, she gasped.

His head hung low, but what froze her blood was his skeletal appearance.

"What...?"

Tripper didn't raise his head or nicker like he usually did. The thought struck her that he appeared as despondent as the first time she had seen him, before she stitched up his wound.

He groaned again.

"Tripper." She moved toward him, gingerly touching his back. "What is it?"

He appeared listless, not even raising his head when she walked behind him. Had his wound become infected? After a brief exam, she saw it was almost healed. She found no other injuries. His feed and water appeared untouched. Why wasn't he eating?

For many minutes, she remained in the stall, unable to fathom what was wrong. Thoughts ricocheted in her head. An unwelcomed idea burst upon her. Had Rhett known about Tripper's condition and not told her? That question settled into a disturbing doubt. Perhaps he did know and hadn't wanted to tell her because of his recent success of getting into Uncle Will's good graces.

"Hang on, Tripper." She patted her horse's neck. As gently as she could, she slipped the halter over his head, then led him from the barn. He stumbled as he walked as though blind. After Ellie put him in the pasture, she stood back to study him. Head still hanging, he didn't move. In the bright light, she could see his coat had grown dull. Some patches looked bare.

"I've failed." The obvious conclusion came to her.

She had overlooked something when it came to caring for the horse.

Did Rhett know and not tell me?

The relentless question continued to build in her thoughts. He said Tripper would make a full recovery. For a while longer, she watched her horse until her heart could take no more. Chest heaving, she marched back to the house to wait for the men.

"That's pert near the ugliest horse I ever seen." Whitey, reining beside Marshall in the yard, spoke loudly enough for the whole group to hear.

Lagging behind the others, Rhett glanced around to see whose mount he meant. He caught sight of a gaunt chestnut in the pasture that looked vaguely familiar.

"Whose bag o' bones is that?" Marshall asked, still astride his mount.

"Tripper." The name escaped Rhett before he had the sense to shut his mouth.

Five pairs of eyes fixed on him.

He had to remind them. "Ellie's horse."

Deafening silence met his pronouncement.

"Looks to me," Bartow drawled, "you ain't been doing such a hot job taking care of him."

Rhett met his gaze, then stared ahead. Something was very wrong here, but he couldn't understand what.

"He's suffering." Marshall's mouth tightened. "It's obvious even from here."

"Want someone to put him out of his misery, boss?" The foreman's tone contained an odd eagerness. When Marshall didn't answer, Bartow tilted his head in Rhett's direction. "Seems to me he should be the one to do it."

"True." Marshall's flinty gaze fixed on Rhett. "You

were responsible for him. I'll not have Ellie seeing him in this condition."

"Yessir." What else could Rhett say?

"Do it now. Before supper."

Transfixed, Rhett didn't move as the men continued their way into the yard.

"Take him up to the woods," Marshall threw over his shoulder. "I don't want my niece more upset than she's bound to be."

Rhett nudged his gelding forward. The others were hitching their horses. As he rode by, Bartow glanced up. A satisfied smirk marked his face before he ducked his head.

Why would the foreman be happy about the death of Ellie's horse? Whatever the reason, the heavy rock that plunged into Rhett's stomach told him this whole incident boded ill.

Especially for him.

Chapter Fourteen ·

A distant pop woke Ellie. Then a second. Were those gunshots? They sounded far away.

Late-afternoon sunshine streamed into her bedroom. Earlier it had gotten so hot, she had opened her window a couple inches. But the warmth had lulled her into taking a nap.

Still groggy, she sat up. Her mother's diary thumped as it landed on the bed beside her. The words Ellie had read earlier jumped off the page.

Lord forgive me for what I've done.

The phrase puzzled Ellie. She couldn't imagine what heinous crime Mama had committed. In the previous entry, she had described what it felt to be in love. For the first time in her life.

Frank, her intended, wasn't the one who occupied Adeline's thoughts, but his younger brother—the dashing and handsome William who had arrived from the wild frontier.

As Ellie read of the dances, parties and theater performances they attended, she couldn't help but imagine what her own life would have been like if she remained in Chicago. What if Rhett had visited her there? Ellie dismissed the silly picture that came to her mind of him attending a ball or lounging in the stuffy parlors of Chicago's elitists. He didn't belong there.

"I don't either." She fingered her mother's diary as she spoke aloud.

Only a few pages remained to read. Judging from the quietness of the house, Rhett, her uncle and the other men hadn't yet returned. According to her clock, supper should be soon. The Johnsons must be delaying the meal until after Uncle Will's arrival.

Time to finish the diary. She found her spot. Her heart began to thump uncomfortably as she learned of her mother's anguish because of something she had done. But what? Ellie had already read of the sorrow when she believed her beloved William had died. Adeline grieved that she would have to face life apart from him.

But from the last entries, some new torment gripped her, evidenced by smeared ink and tear-blotched pages.

Mother insists Frank and I marry as soon as possible. How can I agree to this? But I can no longer consider only myself. God's will be done.

A few more lines followed, then the diary ended.

Ellie closed it, then reopened it to reread the last page. Why would Grandmother Tess insist they marry immediately? More importantly, why had Mama agreed when she was still grieving over William?

Unless, of course, Grandmother already knew he hadn't died. She wanted her daughter wedded to Frank before William reappeared. But Ellie couldn't reconcile that fact with her mother's torment.

Ellie rechecked the date of the entry. June 10. If she

remembered correctly, her parents had wed on the fifteenth of that same month.

A cold prickle of premonition edged down her back.

...I can no longer consider only *myself.*

Ellie reread the line several times. With shaking fingers, she recalculated when her parents had married and the date of her own birth. Almost eight months later.

The truth hit her like a bucket of ice water.

"Dear Lord." Ellie's voice shook as she spoke aloud. "Uncle Will is...is my father."

Heart heavy, Rhett left the shelter of the woods. Taking his time, wended his way back to the ranch. He would have to tell Ellie his suspicions—someone had poisoned her horse. But when could he arrange some time alone with her? And would she believe him?

Never had self-recrimination hit him as hard as it did now. He should have kept a better eye on Tripper. Should have checked his feed. Looked more closely at the gelding. Maybe Rhett could've acted sooner and either caught who was harming the horse or stopped it before the gelding got so sick.

Dusk blanketed the ranch as he paused on a hill and stared at the well-lit house, smoke rising from two chimneys. He was in no hurry. Likely Marshall was waiting for his return, though. What could Rhett tell him?

"Lord, give me wisdom," he prayed aloud. "Please."

He nudged his mount on.

As he drew closer to the yard, his boss rose from the chair in front of the cabin. A couple men by the bunkhouse straightened. One turned his head, as though speaking to his companion, who then hurried off.

Seemed they were waiting for him.

He slid off Wash and slung the reins over the hitching post. Out of the corner of his eye, he could see Marshall stride toward him. But he stopped in the middle of the yard. Obviously he wanted a report.

Gulping, Rhett walked toward him. *Please, Lord, keep me from lying.*

"You take him to the woods?" Marshall asked.

"Yessir."

The foreman arrived. He planted himself beside Marshall while his posse circled Rhett. Instinctively, his palm sought his knife. He didn't like that two of them were standing behind him.

Marshall scowled. "What do you want?" He singled out each of the four men with his glower. "This's none of your business."

Their eyes flicked to Bartow, who dismissed them with a jerk of his thumb.

A chill pooled at the back of Rhett's neck and crawled down his spine at this further proof that Bartow was the true leader, not Marshall. How could the owner not see that?

Only after the four slunk off did Rhett relax.

Best be proactive. He fixed his gaze on Marshall. "I took the gelding past the ridge."

"I heard the shots."

"Two." Rhett licked dry lips. "He's gone."

"Good."

"Shots?" Ellie's question sliced the air. She rushed down the porch steps, wrapping a shawl about her shoulders. "Who got shot? I heard gunfire."

Rhett opened his mouth to answer, but the words stuck. He would not lie to her but dared not reveal the truth—not with this audience.

"Your buddy here killed your horse," the foreman answered.

"What?" Her voice rose as she stared at Rhett. "You shot Tripper?"

Before he could speak, Marshall stepped between them. "I told him to."

Stepping around him, she advanced on Rhett. "How could you? He was *my* horse. You had no right."

"He was sick, Ellie." Marshall spoke again. "Please understand. I can't abide—*won't* abide—letting a wounded animal suffer. Not if I can end its misery. I told Rhett —"

"You should have told me. Asked me first." Ellie glared at her uncle but settled her ire on Rhett. Tears choked her voice. "I didn't even get to say goodbye."

Rhett clenched an impotent fist. Her pain was his pain. He could relieve it in an instant. Regardless of the consequences, he had to admit what he had done.

His gaze flickered to her uncle, who stood beside her, a hand on her shoulder. Rhett lowered his voice as he stepped closer, preparing to admit he had spared Tripper. "I'm sorry, Ellie, but it's not—"

"Go. Leave me." She shook off her uncle's hand as her gaze remained fixed on Rhett. "Leave me be."

Sobbing, she wheeled and rushed to the house. The slam of the door sounded as a death knell.

Rhett gulped air, wanting to run after her and tell her the truth. Tripper was not dead—not yet, anyway. Pete had intercepted Rhett when he had been about to shoot the gelding. One look at the horse and his friend claimed to know what had happened—Tripper was poisoned. Pete asserted it wasn't too late to save the horse.

Assuming he had gotten to the gelding in time.

Tomorrow might be another story. If Pete couldn't help Tripper, the horse wouldn't last the night.

* * *

"Miss?" A timid knock on the bedroom door followed Mrs. Johnson's voice. "Your breakfast is on the table. And a nice, hot cup of tea."

Ellie rolled to her side, pulling the feather pillow over her ear. She didn't want to eat. And she most certainly didn't want to talk to anyone for the rest of her life.

They're all liars.

Every person she had known and trusted betrayed her. Ellie's mother. Father. Grandmother. Uncle Will. Even Rhett. He had promised her Tripper was out of danger. Why had he lied?

Ellie couldn't decide who had wounded her the most.

Another tear—one of thousands—slid across the bridge of her nose. Never before had she felt so alone. Even after Father had died, leaving her world in shambles, she hadn't felt this abandoned.

She hiccupped as she corrected herself. Even after the man she *thought* was her father had died, she hadn't felt this alone.

Pack up and leave.

The unbidden thought came to her. But where could she go? She had no one. Distant cousins resided in New York and San Francisco, but she knew nothing of them. She couldn't just show up on their doorstep. As tears again consumed her, Ellie buried her face into the pillow.

When she finally calmed herself for the tenth time—or the eighteenth?—she sat up in bed. After scooping water from the basin, she cooled her face. Her eyes lit upon her mother's diary.

"You knew what it was like," Ellie whispered.

If what she suspected was true, her mother had faced pregnancy alone.

With me.

The thought shook Ellie anew.

Her palm rested on the embossed leather of her mother's diary. "How did you find the strength to go on?"

Inside on the back cover, Mama had written several Bible verses. In her time of trouble, she had turned to God.

But wouldn't trusting Him only result in more hurt? A lifetime of experience seemed to support her fears. Although Ellie had prayed and prayed, Mama had died. She'd miscarried several times until the last pregnancy killed her.

Then there was Uncle Will. He had done what was right in coming back to the ranch after the attack. While he was away, his love had been married off to another—Ellie's imposter father.

Why hadn't God intervened?

Her fingers traced the delicate paper as hand-written verses jumped off the page.

When you pass through the waters, I will be with you.
Ellie sucked in a slow breath as the words filled her.
I will be with you.

Knees shaking, she slowly sank beside her bed.

Father, increase my love for You. The memory of Rhett's prayer brought fresh tears to her eyes. He knew his true Father in heaven. And trusted Him. Despite the travesty that dogged his footsteps, he had never lost faith in God.

I will be with You.

Ellie looked upward. "Are you with me, Father?"

The image from the barn—of the roof splitting open to reveal the heavens—flooded her mind. The sensations she had experienced once again flowed into her.

She felt as though a soft cloud settled in her soul and buoyed her up.

A long sigh escaped.

Yes. He was there. And with Him, she could face anything.

For the remainder of the day, Ellie sequestered herself. Only by the next morning did she feel ready to interact with anyone. Despite the turmoil in her soul, the Lord had granted her a night of sweet, restful sleep. With a new awareness of God, she started her day with a prayer of thanks for His constant and comforting presence.

Earlier than her usual time, she opened her bedroom door.

"There you are." Will's sad smile met her the moment she stepped out.

He was alone in the great room, sitting at the end of the table.

Breakfast appeared to be long over and no one was in sight. In the kitchen, she could hear Mrs. Johnson puttering at the stove. Ellie sank into the nearest chair, several feet from…

Confusion gripped her. How should she address this man? She had no idea how to share what she'd learned.

Mrs. Johnson bustled into the room and set a plate of food before her.

"Thank you," Ellie said before the woman hurried back out.

"I'm sorry." Will's voice held a gravelly note of regret that she'd not heard before. "I should've told you. About your horse. Before…" He huffed out a breath, then grew silent, lips pressed together.

Ellie held her tongue to keep from saying, "It's all right."

Shooting Tripper without her permission or knowledge was *not* okay, but that wasn't what was uppermost in her mind. The pale, downcast figure before her was.

What if he was her father? Did he know? When Mama was alive, he had visited a few times. After her death, his letters had been sporadic. Ellie couldn't imagine his neglecting her if he knew the truth. Will Marshall was a man of action and passion. She recalled the tone of the letters he had written to his precious Adel. Surely, if he knew she was his daughter, he would have wanted her by his side.

But how to broach the subject?

Ellie picked up her fork and nudged a potato slice toward a chunk of ham while Will looked on. For his sake, she cut off a sliver of meat and ate it.

He appeared a dozen years older. Had her passionate outburst two nights before distressed him that much? She wouldn't have believed it unless…

Perhaps they shared a bond that he was not yet aware of.

As she set down her fork, she prayed for the right words.

Will held up one hand. "Before you say anything, I need to tell you something, Ellie. Something you're not going to like."

Her mind raced, but she couldn't imagine what he might mean.

"Yesterday, after dinner," Will spoke as he sat back, "Guy asked to meet with me. He said he'd noticed cattle disappearing over the last couple weeks. He hadn't wanted to tell me until after he double-checked the numbers. I rode out myself and surveyed the herds. He's right."

When he paused, Ellie asked, "Where'd they go?"

"Stolen."

Her first thought—more outlaw trouble?

She tucked a strand of hair behind her ear. "Do you know who took them?"

"Yes." His voice rasped.

"Who?"

"That's the part you're not going to like." Will reached across the table to cover her hand. "I have irrefutable proof that Callaway is the thief."

Rhett? She jerked her hand back. "Impossible."

"No. It's not." Will shook his head. "I personally talked to the businessman who bought them. Mr. Tesley didn't talk to him personally, but one of his men described what sounded like Callaway. When Tesley found out the cattle might be stolen, he promised—"

"No." Ellie pressed her arms to her sides. "I—I don't believe it. Rhett is…"

She wanted to say, "Rhett is the most honest and honorable man I've met." But Will's expression proved he wouldn't believe her. Only recently had he begun to trust his newest employee. But if he had to make a choice, Will would believe the word of his foreman over a man he'd always been inclined to distrust.

"Tesley also gave me this." Will pulled a yellowed sheet of folded paper from his pocket and spread it on the table.

A wanted poster?

The face on it looked like Rhett, from the cleft in his chin to his neutral expression. The first phrase that jumped off the page was *bright blue eyes*, followed by the bold words *bank robbery, cattle rustling, murder*.

She shoved the paper back toward her uncle. "This poster is nearly two decades old. That can't be Rhett."

"I know." Will's mouth settled into grim lines. "But he's related to this man. Everett Walker. For years, I kept a wanted poster, just in case I ran across him. I memorized every line of that face. I knew 'Callaway' looked familiar, the second I saw him."

"But…" Ellie shook her head. "You can't hold Rhett responsible for the actions of someone—someone who looks like him."

"Blood doesn't lie. The man who calls himself Rhett Callaway has outlaw blood." Will's finger stabbed the paper's visage. "Cattle rustling runs in his family."

Blood doesn't lie.

The significance of those words struck Ellie with such force that they silenced her. What about her own bloodline? She had a father she couldn't claim. Rhett had one he wouldn't. His refusal to talk about his family explained so much.

"You might as well know the whole story." Will's voice gained a flinty edge. "This morning, I told Callaway to clear out. And to not set foot on my property again."

Shoulders slumping, Ellie remained dumbfounded.

"No doubt you think I'm harsh." Will's gaze tore through her. "But I could've had him strung up on the nearest tree. Around here, that's what we do to cattle rustlers."

She could only stare at her white hands, clenched in her lap.

The chair squawked as Will rose to his feet. He strode to the door, then paused to add one final threat. "If he shows up—anywhere on my property—my men have orders to shoot him."

Chapter Fifteen

For the fourth evening in a row, Rhett skirted the edges of the ranch. Of course, Marshall's trigger-happy men might not care that he was technically outside the property. Several times, he had heard them riding the perimeter. Looking for him? Every morning, Rhett made certain to hide the evidence of his presence. His only worry was that Wash might whinny a greeting to the other horses.

How soon before Marshall's men gave up, believing that he'd moved on?

If he had any sense, he wouldn't continue to hang around. However, Rhett was determined to stay. He had to speak to Ellie. Each night he watched and prayed for an opportunity, asking the Lord to protect her, himself and even Will Marshall.

But even as he wished for an occasion to meet with Ellie, he knew it would likely be the last time he saw her. Would she listen? Believe him when he insisted he wasn't a thief? Perhaps not. Many a man had been tempted by greed.

If nothing else, he could reassure her he had not shot Tripper. According to Pete, the gelding would live—as long as the horse remained away from the ranch and the chance to be poisoned again. His friend had taken him to his home, to provide the kind of care Tripper needed. Pete guessed someone had used arsenic. Another couple days and the gelding would have succumbed.

But what weighed on Rhett the most was his need to warn Ellie—she and her uncle were in danger from Bartow and his men.

Would she believe him?

As Rhett crouched on a hill, the evening reached out with long fingers to gather shadows. From a safe distance, he watched the ranch. As he began to rehearse various scenarios of how the evening might play out, Rhett shook his head. Best not plan for a specific possibility. He needed to prepare for any eventuality.

Time to move. He gathered a handful of ashes and rubbed them into Wash's rump to hide the appaloosa's white hairs. Every night he tied his horse with a long, loose lead, so that he would stay put if undisturbed, but could escape if threatened. Remaining low to the ground, Rhett moved closer to the ranch house. He found a dip in the terrain where he could observe without being seen.

As per custom, the ranch hands emerged from the house after supper. Some lingered in the yard. Two men headed for the corral and saddled up. Looked like they were the ones to make the evening's rounds. From Rhett's distance, he couldn't identify who they were.

Ellie, exiting the house, riveted his attention. After pacing one length of the porch, she turned and walked past the open door to the other end. Then she wrapped her arm about one column and stared into the night.

In his direction.

He wished he were close enough to see her face.

Was she thinking of him? Or merely enjoying the cool evening? Didn't matter. Rhett found himself longing to look on her delicate beauty and perhaps even catch a whiff of her lavender perfume. His heart thrummed in longing.

She seemed unaware of the stares of the ranch hands or the dark clouds that rolled across the sky. When Marshall stepped onto the porch, the men in the yard stopped ogling her. Some appeared to bid the ranch owner good-night as they tipped their hats and sauntered toward the bunkhouse. The owner appeared to speak to one man at the bottom of the steps before joining his niece. Soon the remaining ranch hands wandered away, leaving only Marshall and Ellie. Even from a distance, Rhett could tell her uncle was speaking earnestly to her. He laid a hand on her shoulder while she...

The sound of horse hooves sent an icy shaft of alarm through Rhett. Stupid of him to forget the danger of his own situation. The two riders who were checking the perimeter of the ranch drew closer. No time for him to run. No place to hide.

Rhett flattened himself into the earth's depression, praying they wouldn't see him in the gathering dusk. Above, clouds blanketed the sky and covered the moon.

"Hold up," one man called to his partner. Gates might have been the speaker. "This is the area."

Rhett held his breath. Horse hooves drew closer, then paused.

"Ain't nothing here," the second man spoke. McCoy? The creak of saddle's leather sounded mere yards from Rhett.

Body immobile, he slowed his breathing.

"And I'm telling you I saw something." Gates seemed to be farther away.

McCoy growled. "If you ask me, this's a waste of time."

"Ain't your decision, cowboy." Gates's voice grew hard. "We got orders."

"Yeah, from Bartow. Not Marshall."

Gates didn't answer.

"Bartow's lording it over everyone. Like he's the boss." McCoy's voice lowered. "I even heard him and Whitey talking trash about Marshall's niece."

"So what?"

"So…? No man should speak about a lady like that. Bartow should be whupped."

"I suppose you think you're the one to do that?" Gates let loose a harsh laugh.

"I could be." McCoy spat. "If it'd be a fair fight. But Bartow's cronies would make sure it weren't."

"That's a fact. Come next week, there'll be more of 'em to steer clear of."

"What'd'ya mean?"

"Bartow is hiring more men. Fair certain he hand-picked them."

McCoy blew out a disgusted breath. "Figures."

They fell silent.

"Let's move on," Gates said. "We still got a lotta ground to cover tonight."

The sound of retreating hooves met Rhett's ears. However, he stayed where he was, just in case one of them remained behind. It wouldn't be the first time he'd seen that trick. After many minutes of listening, he cautiously raised his head. He truly was alone.

But it was a good reminder that he needed to exercise more care when he stepped on Marshall's land. His life depended upon it.

* * *

"It looks good." Mrs. Johnson inspected Ellie's fabric as they stood by the window. The bright morning sun highlighted the seam, which Ellie had sewn and torn out multiple times. Not until the piece was nearly perfect had she shown it to the housekeeper.

"Thank you." Smiling, she fingered the placemat. A small accomplishment, but one that filled her with satisfaction. Ellie set aside her project. "And have you thought about my request?"

The woman threw her a sideways glance as she continued to gather the dirty dishes from breakfast.

"Last time I was in town, I bought some real work clothes." Ellie followed her as she spoke, picking up a few items from the table. "I'm not afraid to try something new."

"Hmm." The woman went about her work. When they reached the kitchen, she took the plates from Ellie. "I'm not just concerned about your pretty clothes getting spoiled, but your hands."

"My hands?" She studied her palms.

Mrs. Johnson wiped hers on a towel before holding them up. "Do you want yours looking like mine?"

As she inspected the housekeeper's calloused skin, broken nails and the permanent dirt etched into the surfaces, she tried to maintain a neutral expression. True, she didn't want her hands appearing as rough as that, but she also didn't want to sit around and sew all day.

"I want to be useful." Ellie inserted determination into her voice. "Doing something that'll help my uncle."

That something would keep her from melting into tears, especially as she grieved Rhett's departure.

Mrs. Johnson met her gaze. "Take care of Will. He's most important."

Yes, he was. And Ellie grew aware that she had done little for him over the last several days. More and more, she found herself staring into the distance, thinking of Rhett. Instead of diminishing over time, her longing for him had grown more intense. Where had he gone? She had made a few quiet inquiries in town to no avail. Even Pastor Charles said he hadn't seen Rhett.

If not for the man who called himself her uncle, Ellie might have relocated to Casper by now. Or even Cheyenne to try to find Rhett. Someone would know something. She wanted to make certain he was well and had enough money to survive.

To that end, she spent a lot more time praying. Praying for Rhett's safety. Praying for wisdom about what she should do. Praying for the perfect time to confront Will about her parentage.

Because her vigilance in watching over Will had grown lax, he had begun riding out to the range for longer hours. That resulted in his coughing more.

Ellie drew herself up. "I still want to help with the chickens. Maybe the garden too. I'll wear gloves."

The frown on Mrs. Johnson's face slowly gave way to a small grin. "Very well. We'll start tomorrow after breakfast."

"Why not now?"

"Got my hands full today."

"All right." Ellie gave a nod. "Thank you."

Arms full of dishes, the woman ambled out the back door.

Ellie had just returned to the main room when footsteps stomped across the porch. From the sound, she knew it was Will. He paused to scrape mud from his boots, unlike most of the men who carried in half-dried clods with them. The night's rains had made a mess inside the house.

Ellie met him at the door.

"There you are." Will smiled down at her. "I wanted to let you know I need to take a quick trip to town. I shouldn't be gone too long."

"Would you like me to go with you?"

"Nah." He shrugged and looked away. "I'm going by horseback. Faster that way."

His odd secrecy struck her. Besides, they'd gone to town only a few days before. "I can keep up with you on horseback."

"I know." He patted her shoulder. "I won't be gone long."

"Are you going alone?" A vague uneasiness gripped her.

"Yeah."

"Not taking Guy?"

"No. He's out on the range today."

She absorbed the news in silence, disliking the thought of Will traveling anywhere alone, especially in his state of health.

"I know Guy's a bit rough." Will's hand lingered on her shoulder. "But I cannot impress upon you the strength of his leadership. Because of him, we survived the worst winter in our history. The ranch has flourished under his care."

She managed a small smile. "I'm sure he's a great foreman."

"All he needs is a good woman. To help smooth his rough spots."

Ellie drew back. Surely he wasn't thinking *she* could be that woman.

"I see my hint doesn't set well with you." Will made

a wry face. "Chalk it up to your uncle's crazy fancies and a desire to look to the security of your future."

Openmouthed, she could only stare at him.

He pulled on his hat's brim in a salute, then stalked out the door.

"Be careful," she called. Dark clouds roiled overhead, warning of the possibility of more rain.

Will waved. In no time, he'd mounted his horse and thundered out of the yard.

For a long time, she watched after him, considering their conversation.

Why would he think Guy Bartow could be her suitor? Ellie thought she had made it clear she had no interest in him. Since Will apparently had missed her indicators, she needed to flat-out tell him she would never entertain a future with the foreman.

As she watched the wind whip the strands of grass, she realized why she would never consider Guy. He couldn't hold a candle to the one man to whom she compared all men. As the breeze brushed her cheeks, she closed her eyes, daring to give free rein to her emotions.

I love Rhett. And I always will.

Chapter Sixteen

From the safety of an outcropping, Rhett stared at the ranch below. Nearby, a small cave had turned out to be an excellent hiding place. He not only was able to stash his belongings there, but it provided shelter in inclement weather.

He squatted as he considered his circumstances. A week had passed since the ranch owner had ordered him off the land. By now, both Marshall and Bartow must believe he was gone. For the last two nights, no riders had checked the perimeter. Everything in Rhett said to relax his guard, but common sense told him to stay cautious. He needed to wait until darkness fully covered the land before he dared move closer.

But to what end? Lately he'd berated himself for hoping to speak to Ellie. He told himself tonight was the night. He hoped and prayed that he *would* be able to talk to her after all. If for no other reason than to tell her goodbye.

Rhett looked to the heavens. "If it is Your will, Father. So be it."

However, his heart felt like a knife pierced it. Would the Lord command him to move on?

Regardless of what happens, I will never forget her.
Rhett would carry his love for her to his death.

As usual, he waited until the full cover of darkness before approaching Marshall's land. The lights inside the main house proved that the men were still at supper. But they would emerge soon. He had to move fast.

Crouching, he ran from trees to shrubs, staying hidden as best he could. Out of breath, he finally reached a small knoll where he could hide. Just in time. The front door burst open and a couple men exited into the yard. As they were wont to do every evening, some lingered, their voices echoing in his direction. Rhett could hear laughter. After many minutes, most shuffled toward the bunkhouse. A little while later, Bartow emerged, then Marshall, who paused on the porch to cough hard. They spent a few minutes talking, then the ranch owner walked to his cabin.

With the door to the house still open, light streamed onto the porch. Bartow seemed undecided about something. Ellie? Rhett imagined he wanted to go back inside. Leaning against the porch's column, the foreman stared into the night. Another two men emerged and passed Bartow, intent on the bunkhouse.

Rhett focused on Marshall, who paused on the small porch of his cabin. He too seemed reluctant to retire. Several times he coughed. After a minute, he disappeared. A light appeared in the cabin, proving he prepared to retire.

Bartow rested his boot on the railing's lower rung and struck a match before bending forward to light a cigarette. However, Rhett recognized the stalling tactic as Bartow propped his elbow on a raised knee. Rhett sucked in a slow breath as he grew anxious about Ellie being alone with the foreman. Before thinking through the ramifications, Rhett moved toward the ranch yard, using whatever cover he could find. He flattened himself against the backside of Marshall's cabin, taking huge, silent gulps of air. The dogs bounded out of the darkness, but they didn't bark. They nosed Rhett's hand but he had no food to offer. After a pat to their heads, they soon wandered off.

"It's a fine night." Bartow's voice reached Rhett in his hiding spot.

Ellie's reply was slow to come. "Yes, it is." Her soft booted feet moved across the porch. Away from Bartow?

The foreman's heavy steps followed.

Rhett peered around the building. Ellie stood at the corner of the porch, with the foreman nearby. Too close.

An odd sound reached his ears, like creaking metal. After listening, Rhett realized that Marshall was slowly opening his window. So he could eavesdrop on Ellie and Bartow's conversation? Rhett's cautious glance around the cabin proved his suspicions to be true. The tip of a curtain fluttered out of the window's gap.

The proof that Marshall kept an eye on his niece eased some of Rhett's worry. However, he reminded himself that the owner was only one man against at least five—Bartow and his four friends, who were never far from his side. No telling how many of the other ranch hands would become traitorous should the situation turn into a showdown.

"Tomorrow, we got us an early morning. We start branding cattle." Bartow took a long draw on his cigarette. "Ever seen that before?"

"No." Ellie coughed, then pressed her fingers to her nose. "Can't say I have."

"Quite a sight. You should come watch." He gestured toward one corral. "We'll be working over there."

"I'll think about it." She cleared her throat when his cigarette smoke wafted her way.

He scratched his head, looked away, then studied her again. "Next week, sometime, I plan on taking a trip to Cheyenne. For your uncle. Y'might consider coming along. I'd love to show you the Cheyenne Club. They got some of the finest food in the country."

"I'm sure."

"So, what'd'ya say?" Bartow's voice rang with eagerness.

Again, Ellie took her time answering. "Next week's a long ways away."

"Ain't too early to plan."

She fell silent, then sighed. "It's getting late. Didn't you say you had an early morning?" Skirts swished as Ellie retreated. "Good night, Mr. Bartow."

The sound of the door closing seemed to end the conversation.

In the darkness, Rhett heard the foreman mutter under this breath. Footsteps finally moved down the steps and tromped across the yard.

With Ellie safely inside the house, Rhett could breathe more easily.

Still flattened against the building, he waited until the window in Marshall's cabin closed. Only when the coast was clear would he move to a better hiding spot.

His stomach grumbled in protest. Sometime soon, he would have to go hunting again to scare up small game. The food Mrs. Johnson had given him the day he'd left had grown scarce.

Scratching at the unfamiliar scruff on his cheeks, he considered visiting the root cellar. He shunned the idea of stealing, but worried about the alternative—asking for a handout. The Johnsons might have to shoot him on sight as Marshall ordered.

No, best to scrounge up food on his own. He'd done it before. But not tonight. Since he'd gotten this close to the ranch house, instinct told him to hunker down and wait. This might be the only chance he would have of seeing Ellie again or saying goodbye. It was tonight or never.

Taking the usual precautions, he slunk more deeply into the shadows.

Ellie rolled over and sighed. A bright beam of moonlight, skirting around the parted curtains, danced across her blankets. Every time she moved, the glow disturbed her. She flopped one hand on the bed, admitting to herself that she had only been dozing. For hours.

No use. She couldn't sleep.

The wanted poster she saw of the man that looked like Rhett continued to trouble her. Was Rhett the son of an outlaw? Or a brother? He was related somehow, the similar features making that obvious.

She sighed. It didn't matter. His bloodline did not define his character. Or guilt. He was his own man, definitely not a cattle rustler. Or murderer.

Arising, she slipped a shawl about her shoulders. She parted the curtains and peered out.

What a glorious night. Earlier, she had wanted to linger on the porch, but Guy wouldn't leave her alone. Ever since Rhett had left, he had grown more persistent in his attentions. Short of being rude, Ellie had no idea how to discourage the foreman. He seemed incapable of taking a hint.

With care, she unlocked her bedroom door, then cautiously opened the front. Because the Johnsons took such good care of the property, the well-oiled hinges didn't squawk. Ellie sought to keep from disturbing her uncle or the ranch hands. Especially Guy.

Aware that her cream-colored nightgown would glow in the moonlight, she spread her dark shawl over her clothing. Then she moved to the side of the house that was swathed in shadows. Staring into the night, she wrapped a hand around a porch column and breathed deeply.

Eight days. Eight torturous days without seeing Rhett. Her soul longed for him.

Where was he? Ellie imagined he could be anywhere by now. Had the gold in the Black Hills called him to try to strike it rich? Or was he drawn to the bustling city of San Francisco, despite it being prone to earthquakes? Perhaps he had traveled east.

"God…?" Breathing a one-word prayer, she lifted her face skyward. Though she had begun to call out to the Lord on a regular basis, she wished she could pray with confidence the way Rhett did. Most of the time, she didn't know what to ask beyond acknowledging the Creator of the universe. For now, that seemed enough. She basked in the peace that cocooned her.

Please care for him, Lord. The bold request came unbidden to her mind. *Watch over him.*

But anxiety crept into her small sliver of peace. If only she could be certain he was safe. If only she knew where he was. The idea of writing to him struck her. They could correspond. Then she could hear about his life. If he was happy.

But where would she send letters?

Lord, please let me know how I can reach him.

"Ellie." The faintest whisper pierced the dark.

Startled, she gasped. When nothing more sounded, she squinted into the blackness. "Who's there?"

The faintest rustle met her ears. "It is I."

Were her ears deceiving her? It sounded like...

Rhett emerged from the side of the building.

Joy flooded over her. But as quickly, fear trampled it.

"You shouldn't be here." Ellie tempered her whisper. "They'll kill you."

He stopped below her, face lifted. "I had to speak with you."

Gripping the railing, Ellie leaned over to lower her voice even more. "You aren't safe."

He appeared not to listen. "I'm not a thief. You must believe me."

"I do. I never thought it for a moment." In the faint light, she could make out his grim smile and nod.

"Good."

Her rising worry for him warred with her desire to keep him near as long as possible.

He moved closer. The drop from the porch put him several feet lower than her. "And I had to tell you. I didn't shoot Tripper."

"Wh-what?"

"He was sick. But not dead. I fired the shots in the air so your uncle would assume I obeyed his orders."

The news confounded her. "Where is Tripper?"

"In town. Safe. Someone poisoned him, but we think he'll recover."

We? Before she could ask who Rhett was talking about, he went on.

"You and your uncle are in danger." Iron edged his voice.

"Danger? From whom?"

"Bartow. And his men." Rhett's mouth tightened.

"Guy?" Though a dozen questions crowded her mind, what he said made sense. She had never trusted the foreman. Or his shady friends. Her mind raced ahead. Had Guy stolen cattle and pinned the crime on Rhett just to get rid of him?

"I saw a wanted poster. The face looked like yours." The words were out of her mouth before forethought. "Who was it?"

For the longest time, he appeared to wrestle with himself. "My father."

"But not you. I mean, you never…?" She couldn't help her question. Though she didn't believe Rhett capable of robbing or killing anyone, she needed to hear it from his own mouth.

"You have my word." He backed up as though readying to leave.

She panicked. "Wait."

He paused.

"Wh-where are you going?"

"For now, back into the hills." A wry smile twisted his mouth. "All I have to worry about there are cougars and bears."

"But…" She sucked in a quick breath. For now, the hills, but then where? She didn't want him to leave, but how could she ask him to stay? Every second he remained on Will's property, he risked his life. The desperate question burst from her. "When will I see you again?"

For endless moments, he stared up at her. A slow smile creased his lips. "I'll be close."

Her heart thumped so hard that she thought it would burst through her chest. An idea—one that originated from her own mother—entered her mind. "If I put a candle in my window, would you come here? To me?"

She heard his sharp intake of breath, as though he couldn't believe she asked.

"I'll watch for it." The intensity of his whisper sent a jolt through her. "I promise."

The spinning of the earth and heavens seemed to slow. Any second, he would turn and leave.

Ellie couldn't let him go.

Her body began to shake. Gripping her railing, she steadied herself. She gulped, terrified of her daring. "What—what if I put a candle in my window. Every night?"

The sky had grown so black, clouds rolling across the moon, that she couldn't read his expression. She waited for his answer, her fingernails digging into the wooden railing. Did he understand what she was asking? Did he know she loved him with every ounce of her being— that she wanted him with her always?

One moment he stood below her on the ground. The next he vaulted noiselessly over the railing. But he didn't step closer.

"Rhett." Her whisper danced on the breeze.

Despite the dark, she could see the glitter of his eyes. His hand inched toward hers as it rested on the railing. With a gentleness that sent delightful shivers through her, he took her fingers in his, then bent to kiss them.

Her head swam. She couldn't breathe. Every ounce of her being longed to be with this man. Every hour apart tortured her.

Still holding her fingers, he moved closer until he was mere inches from her.

"I'm here now." His soft breath brushed her cheek.

She couldn't help but lean into him. His other hand smoothed over her shoulder, then edged around her back, finally resting on her waist. The touch remained gentle and respectful. Ever a man of honor, he would not take advantage.

Stepping closer, she raised her lips to his. His head tilted, meeting her halfway.

Warmth, sunshine, grassy plains—all flooded her in his kiss. But one was not enough. Would never be enough. They kissed again, each one satisfying, yet proving that she would never be content as long as they remained apart.

With a slow exhale, she rested her forehead against his chest as his arms encircled her. Rhett's pounding heart reassured Ellie that he felt as she did. For many minutes, they stood in silence. As his lips nuzzled her forehead, she sighed.

"Thank you," she breathed, not entirely certain if she were thanking God or Rhett. It mattered not because she was grateful to both.

He gently squeezed her.

How long they stood together in silence, she didn't know. Didn't care. He was with her now. That was enough. But all too soon she realized that the sky to the east brightened, the black fading to purple.

Rhett raised his head.

"I don't want you to go." Her simple plaint escaped as she snuggled more deeply into his arms.

"I don't either." He smoothed back a strand of hair as she looked into his face. In the growing light, she realized several days of growth covered his cheeks and chin. But she also noticed how thin he appeared.

The thought troubled her. "Do you have enough food to eat?"

His fingertip traced her cheek. "Being with you is food enough."

"I can find a way to get some to you. I'll borrow a horse and—"

"No. Bartow, or one of his men, would follow you. It would be too dangerous."

The implication seemed clear—dangerous for them both.

"I'll find a way." Ellie considered leaving a food parcel in one of Will's burned-out buildings. As she stared into Rhett's face, she again grew aware that his features became more visible in the growing light. Her selfishness in delaying his departure endangered him. "You'd better go."

He nodded. Cupping her jaw, he kissed her one last time. Then he leaped over the railing onto the ground.

"Wait." Her breathless call stopped him. When he turned, she dared to whisper, "I love you."

The tense look on his face instantly gave way to a smile. It didn't last long. Something must've caught his attention because without answering, he disappeared into the brush. A moment later, she heard it too. The sounds of horses stirring in the distance. Was someone up already?

Ellie knew she must not linger on the porch. With the speed borne of anxiety, she slipped into the house.

Not until she was inside her bedroom, fingers shaking as she locked the door, did she exhale in relief. As she leaned against the panel, she prayed, "Please, God, please keep Rhett safe."

She crawled into bed, drawing up her chilly feet. As she burrowed under the quilt, she shivered from the dual emotions of excitement and fear. While she relived the joy of his arms about her and his lips against hers, she also worried. Had he gotten safely away from the ranch?

Not until she heard the men enter the house in search

of breakfast could she relax. No tension rang in their voices as they joked with each other. Benches scraped the floor and dishes clattered. No one referenced Rhett or a mysterious intruder. Her mind settled. Despite the noise, Ellie succumbed to sleep.

Rhett filled her dreams.

Chapter Seventeen

Ellie rose late, much later than she had intended. However, she couldn't help but linger over her toilette as she basked in sweet memories. Rhett loved her. Although he had not spoken the words, she had no doubts. Every kiss, every soft caress shouted that truth. After all, hadn't he risked his life to meet with her?

With extra care, she washed her face, styled her hair and chose her most flattering gown. Because she hoped to see him later? She smiled at herself in the handheld mirror. Her pink cheeks and sparkling brown eyes gave her away.

"I love him," she whispered to her reflection. "So very much."

She was about to open her bedroom door when approaching voices caused her to hesitate. Two men, speaking loudly, sounded as though they were arguing. One was Will.

Pressing her ear to her door, she tried to discern the words.

"...not possible...long gone." The rest of Will's words were lost.

"And I'm telling you, Whitey saw him. Just this morning. Sneaking off into the woods."

Ellie's heart stopped. Were they talking about Rhett?

Will spoke. "How early was this?"

"Before dawn. No mistaking it was him."

Several moments passed while she waited. Ellie heard nothing more. Had they left?

She opened her door to look.

Will's frame filled the doorway. Guy stood just beyond him. Both turned. Two sets of eyes met hers.

No use hiding since they'd already seen her. Besides, she wanted to know if her suspicions were true.

Will turned back to his foreman. "All right. We'll do it. Tomorrow. We've work today."

"Do what?" Ellie strode toward them. If Will's orders had anything to do with Rhett, then she needed to find out.

"Whitey saw Callaway. On my land." Will's jaw jutted. "I gave him a chance to leave. And he didn't. First thing tomorrow, Guy's going for the sheriff to get together a posse."

"To hunt him down?"

Will held up a hand. "Ellie, I take the law seriously. If he's stolen his last cattle, he needs to be brought to justice. He's crossed me for the last time."

Stricken, she could only stare at the man who called himself her uncle.

"You know why he was here?" Guy stepped forward. "Looks like you got somethin' to say."

Feeling her cheeks warm, she pressed her lips together.

Guy's mouth flattened. "Whitey thought he came from the direction of the house. Is that 'cause he was here?"

No mistaking his vile insinuation.

"How dare you." Ellie glared at him.

He pushed past Will. "I asked you a question."

"And I have no obligation to answer." She spoke through clenched teeth.

"Why, you little traitor."

"Guy. Enough." Will's arm came up like a barricade between Ellie and his foreman. It seemed to take several minutes for Guy to back down. Will went on. "Let me know when you finish branding."

"Yessir." The foreman hissed the words with a sneer. After shooting a look of hate in Ellie's direction, he stomped away.

She stared after him, aghast at his rudeness. Why hadn't Will said anything? Why let his foreman insult her?

"Well?" Will crossed his arms. "Any truth to what he said?"

She took her time answering. "Any truth to *what* exactly?"

"Was Callaway inside my house?"

Lifting her chin, she spoke with as much coldness as she could muster. "No."

"Girl, you lying to me?"

She drew herself up. Her voice shook as she spoke. "From the moment I arrived, you've treated me little better than a stranger. No, worse. Time and again, you've dismissed me, my opinions, my feelings. Now you act like an outraged father—not to protect your daughter, but because you need to save face with your foreman."

Will went white. "Daughter?"

Suddenly realizing what she'd admitted, Ellie decided to tell all. "I love Rhett. He's been more of a gentleman than…than your foreman ever could be. But I warn you—harm Rhett and you'll destroy every tender feeling I have for you."

Will staggered back as if she had gut-shot him.

Without waiting for his response, Ellie stalked back into her room and slammed the door. She locked it with one savage jerk. Then she paced across the room, fury and frustration driving her steps. Finally, she ended up at her small desk, fists pressed to the surface.

She had nowhere to go. The bitter truth crushed her. She couldn't ride into the fields to clear her head. She couldn't escape into town and visit friends or seek pastoral counseling. She couldn't even go to a relative's home where she could ask for haven. She was not only isolated but trapped.

As her breathing slowed, she realized there was only one man she wished to see. One person in whom she could confide and find comfort. And he was a dead man walking.

Knees shaking, she tottered to the window and leaned against the sill.

Don't let him come here tonight, Lord. Please, please *keep him away. For his sake.*

A distant thought struck her of one other time she had prayed in desperation—for her mother on her deathbed. The devastating memory came back in full force. She had prayed, but Mama had died. She wanted to have faith, wanted to believe…but God hadn't listened then. Why did she think He would listen now?

Ellie slipped to her knees.

For many minutes, she remained immobile. Clasping her hands, she bowed her head as she wrestled in her soul. She felt like she had come to a crossroads—adhere to the God with whom she was raised, the faraway God who was only to be feared and served.

Or cling to Rhett's God—the Father who would never leave her or forsake her. The One who promised to walk beside her in difficult circumstances, through the valley of the shadow of death. The One who would always love her.

"I choose You, Father." She raised her eyes heavenward. "I choose You."

Her anxiety slowly ebbed. An inexplicable peace settled over her. Her perception of the world seemed to expand, as though the blinders fell away.

She didn't know what the future held, but the God she called upon did. For the first time since her mother died, Ellie did not feel alone.

Something has changed.

Crouching at his usual post, Rhett stayed well away from ranch property. After watching almost an hour, he noted that the yard remained empty. Where were the men? Peering at the sun's position, he ascertained it was a little after noon.

Though he tried to concentrate, his mind drifted to Ellie and the tender moments they'd shared. Had it been a dream? Impossible. With vivid clarity, he recalled her lips, the way she whispered his name, her softness as she leaned into him, the heady lavender fragrance.

She loves me.

For several sweet minutes, he basked in the knowledge, aware that his future had irrevocably changed.

Several quail exploded from the brush nearby, startling him. The thunder of hoofbeats snapped his attention back to the here and now. A band of men rode up the hill, in the general direction of town. When they paused below his position, he hunkered down. The leader pointed to the east, then to the west. Three men went one way and the remainder traveled the other.

Obvious what they were doing.

Looking for me.

In seconds, Rhett scrabbled backward toward his temporary camp. He piled stones over his cold fire, then shoved his bedroll under some rocks. He grabbed Wash's bridle and, rather than riding him, led him off the rugged terrain, to keep the sound of the horse's hooves from alerting Marshall's men to his location. Rhett vacillated between heading for the grassy plains or doubling back to the small cave where he had hidden his saddle and some other gear. Both he and Wash could fit inside, where they could hide out until the evening.

In seconds, he chose the cave. Being a target as he made a run to the plains didn't appeal to him. Besides, he wanted to stay close. Tonight, he planned to see Ellie again.

He moved along his prechosen paths, familiar terrain after the last week and a half. When he reached the bottom of a ravine, he traveled by horseback, keeping Wash to a walk. Footprints in the soft dirt might give him away, but Rhett couldn't take the time to cover his tracks. The sound of shots being fired drew him up short. No doubt they came from a rifle.

However, the gunfire was nowhere near him. Who or what were they firing at? He dismounted, quieting his gelding as he listened.

The unmistakable sound of a man yelling reached his ears. Was he speaking a foreign language? Rhett concentrated, but from this distance, it sounded like gibberish.

Dropping Wash's reins, Rhett moved along the ravine bed toward the speaker. When he found a spot he could climb, he ascended with care. He had just reached a ledge when he heard Marshall's men. The jingle of bridles and the chuffs of horses indicated the group of three. From the sounds they made, they were close. Rhett could hear them arguing among themselves.

Finally, one man ended the discussion. "We're done here."

A horse squealed and then came the clatter of hooves. The sound of riders receded.

Clinging to the rock face, he continued his way up. Long before he reached the summit, he knew he was being watched. But he had no fear of the watcher.

Rhett rounded one corner, then peered up and met a familiar, green-eyed gaze. "Pete!"

His friend was dressed in dark clothing with a heavy coat for the cool nights. His beard and mustache were blackened, likely to hide his identity, but more importantly, he carried a rifle in one hand. Was that why the men had left?

"You pretending to be a cougar?" Rhett asked. "Sitting up there on the rocks?"

"If I were, I would have pounced on you long before now and eaten your liver." Then Pete's eyes narrowed. He stroked his own bearded chin, then pointed at Rhett. "And are you pretending to be a bear? You look a bit shaggy."

He accepted the hand that pulled him up to safety. "I have few luxuries out here."

Pete broke into a grin.

Rhett dusted off his hands, then clothes. "I didn't know you were going to come back."

"I wasn't. Not until yesterday. Overheard a discussion that told me I needed to."

"And that was?"

"One of Bartow's cronies, all cozy with Tesley." Pete made a face. "Sounds like they are very interested in you being dead."

Growing solemn, Rhett held out his hand. "Thank you for saving my life."

His friend clasped it. "I haven't. Yet. I just acted like a crazy man. Told 'em this was my mountain. Then I began reciting a children's tale. In Irish."

With a tilt of his head, Rhett indicated the rifle, still in his friend's hands. "That didn't hurt either."

Pete nodded. His grin slowly faded. "They may not give up so easily next time. You gonna be ready for 'em?"

As the memory of Ellic filled his mind, he shrugged. Darkness shrouded what lay ahead. Now that he knew she loved him, could he leave her?

Pete drew closer. "I don't know what's going on with Marshall, but it has something to do with Tesley."

"He and Bartow are business partners. Cattle rustlers." Rhett then went on to explain what he'd seen. But as he talked, his gut told him Bartow had something more planned for the ranch than just stealing cattle.

"We should go to the sheriff. Right now."

"I have no proof beyond my say-so." Rhett shook his head. "Bartow can claim anything he wants since he's Marshall's foreman. Besides, my word isn't worth spit."

His friend crossed his arms, considering.

"One other thing." Rhett took a deep breath. "Somehow or another, Marshall got a hold of an old wanted poster."

Pete's eyebrows shot up. "I didn't think you were on any."

"I'm not. It was one of my father's." He ran a hand over his rough cheek and chin. "All Marshall has to do is show it to a few people and I could very well swing from a rope. Or get shot in the back."

"Then come away. Leave this place." His friend laid a hand on his shoulder.

Rhett stared into the vast open sky, then in the direction of the ranch. "I can't. Not without Ellie."

With a jerk, Pete straightened, his hand falling away. "Is she worth dying for? They catch you, they'll kill ya f'sure."

The words cut through Rhett's murky future. He had a decision to make—leave or stay? If he stayed, he might end up dead like Pete warned. But to go without Ellie? Rhett shook his head at the thought of life without her. Impossible.

His friend pursed his lips. "Ah, I see the lay of the land." He exhaled noisily. "Okay. Count me in."

"What? You'll help?"

"Do ye na' ken," Pete said, laying on a thick brogue, "the Irish are romantic at heart."

Chuckling, Rhett slapped his friend's back. He soon grew subdued as he considered his course of action.

Tonight he must convince Ellie to run away with him. But would she consent to be the wife of a wanted man?

Ellie inspected her bedroom, making certain nothing was out of place. Her small, packed valise was under the bed. She put in only the most basic supplies, along with money, the photo of her mother and her Bible. She rearranged the surface of her dresser where the frame used to be. It was imperative that she not give away her intentions.

Her mind was made up. Nothing would divert her plans now.

On her desk sat a candle, ready to be lighted when she

was certain the coast was clear. As soon as Rhett came, she would slip away with him. Someday in the future, she might send for the rest of her belongings. Someday.

Would he want her as his wife?

If not, she would travel with him to a big city where they could part ways. There, at least, she would know he was safe. She would write to Will, and then…

Ellie shook the speculations from herself. Right now, she could see no future without Rhett. But she had to make certain he would not be hunted down like an animal and shot. Or hanged as a thief.

The sounds of the men gathering for supper reached her ears. She must eat with them as per her habit, pretending nothing unusual was about to happen.

After smoothing her hair and gown, she opened the door. Seated at the table, the ranch hands threw her barely a glance as they helped themselves to food. She noted that Will and Guy were missing. Not uncommon as they finished up chores and planned for the morrow.

Mrs. Johnson carried in a large platter of meat. As Ellie's gaze met hers, the woman threw her a meaningful look. What did that signify?

It was then Ellie noticed how empty the room was. She did a quick headcount. Seven men, excluding Will and Guy, were missing. Only five had assembled for their supper.

The housekeeper brought in a bowl filled with boiled potatoes.

Where? Ellie mouthed, but the woman shook her head. Did that mean she couldn't speak or didn't want to?

Nodding her head in greeting to the men, Ellie sauntered to the front door and looked out. The yard appeared empty. By the back corral stood Guy and two of his friends. Where was Will?

She followed Mrs. Johnson to the kitchen, staying out of the way while the woman bustled to and fro serving the men.

"Your uncle's feeling poorly this evening." The housekeeper ladled thick gravy into a bowl as she spoke. "Cookie took a meal to his cabin earlier."

The news undermined her carefully laid plans. Before she retired for the night, she needed to bid Will goodbye. To leave him a note seemed too cold. Especially since he might be her father.

She couldn't think of that right now.

"What about the others?" Ellie lowered her voice. "Where are they?"

"Guy Bartow fired three men earlier."

"Why?"

"Heard-tell they wasn't doing their job. A'sides, he's got some new fellers coming next week. He told the boss this afternoon."

Told? Not asked? But Ellie kept the question to herself while Mrs. Johnson scurried back into the main room.

Three men gone? That didn't make sense considering how much work there always seemed to be. Remembering Rhett's warning, she couldn't help thinking that Bartow was planning something evil—perhaps taking over the ranch?

She wanted to warn Will…but would he even listen? Above all, she would do nothing that would jeopardize her plans to leave undetected. She hardened her heart. After tonight, that would no longer be her concern. By Will's own shortsightedness and stubbornness, he had brought this upon himself.

Taking a seat at the table, Ellie nibbled at her dinner. As the thought crossed her mind that this might be her last meal for many hours, she tried to force herself to eat more. But the men around the table seemed to have lost their appetite too. Their usual banter was missing.

When she heard heavy footsteps outside and Guy's voice, Ellie picked up her plate and hurried into the kitchen. She couldn't abide the idea of spending her last evening on the ranch anywhere near him. As she stood in the kitchen, scraping her plate, the door in the main room banged open.

"Why didn't you just shoot him?" Guy's irate voice rose.

"He weren't hurting nothing," Dietmeyer answered. "Just raving in some foreign lingo."

Whitey snickered. "His skill with a rifle helped convince you to move along, I'm sure."

"We was looking for that chucklehead, remember?" Dietmeyer answered with heat. "You didn't tell us to go around shooting anyone we saw."

Guy growled, "I don't like strangers on our land."

Our? Ellie stiffened at his word choice.

"He wasn't. He was up in the foothills a little ways."

"So no sign of the skulker?" the foreman asked.

"Nope. Maybe he really is gone."

Guy blew out his breath. "Tomorrow, we'll make sure. Got it? What'd you think about us having a lil' hanging?"

"Fine by me." Sounded like Whitey was cracking his knuckles. "I'm looking forward to it."

Cold dread slipped down Ellie's spine. His words confirmed her determination to leave the ranch as soon as possible.

Silence, amid the clatter of dishes, fell over the group.

"What're you all staring at?" Whitey's voice cut through the room.

The scrape of benches responded to his snarl. Several men muttered their good-night. From the sounds they made, most hastened out the door.

Ellie remained in the kitchen, undecided about what to do. She dreaded the idea of walking through the main room, even to return to her bedroom. Without Will there, she feared what might happen. Guy sounded like he was already taking over.

Two other men entered the main room. As soon as one spoke, Ellie recognized Hoskins—another of the foreman's close cronies. "Everything's buttoned up for the night."

"Good." Guy spoke with his mouth half full.

"Marshall's in his cabin." Blade was the speaker.

"Huh." Guy smacked his lips. "Pass me the potatoes. This all there is to eat?"

"We got more." Mrs. Johnson hastened to say.

She rounded the corner, startling Ellie. After glancing over her shoulder, the housekeeper drew closer.

"Go check on your uncle, miss." The woman spoke in a whisper. "I'll tend to the men."

When she remained frozen in place, Mrs. Johnson jerked her head at the back door. Heart hammering, Ellie grasped the handle.

"Hurry it up, woman," Whitey yelled.

"Hold yer horses, I'm a'coming." Mrs. Johnson's voice rang out, covering any sounds Ellie made as she slipped away.

The warm evening wrapped around her, a red beam from the setting sun filling her vision before blinking out of sight. She paused, debating which way to go to her uncle's cabin. Definitely behind the house, rather than through the yard, in case Guy or his men exited. When she reached the side of the building, her feet slowed.

The minute she rounded the corner, she would be visible to anyone on the front porch before reaching Will's cabin. But why go there at all? As she lingered by the spot Rhett had stood the night before, she wrestled with herself. She had nothing more to say to Will Marshall. If she were brave, she would escape to the hills right now. Rhett would find her.

But as darkness descended, the night sounds awakened. Creatures scurried in the murky fields nearby. A large bat flew in the cerulean sky. The mournful hoot of an owl chilled her. Brave? No, she would be foolish to strike off on her own.

She reminded herself that she had no sense of direction. No way to protect herself. No outer clothing for the changing elements. She needed to wait for Rhett. Tonight.

But she could not, would not, go back into the main house while Guy and his henchmen were inside, acting as kings of the castle. Over the past few days, their attitude toward her had subtly shifted. The foreman openly studied her while his friends treated her with veiled contempt.

Ellie shivered again, but not from the breeze that brushed her. Wisdom told her to go to Will's cabin. Perhaps wish him well to hide that she was really saying goodbye. But as she made her plans, she worried she would inadvertently give herself away. While she and Will talked, she needed to guard her words. And her heart.

Then tonight, when Rhett came for her, she could leave with no regrets.

Chapter Eighteen

All through the afternoon, Rhett had watched the ranch. He and Pete had moved closer, staying just outside Marshall's property, but the worry kept returning to his mind. Something had changed. And not for the better. The way the ranch hands acted seemed out of character. He saw no signs of their usual activities. They weren't working, and yet there was no horsing around. Instead, they lingered in the yard, going out to the fields in groups of two or three. The atmosphere at the ranch felt somber.

A chilling memory struck him.

Soldiers gather in clusters. As they talk in low voices, they throw glances over their shoulders. Their movements are slow. Measured. Eyes always prowling. Mouths set in hard lines. Their fingers tighten around their weapons. The slightest noises cause them to flinch.

Rhett recalled the soldiers' behavior the night before the incident that claimed so many lives, including his stepfather's. Before his and Ma's world crumbled into tears and pain.

He flexed his back, hating the way the memory felt. Instead, he sought to concentrate on the sounds around him. Pete remained at their makeshift camp, consuming the provisions he had brought, ones he had shared. Again, Rhett found himself praising God for the man he was proud to call friend.

As the sun set, three riders crested the hill, riding toward town. Easy to see they weren't looking for Rhett, but what filled him with anxiety was what they wore and carried. Their coats and gear seemed to indicate they were leaving. For good? Rhett identified them as men he knew to be good workers. Loyal to Marshall. Handy with cattle and horses.

Then it struck him.

Bartow was getting rid of anyone he didn't control. Anyone who might rebel.

Rhett's anxiety turned into full-blooded fear.

The sound of Pete, crawling his way, met his ears.

Settling beside him, his friend studied him. "What's the plan?"

He shook his head. "I don't have one. Yet." He licked dry lips, tortured with indecision. Everything inside himself said to shoot his way into the yard, find Ellie and run.

As though you'd get within twenty yards of her before getting cut down.

Pete scratched at his ribcage. "You wanna share what you find amusing about our situation? Or that not a grin I just saw?"

He confessed his crazy idea, then added, "I have no gun. You have a limited amount of ammo. I count at least eleven men below. What good are two blades and a rifle?"

Pete's slow smile proved the news left him undaunted. "When has that ever stopped you?"

"True." He recalled telling his friend about childish pranks, like untying horses, barricading the outhouse door with someone inside, stealing items—which he always returned. Mischief for which Mr. Callaway thoroughly chastised him—when his deeds were discovered. But the fun came from *not* getting caught.

Perhaps youthful games held the answer to this situation.

He and Pete had no need for guns. Stealth was by far the better choice. That way, fewer people would get hurt. Especially them.

"Promise me—" Rhett gripped his friend's arm as he spoke "—promise that if matters get out of hand, you'll save yourself."

"And leave you?"

Rhett nodded. "I don't want your blood on my conscience."

Pete's gaze returned to the scene below. "I doubt they'd waste a bullet on us. I'm thinking they'll string us up in the nearest tree."

Chilling words. Likely true.

"We'll move when it's full night." Rhett stared down at the ranch as he spoke. "After I speak with Ellie, I'll know what to do."

He didn't add that they had already worked out a prearranged signal. Although she said she would put a candle in her window, perhaps she had changed her mind in the light of day. It didn't matter. Tonight, Rhett would give her an ultimatum—leave with him or stay. If she refused to go, he would bid her farewell.

But where would he find the courage to leave? If he was forced to roam earth for the remainder of his days without her, how could he live without his heart?

Ellie knocked at Will's door. Before he answered, she could hear him coughing. It sounded bad.

"Be right…there." His hacking seemed to go on indefinitely.

When he opened the door, he held a dark handkerchief to his mouth. He frowned. "What brings you here?"

She blurted the truth. "Guy and his men are in the house. I felt uncomfortable. Without you there."

That struck a nerve. She could see it in his narrowing eyes.

Will turned. "Come in. Sorry for the mess."

As Ellie stepped inside, she grew aware that she'd never been in his one-room cabin. Besides the narrow bed, the place contained a small writing desk, a chest of drawers and one lone chair beside the fireplace.

"Have a seat." After closing the door, her uncle perched at the edge of the bed.

She did as he bade. After sitting, she realized she had no idea what they would talk about. She doubted Will would bring up their conversation from that morning.

He wheezed a little as his gaze met hers. "You probably shouldn't be in here. It's not safe because of my condition."

"I know." At this moment, she feared his illness less than she feared Guy and his men. The sooner she left, the better for her and Rhett. But would anywhere be safe?

For several minutes, she and Will sat in silence.

He stared at his hands as though seeing them for the first time. "After the outlaws burned the place—almost twenty years ago now—not much was left. Except this cabin. And the shed. As soon as it was decent, I started rebuilding. But I wanted the house to be in a new location. I planned the place, you know, for Adel. And me." A sad smile touched his lips. "I never thought I'd end up·in the cabin again. But it's best. For everyone."

As though to emphasize his words, Will coughed, turning his head aside.

He sounded worse than he had in some time. As was his habit, he hastened to fold the fabric to hide the splotch of blood.

Hands clenched in her lap, Ellie didn't know how to reply.

"Your hair is about the same color as your mother's." His raspy voice fell on her ears, full of wistful longing. "Maybe a little more golden."

Ellie's breathing slowed. Never before had she seen this man's soft side so openly displayed. Except when she was a child. When she thought the world revolved around herself.

"You've definitely got Adel's spunk." He chuckled mirthlessly to himself, then grew somber. "And I loved her all the more for it."

"Are you my father?" The question burst from Ellie.

Will's gaze slowly raised to meet hers. "I don't know. I honestly don't know."

"How could you not?"

"I suspected." Mouth flattening, he shook his head. "But Adel wouldn't tell me. No matter how much I pressed."

Why not? Ellie sat back, confounded.

"My last visit to Chicago, when you were a child. I knew my brother would be gone. That's when I asked her."

Of course. Frank had been conspicuously absent. That detail had never struck her as forcefully as it did now.

Will's eyes again got a faraway look in them. "I think

Adel knew if she admitted the truth, nothing would've kept me from taking her—and you—away from Frank. But we both knew my brother would've hunted me down. He had the law, the power and, of course, Tess behind him with all her money and influence."

Gulping, Ellie stared at her hands, clenched in her lap. Now that she knew what Will was like, she believed he would have done as he claimed. Frank Marshall, the man she'd once called her father, would not have stopped until he'd gotten his revenge. How well Ellie remembered his vindictive and tenacious nature. He had proven it on many occasions.

When she met Will's gaze, she saw that he was staring wistfully at her.

"But regardless." He visibly struggled with what he wanted to say. "I'd be honored to claim you as my daughter."

Would he really? Despite her determination to remain detached, Ellie's eyes stung with tears. What would it be like to have a man like Will as her father? No doubt they would continue to have their differences. But somehow she sensed she would never have to prove herself every day in an attempt to win his affections like with Frank. She and Will might argue, but Ellie would have no fear of speaking her mind.

With painful clarity she recalled the times Frank had slapped her when she dared voice her opinion. Afterward, she learned to stew in silence.

That had never happened with Will. Even when he disagreed with her, he had never laid a hand on her. He had never shamed her.

But however much she wanted to agree to Will's tender offer, she must make one demand. Otherwise, he would prove he was all talk.

"If I mean anything to you, if I matter the tiniest bit, believe me when I tell you Rhett is not a thief. Please allow him the chance to speak in his own defense."

Brow lowering, Will's chest rose and fell as he considered her request.

"But even if you won't," she continued, gathering her courage, "I beg you not to go through with your plans tomorrow. Don't hunt him down."

Will's eyebrows shot up. "I wasn't going to. And I told the men so."

His words confounded her. "But that's not…" She paused.

"I need to personally verify the facts before I hang a man for theft."

The news relieved her on one level but distressed her on another. "I heard the men talking about forming a posse." She paused, trying to recall the exact wording of Guy's conversation with his cronies, after they had arrived for supper. "Whitey said—no, it was Guy. He said something about making sure Rhett was gone. Tomorrow."

"What?" Will shot to his feet. "I told him specifically to call it off."

Ellie rose, as well. "I think he's still planning to. He mentioned a hanging."

Will's jaw jutted. "You know, he's been pushing me a little too much lately. I think it's high time he and I had a chat."

Although the news thrilled Ellie, it also frightened her. As far as she knew, Guy was inside the house with his four buddies. Did Will still have the authority to control them?

She hadn't time to caution him because he yanked open the door and headed out. Knees shaking, she followed. He strode across the yard and was halfway up the steps when Guy exited the house. His raucous laughter abruptly ended when his gaze lit on Will. It skipped to Ellie, then back to the ranch owner.

"You and I need to talk." Will stepped to within inches of his foreman. "Now."

With studied nonchalance, the foreman hooked a thumb into his belt. With the light at his back, Ellie couldn't see his face clearly.

"Sure thing, Mr. Marshall."

Something about the way he drawled the name made her skin crawl.

With an elaborate gesture, he waved for Will to precede him into the house. Ellie hurried to join them. As she reached the porch, she caught the smirk Guy threw his men.

"You boys can wait outside," he instructed.

But his next gesture confused her—the way he jerked his head at his men. Was he signaling them? To do what?

Her curiosity leaped to alarm when she caught sight of Whitey and Blade slink around the back. Why?

"After you, Miz Marshall." With an innocent smile and outstretched arm, Guy waited for her to go inside.

Ellie couldn't help but feel that she stepped into a predator's lair. When Guy slammed the door behind her, she jumped.

"What's this I hear about you getting together a posse?" Will didn't waste any time.

"Don't know what yer talking about." Guy leaned against the door.

Will crossed his arms. "I think you do."

The foreman spread his hands and shrugged. "You musta misunderstood."

Ellie studied Will, but he didn't appear to believe Guy's story.

Pursing his lips, the foreman held one finger in the air. "Ah, I think you heard about the hunting party I'm getting together tomorrow. Mrs. Johnson said we're getting low on venison."

"We're cutting calves tomorrow." Will glowered at him. "And since when do you go hunting?"

The question hung heavily in the air.

Guy said nothing as he scratched his neck. "Guessin' from now on, I'll do it when I want."

Ellie sucked in a quick breath. Guy was openly defying his boss?

Will planted two fists at his hips. "What'd you say?"

"You heard me." Guy's lip curled. "I don't need your permission."

"That's it. You're fired."

"What if I don't wanna be? How 'bout I fire you?" The foreman's sneer appeared to push Will over the edge.

"I want you off my land. Tonight."

"Ya mean, *my* land? I've slaved for you twelve years. I've earned it."

"Why you…" Will charged the man.

Before Ellie knew what happened, Guy drew his gun. She shrieked, slapping hands over her ears as the boom reverberated in the room.

Will staggered back. When his clothing blossomed red, she screamed, "Daddy!"

"Was that gunfire?" Pete's gaze met Rhett's.

From their distance, the popping sound seemed to have come from inside a building.

A cold hand clenched Rhett's gut. It was happening.

The evil premonition that had dogged him for days was now playing out.

When his friend rose, Rhett clasped his arm. "Wait."

Someone emerged from the bunkhouse, yelling a question. Two people joined him in the yard. In the uncertain light, Rhett couldn't tell who was who. The clouds, intermittently covering the moon, further disguised their identities. Someone stepped off the porch and approached the group. Strident voices rose, proving they were arguing. Another man, coming from the back of the house, ran toward them.

Several minutes passed while the crowd backed toward the bunkhouse. Two men appeared to be herding the others in that direction.

Bartow's cronies—Rhett had no doubts. The foreman now appeared to be in control.

But what of Ellie? And her uncle?

"Let's move closer." Rhett didn't need to warn his friend that they couldn't risk being seen. Even in the uncertain light, he could tell that a couple men now carried rifles. And he didn't need to be able to see their faces to know that only the foreman's friends had them.

He and Pete made their way down the hill until they reached the field where Sugar had been pastured. Using hand gestures, Rhett indicated they should move toward the blackened building. They progressed steadily toward it. So far, they remained undetected.

But that was likely because all attention was focused on what was happening at the main house. Several times, three of the four henchmen gathered to consult with each other, then move back into what appeared to be prearranged posts—two at the front of the house, one at the rear. The fourth took up station by the bunkhouse.

Rhett and Pete reached the burned-out house. A

whoosh above startled Rhett, but it was only an owl, disturbed by their presence.

His friend grinned, white teeth flashing in the dim light. "Still don't like birds?"

"Only for dinner," Rhett whispered.

Pete clapped him on the back.

With care, they made their way up to what used to be the building's second story. Balancing on a great beam that hadn't burned completely, they had a good view of the yard.

"I count four men." Pete kept his voice low.

"Bartow's closest friends." Rhett took a minute to explain who the people were at the ranch.

"Marshall and his niece are in danger," his friend concluded.

Rhett could merely nod, refusing to believe that Ellie was the one who got shot. Even so, worries clouded his thinking.

Pete gripped his arm. "Look."

Below someone rushed toward the corral full of horses. From the man's gait, Rhett determined it was the old cook. A shout rose. The crony who was guarding the bunkhouse—Dietmeyer?—ran to intercept him. With one blow, he felled Cookie. Blade joined Dietmeyer to stand over the prostrate man. They seemed to reach some agreement because Blade grabbed the cook and dragged him toward the house. They disappeared inside.

That meant at least two injured people.

"I need to get closer." Rhett didn't realize he had whispered aloud until he felt his friend's hand on his shoulder.

"We go together."

"Bring some of your food."

"For what?" Pete spread his hands.

"The dogs. We don't want them barking."

His friend pulled something from a coat pocket—jerky. "I never travel far without some."

"That'll do." He studied Pete. "Remember that promise I exacted from you earlier? About not endangering yourself?"

After shrugging out of the heavy coat, his friend rolled up his sleeves. "What promise? I don't remember saying nothing."

Rhett sucked in a slow breath.

Pete's eyes glittered in the low light. "Trust me, my friend."

"I do." Rhett's throat tightened. "With my life."

Chapter Nineteen

"What kind of monster are you?" Ellie shrieked as Guy blocked her from going to Will.

The foreman merely scowled at her.

From across the great room, she stared at Will, prostrate on the floor. Face ashen, he clutched his bloody thigh. Red bubbled up through his fingers. Next to him slumped Cookie, hand clasped to his gory head. Earlier, Blade had dragged in the elderly man and shoved him next to Will. He stood sentry over them.

"I need to attend to them. Now." Ellie's voice rose despite herself. Since pleading wasn't working, she tried to push past Guy.

He grabbed her wrist and shoved her into a chair so hard that she yelped.

"And I said no." Guy stood over her, mouth hard. "Try that again and I'll make you sorry."

She shrank from him.

Why wouldn't he let her tend to the men? Every time Will groaned, she thought she would scream. Cookie whimpered. With his palm pressed to his head wound, he rocked as though trying to escape the pain.

She rubbed her sore wrist. "Will's going to bleed to death."

This time Guy grinned. "Then you should thank me. He'll die quicker. Well, quicker than from consumption."

Overwhelmed with that possibility, Ellie buried her face in her hands.

"What do you want us to do, boss?" Blade posed his question to Guy.

"That's what I'm deciding." His tone contained an element of satisfaction as he rested his muddy boot on a bench. "What's going on outside?"

"Whitey's in the yard. All the ranch hands are in the bunkhouse. Hoskins is guarding 'em."

"Have them roll a couple barrels in front of the door. Just to make sure. Where's Dietmeyer?"

"I just sent him to ride perimeter."

"Find him. Tell him not to wander too far." Guy's gaze passed between his three captives. "And tell Whitey to hunt up the old woman. I don't want her causing trouble."

"Got it." Blade strode out of the house.

The foreman went back to musing.

Ellie gripped the armrests of her chair, fighting to calm herself. "Why won't you let me help Cookie? Or Will? For pity's sake, let me do something."

"You speaking about your father?"

Ellie blinked. "What?"

"You ain't gonna pretend he's jes' your uncle now, are ya?"

Her mind remained blank.

He swiveled and drew closer. Hands pressed to the armrests, he leaned into her face. "You called him 'Daddy.' Don't try to deny it."

She had?

"And since I know," Guy said, straightening, "that changes a few things."

Ellie shivered, not merely because she had accidentally betrayed her and Will's relationship. The glee in the foreman's voice terrified her.

"I don't…" She gulped, trying to form words as she glanced at Will. "I don't know for certain if he's my father."

"Don't matter." Guy paced back and forth in front of the injured men before stopping in front of Will. "Did you make Ellie the heir to your ranch? The other day when you rode alone to town. Did you make it official?"

When the injured man ignored the questions, Guy kicked his wounded leg. When Will cried out in pain, she leaped from her chair.

"Stay." Stabbing a finger in her direction, Guy glared at her.

Knees shaking, Ellie sank down.

The foreman squatted in front of his former boss. "You get that I'm serious? When I ask you a question, you answer. Is she your heir?"

Teeth gritting, Will merely glared at him. Several seconds passed before he nodded.

"You talk to a solicitor?"

Again, Will nodded.

"Good." Guy rose. When he turned, his smug expression caused Ellie to shrink back into her chair. "It'll be easier to keep all this nice and legal."

She shivered when he stationed himself in front of her.

"You want to watch 'Daddy' bleed to death, or are you willing to negotiate?"

Her chest felt as though a boulder rested on it, making every breath torturous. "What—what do you want?"

"For you to say one tiny word. 'Yes.'" He tilted his head as though waiting.

"You can have the ranch. I'll sign—sign anything. Just let me save him." Out of the corner of her eye, she could see Will shake his head and mouth *no*.

But what was a ranch in comparison to him? Now that she knew he wanted her as a daughter—that he loved her—she would not risk losing him.

She met Guy's gaze. "He's more important than anything else."

His eyes narrowed. "You keep telling yourself that." Backing away, he jerked his head in Will's direction.

Did that mean she could tend his wound?

She rushed to her father's side. Kneeling beside him, she pried his fingers away from his thigh. Blood gushed from his wound. She immediately pressed her palm to it to slow the bleeding.

"No, Ellie." His voice rasped. "Don't...don't agree. To anything."

She choked back tears. "I can't lose you."

The front door banged open and Blade strode in. "Found her. I locked her in the root cellar."

They could only be talking about Mrs. Johnson. In an instant, Ellie came up with a plan. But would the housekeeper cooperate?

"I need her." Ellie raised her voice.

Guy turned to study her.

"I can't do everything myself. I need her help."

He turned back to his man. "Bring her. But first..." He grabbed Blade's arm. "Tell Whitey to go get the preacher."

Ellie gaped at the men.

Blade's eyebrows shot up. "Someone needin' burying?"

"Maybe."

"What if he won't come?"

The foreman hooked one thumb at his waist. "Whitey'll convince him. But tell him not to harm the preacher." When his crony scratched his head, Guy added, "We're gonna have ourselves a lil' wedding."

Rhett and Pete made it to the barn without being seen. The dogs had been no trouble, especially when they smelled the jerky Pete had. They wolfed down the chunks of dried meat.

"Good boys." Rhett kept his voice low as he patted each one, but he wouldn't allow them inside the barn. Someone would notice their absence.

From the upper story, they watched the ranch yard. A tap at Rhett's shoulder drew away his attention. His friend pointed to the corral, where a man grabbed a horse, then leaped into the saddle. Rhett squinted, but the minimal light didn't help much. Looked like Whitey.

"Git up." His cry spurred the horse into a gallop. He thundered out of the yard, heading toward Casper.

"Should I follow?" Pete's whisper cut through the dark. "Stop him?"

Rhett considered the situation. "No."

They needed to stick together until they found out what was happening inside the house. Though he didn't know where Whitey was going, or why, nothing was more important than Ellie.

If the man was riding to Casper, they had about four hours before the man returned. Not much time.

Rhett kept his voice low. "We need to find a way into the house."

"Agreed. Plan?"

"With Whitey gone, only three of Bartow's men are left." As he spoke, he studied the yard. Blade remained on the porch. "Hoskins is guarding the bunkhouse. Looks like he barricaded the door."

So the other ranch hands wouldn't interfere?

"Dietmeyer's around somewhere." Rhett calculated that the henchman wouldn't be far.

"What about Marshall and his niece?"

"In the house. Likely with Bartow." Rhett's idea took shape. "We take out his cronies first."

"All right."

Even as he spoke, he knew his plan was risky. What if the foreman called to one of them for a report? Or checked on them?

Give me wisdom, Lord. I need direction.

Though Rhett could not see, the God of the heavens saw all. And He could be trusted.

The *clop-clop* of a horse sounded in the yard. Dietmeyer rode by the porch and, still mounted, chatted with Blade. From where Rhett was, he couldn't understand what they were saying. A little while later, Dietmeyer nudged his horse toward the bunkhouse. But he kept his horse to a walk, as though he hadn't a care in the world.

"Him." Rhett spoke to Pete as he pointed to Dietmeyer. "We capture him. Quietly."

Pete's teeth flashed in the dark. "Consider it done."

Together, they scrambled down from their post. Before they left the barn, Rhett grabbed some rope.

Maintaining their distance, he and Pete kept the mounted man in sight when he stopped to speak to

Hoskins. With hand gestures, Rhett indicated that Pete should stay away from the bunkhouse windows. He didn't want one of the ranch hands to look out and see them. No telling how they would react.

After a few minutes, Dietmeyer moved on. He checked on the stables, then the granary, never dismounting. When he rode toward the barn, Pete gripped Rhett's arm. *Take him here?* he seemed to be asking.

Rhett shook his head. The man was too close to the yard. Someone would hear the scuffle. He pointed toward the hills.

As they moved away from the buildings, they kept an eye on the rider. Because his path was unpredictable, Rhett readied himself to take him out when the opportunity came. Dietmeyer meandered on the yard's fringe before urging his horse to move farther afield, checking the corral and then wandering along the fence lines.

Rhett determined the perfect place for an ambush outside one pasture, beside a small knoll, but Dietmeyer had to be lured there. Rhett indicated the spot to Pete, then pointed to his own lips. Teeth gleaming, Pete nodded in understanding before he slunk away. Rhett clambered over the knoll. Slowing his breathing, he forced himself to be patient. An eternity seemed to pass.

Finally, the sound he was anticipating came—the mewling of an injured animal. He smiled when he recognized his friend.

As planned, Dietmeyer followed the noise. When a rustle, directly below Rhett, sounded in the dark night, he tensed. After a quick look, Rhett launched himself from his hiding place, knocking the rider off his horse. Their brief scuffle ended when Rhett pinned him and held a knife to his throat.

"Make a sound," he hissed, "and you die."

Dietmeyer's eyes widened, their whites stark in the uncertain light.

An out-of-breath Pete showed up seconds later to help bind and gag Dietmeyer. A short while later, they secured the trussed-up man in the burned-out building.

"I'm going to ask you some questions." Rhett got close so Dietmeyer could see his seriousness. "Tell the truth and live. If not…" He held his knife so that the blade flashed.

At his nod, Pete unbound the man's mouth.

Rhett came within inches of Dietmeyer's face. "Tell me what's going on at the ranch. Everything."

The cowardly man needed little urging to blurt all he knew. After Pete replaced the gag, they huddled together to plan.

"We have to move fast." Rhett considered how much time they had and how much they must accomplish before Whitey's return. Somehow Rhett and Pete would need to incapacitate two other men without alerting Bartow inside. And soon.

However, Rhett hesitated to leave Dietmeyer. Even with the bindings, he had no guarantees the man would not escape. Instinct urged him to leave Pete behind, to guard him. But Rhett needed his help with the men at the ranch.

I will not take a life, Lord.

Not unless absolutely necessary.

"I can tie him in such a way that he'll not want to escape." Pete's quiet suggestion seemed to indicate he read Rhett's mind. "A rope'll go here," he said, pointing to his own neck and then feet, "and there. Every time he moves, the noose will tighten."

Encouraged by the news, Rhett nodded. "Good. Then the plan might work. But I'll need some of his clothing."

Pete chuckled. Once upon a time, Rhett had told him about a game he had once played as a half-grown man—"borrowing" a soldier's coat to infiltrate the fort in the darkness.

Wearing Dietmeyer's clothing, Rhett would be able to get into the yard without raising suspicions. He could take out Hoskins by himself, but the next part involved his friend.

Rhett told him to meet him at the back of the house. There, they could access Ellie's room. Once inside, they could rush Bartow. When Blade entered, one of them would break away and attack him.

After Ellie and the others were safe and the house secured, they could hole up and decide what the next course of action would be.

Pete nodded.

Rhett rose. "Let's go."

"The bleeding won't stop," Mrs. Johnson worried aloud about her husband.

With shaking fingers, Ellie tore more strips of fabric to use to staunch the men's wounds. They were running low. All the while, her mind frantically searched for a way to end this nightmare.

Nearby, Guy watched with an expression of mild amusement. He leaned against the large table in the room as he bit into slice of bread, slathered with jam. Several times he had made snide comments about nature taking its course—giving up on Will and letting him die. Then apparently changing his mind, Guy started admonishing her to hurry to finish up before the preacher returned. Unless she didn't mind getting married in a bloody dress.

Her heart froze at the thought. She could not think about being his wife—had not considered that possibility—when she said "yes" to him.

"Cookie needs to be stitched," Ellie told the woman. "If you apply pressure to Will's leg, I'll tend to him."

Mrs. Johnson shook her head. "Your uncle needs help first."

Guy snorted, probably because the housekeeper did not yet know that Will was Ellie's father.

"I cannot tend to him while worrying about Cookie." She indicated that Mrs. Johnson should take over caring for the ranch owner. "Press here. Hard."

As soon as Mrs. Johnson did as she bade, Ellie rose and wiped her hands.

"Where you going?" Guy stepped in her way.

"To my room. I need my medical supplies. And more fabric."

"Oh no you don't. You'll disappear out the window."

She planted one fist at her hip. "Do you really think I'd leave now?"

His eyes narrowed.

"Besides," she added through clenched teeth, "it's the middle of the night. Where would I go?"

"Okay, but to make sure you don't…" He pulled out his gun and aimed it at her father's head. "Leave the door open so I can see you."

Gulping, she went into her room. Ellie knew exactly where her bag was, but she needed to stall so that she could put a candle in the window. The idea struck her to pull down the curtains.

"What're ya doing in there?"

"Getting more material. For bandages." She dared

not meet his gaze or Guy would know she was up to something.

After she removed the curtains, she lit a candle, then pretended to search for the items she needed.

"What's taking so long?" The distinct click of the gun's hammer filled her with terror. Guy would have no qualms about ending Will's life.

Taking a deep breath, she set the candle on the windowsill then marched to the doorway of her bedroom. "Stop distracting me with your yammering. How do you expect me to find anything?"

She was taking an awful chance, challenging him like that.

His mouth settled into a hard line, then he unexpectedly uncocked his gun and holstered it with a chuckle. "I like a plucky woman. We're gonna get along just grand."

The reminder of his marriage plans sent a shaft of fear through her. She would not—could not—dwell on that.

Ellie soon retrieved her bag and carried it and the fabric back into the main room. But she left the candle. As she crouched before Cookie, she could see the flickering flame, reflecting off the glass.

Would Rhett notice it in time?

"Please, God…" she whispered as she retrieved her astringent powders to deaden Cookie's pain. "Please help."

The older man's gaze met hers. He whispered back, "Amen."

Working as quickly as was wise, she stitched Cookie's head. Her gaze kept returning to the candle, but when she realized Guy watched her, she forced herself to stop.

"There. I just need to bandage your wound." After

nicking the edge of the curtain fabric with small scissors, Ellie tore the material into long strips. Soon she bound Cookie's head. All the while, she was aware of the three people who stared at her while she worked.

Mrs. Johnson was about to leave her post by Will's side when Ellie shook her head. "Wait. I need to tear more bandages."

"I'll do that. You care for Will."

They traded places.

Pressing her hand to his wound, she studied her father. "How're you doing?"

Skin gray, he could only manage a faint smile. Under her fingertips, his pulse raced. His symptoms indicated that he would die if she didn't do something drastic soon.

"Get my pillow," she directed Mrs. Johnson, glaring at Guy to keep him from challenging her. "And blankets. We need to lie him down."

The woman was soon back with the items. They maneuvered Will so that his legs were propped up. Mrs. Johnson covered his torso with the quilt, then rolled the smaller blanket for under his neck.

With care, Ellie cut the material from around his wound while Mrs. Johnson tried to keep pressure on it.

"Light." Ellie squinted at the ragged hole. "I need more light."

The woman again complied, bringing a candle.

"Better."

But as she peered past the woman, her heart stopped. Mrs. Johnson had grabbed the lighted candle from inside her room. The door stood ajar, revealing a dark room.

Ellie gulped. No candle meant no signal. He wouldn't

know she needed him. *I can't think of that right now.* Her father's life hung in the balance.

After she cut away the pants material, she felt around his thigh, but could not find an exit wound. That meant the bullet was still lodged in his leg. The powders she'd used on Cookie would do no good because of the un-stemmed flow of blood. She had to remove the bullet. Breathing hard, she plunged her fingers into the wound. Spasming, Will let out a loud groan.

"Hold him," Ellie commanded.

Cookie scooted across the floor to assist his wife.

Tension engulfed Ellie as she searched for, then found, the hard, jagged metal. Grunting in disgust, she dropped it to the floor. After making certain no fabric from his pants remained in the wound, she washed away the gore, then sprinkled the powder liberally. Working quickly, she placed a large compression bandage on his injury, held in place by long cloth strips around his leg.

Exhaling in relief, she sat back on her heels. The older couple met her gaze. Cookie gave her a small nod. "You done good, miss."

"I hope so," she managed to whisper.

Guy's raucous laughter broke the silence. "Yeah, you done *real* good, Ellie. But what's the point if he's gonna die anyway?"

She glared at him. "We all die. But God decides when and where. Not you."

He snorted.

With shaking limbs, she rose. Brushing by Guy, she washed her hands and forearms in the basin by the kitchen. Ellie had just dried them when the sounds of footsteps on the porch made her blood run cold. Was Whitey back already? She had been so intent on Will, she had not heard the horses.

"Time for a wedding." Guy winked at her, then turned as two men entered the house.

Blade came in, expression stony. Behind him, with his head lowered, a man in a coat and hat followed. The preacher? Her befuddled brain told her Pastor Charles looked different. This man seemed too tall. Were her nerves so frazzled that she was seeing things?

Feeling faint, Ellie grabbed a cloth and rubbed at the bloodstains on her gown. *God, please do something. I can't marry Guy.* With renewed vigor, she scrubbed a red splotch. She was so intent on her task that she didn't even look up when the back door slowly opened.

"Dietmeyer?" The foreman barked. "What're ya doing in here? You're supposed to be—"

"Guy, it's a trap!" Blade swiveled, then grappled with the man behind him.

Someone charged by Ellie, knocking her against the wall. She shrieked.

Guy was reaching for his gun when the newcomer rammed into him. Together they rolled on the floor, smashing against chairs and knocking over a bench. Blade and the preacher were also fighting.

Rushing to her father, Ellie covered him with her body. The struggling men grunted and yelled. The sound of splintering wood and shattering porcelain filled the room. When a shot rang out, she screamed.

In an instant, the room grew quiet.

When she raised her head, she fought to take in the sights around her.

Huddled on the floor, the Johnsons clung to each other. Across the room, Guy lay unconscious, sprawled across a broken chair. Several feet from him, a man who seemed familiar stood over Blade. Prostrate on the floor, he slowly raised his hands as he stared at the gun pointed squarely in his face.

But the man who held the gun riveted her attention. "Rh-Rhett?"

He didn't move while his companion bound Blade's hands. When Rhett finally looked her direction, Ellie shivered at the expression on his face. One other time she had seen that look—when he had crouched on the overturned stagecoach.

Relief and residual fear bubbled up inside her. She clapped one hand over her mouth as she burst into tears.

The Johnsons drew closer and put their arms about her. Ellie shook her head, trying to let them know she was all right, but she was too distraught to speak. By the time she gathered herself, both Blade and Guy were tied up. When Rhett's companion turned, she realized who it was—Pete, the stagecoach driver. But his face and hair appeared blackened with soot. He guarded a collection of weapons, arms crossed as he glared at his prisoners.

When Rhett turned to her, his face relaxed. She saw a welcoming, eager smile that she had learned to love.

She rushed into his arms. For the longest time— though not nearly enough—he merely held her.

When she pulled back her head, all she could say was, "You came."

A small smile graced his lips. "I saw the flickering candle. Didn't you tell me that was the sign?"

"Yes, but how…?" She shook her head, unable to comprehend how he had arrived so quickly. And how he had subdued Guy's men.

"Explanations must wait." Rhett gripped her shoulders. "Whitey will be arriving any minute. We need to be ready."

How did Rhett know? Through fresh tears, she merely nodded. "Tell me what to do."

"You, all three of you," he said, pointing to her and the Johnsons, "get into Ellie's room. After Whitey arrives—"

"I won't leave my father out here." Ellie lifted her chin.

Rhett's eyebrows rose. After studying her face, he nodded as though her announcement was the most natural thing in the world.

"We'll carry him to your room. Is that acceptable?"

"Yes." The escaping word was barely above a whisper, she was so overcome with emotion. "Let me prepare the bed." She grabbed the still-lit candle.

In moments, she was ready.

The three men carried Will, then stepped back so that Ellie could make him comfortable. Mrs. Johnson joined them, crowding into the room.

"Stay in here," Rhett instructed them, "No matter what happens in the next room."

Retreating, he and Pete shut the door behind them. Ellie sat beside her father on the bed, holding his hand. Under his waxen skin, he appeared to have regained some color, but his eyes remained closed.

From the other room, she heard furniture scraping the floor, then what could only be a body being moved. Blade began to curse, but the sound abruptly stopped. A muffled growl soon followed, indicating that they had gagged him.

"The foreman stays," Rhett's voice commanded behind the door. "Lock Blade in the root cellar. And make certain the bunkhouse door is still barricaded."

Blade's muted profanity faded and the kitchen door banged. After a few minutes, Ellie again heard Rhett speaking to his friend. "Let's put Bartow in front of the fireplace, back to the door."

Shuffling sounds and grunts of exertion ensued until the room grew quiet.

Were they now ready for Whitey?

For many tense minutes, Ellie merely listened, the Johnsons' scared eyes staring back in the shadowy room. She gasped at the sound of horse hooves. Two sets? Or more?

Scarcely able to breathe, she waited. The riders slowed as they reached the house.

"Go in." Whitey's gruff voice ordered from outside.

Reluctant feet climbed the steps, then the door banged open.

"He's here, boss." Whitey's voice grew louder.

Footsteps moved into the room.

"Boss? I said...hey!"

Another tussle ensued. From the sounds, it didn't take long for Rhett and Pete to overpower Whitey.

Another voice arose, that of Pastor Charles. "Would someone please explain what is going on?"

Murmuring voices followed, then the bedroom door opened. Rhett's visage appeared. He motioned for Ellie to come out, but she shook her head. "I'm not leaving my father."

His smile let her know he understood the double meaning. But did Rhett understand she couldn't let him go either?

Holding out her hand, she waited for him to join her. He hesitated a mere second before lacing his fingers with hers.

"We'll get more light," Mrs. Johnson volunteered. She and her husband left, bringing in more lanterns to dispel the darkness.

As soon as the pastor entered the room, his eyebrows shot up. His gaze took in Ellie's patient as well as her hand linked with Rhett's.

"Guy shot my—my father." Ellie choked on the words that were beginning to mean more to her than ever before. Rhett squeezed her fingers.

The news didn't seem to faze Pastor Charles. "I see."

"I got the bullet out. Bandaged him." She looked at Rhett, recalling that not too long ago, she had done a similar procedure on him with a thorny twig.

The pastor stepped closer. "Will he make it?"

"I hope so." Her words came out barely a whisper.

Her father's eyes fluttered open and fixed on the man standing at the foot of the bed. "Charles."

"Haven't seen you darken the church's door for years." He moved closer. "So the only way to see you was for me to get kidnapped at gunpoint in the middle of the night? Oh, and for you to get yourself shot?"

A faint smile passed her daddy's lips. "I reckon."

"As soon as he's well enough, you'll see him more." Ellie spoke with certainty.

Pastor Charles tilted his head toward her father. "I'd like it to be up to him."

"Will you go to church with me, Daddy?" She stroked his hair from his forehead.

Her heart soared at his awkward nod. "I promise, Sunshine."

Ellie swiped a tear that slipped down her cheek.

"You know I'm gonna hold you both to your word." Pastor Charles grew silent, gaze flickering from Will to her.

She turned to Rhett. "You too, right?"

His eyes twinkled as he grinned. "It'd take more than

a lil' old posse to keep me away—" he leaned closer and whispered "—from you."

Heat blossomed in her cheeks at his soft expression. Only the clearing of a throat reminded her they were not alone.

Pastor Charles was studying them. His gaze again drifted down to their entwined fingers. "I was told I'd be performing a wedding. That still true?"

Ellie inhaled sharply, then stared at Rhett. Would he want her after all the trouble she'd caused him?

The intense look in his eyes left no doubts in her mind.

"I'd like that." His gentle voice caressed her. "Very much. If you agree."

Unable to speak, she could only nod.

The light in Rhett's eyes dimmed. "But I need someone to give us his blessing."

From the bed, Will Marshall stared up at them.

Rhett stepped forward. "Sir, may I have the privilege—and exceeding honor—of wedding your daughter?"

The man she had grown to believe was her father visibly struggled to answer. "Only if you first tell me your name. Your *real* name. And who you are."

Rhett drew a slow breath, as though the words were too sacred to utter. "Everett Michael Walker Callaway." One corner of his mouth creased as though he attempted to smile, but his expression remained sad. "My mother's second husband—Russell Callaway—may not have legally adopted me, but I consider him my true father."

Our stories are so similar. Ellie studied the two men dearest to her in the world. Even though Frank Marshall was legally her father, she would honor Will with that title for the remainder of her life.

"Who I am," Rhett continued as he took both her hands in his, "well, that is up to you, sir. Regardless, I will never stop loving Elinor Marshall."

Her daddy took his time answering. "Then, yes. You may marry my daughter. But you must do it now. While I still have breath in my body."

Though his words sounded ominous, Ellie had no doubt he would recover—as long as she could watch over him.

However, as she studied Rhett, her joy melted into shock. He was covered in dirt and a raised bruise darkened the skin above one eye. No doubt she looked equally a mess with her filthy, blood-streaked gown and hair askew.

"I—I…" she stuttered as she spread her hands. She couldn't ask everyone to leave so that she could take a bath and change clothing.

Apparently guessing her dilemma, Pastor Charles grinned broadly. "Welcome, m'dear, to the wild frontier. You belong now."

A near-hysterical giggle escaped her. Had she truly once been offended by dirt?

"Shall we?" Pastor Charles stepped closer. "I'd like to get back to my family. Right after Pete and I deliver a bunch of outlaws to the sheriff."

Pete stepped forward. "And let's not forget our friend, Mr. Tesley."

"Right." Rhett's jaw tightened. "I'm going with you."

"Take a few more men with you," Will ordered.

"Then it's settled." Pastor Charles motioned to Pete and the Johnsons. "Gather round."

Rhett slipped his arm through Ellie's. As he drew her closer, he murmured, "I can't promise you a life free of hardship, but I can promise a love for you that is anchored in the Lord above."

Somehow she managed a tremulous smile. "Your God is my God."

With a gentle finger, he traced her cheek.

Clearing his throat, Pastor Charles retrieved a small, worn book from his pocket. Face growing solemn, he opened to the first page. "Dearly beloved…"

Epilogue

With care, Ellie straightened, apron full of eggs. After balancing it with one hand, she lifted the basket beside her that was full of more. Who knew chickens could be so productive? Had to be because of Mrs. Johnson's tender care, which Ellie daily tried to emulate.

A number of hens clucked and scratched about her feet, hoping, no doubt, for the treats she sometimes brought. As she watched their antics, she giggled. "Pecking order" and "henpecked" were phrases she now understood in a whole new way.

Tiptoeing through the brood, she took her haul to the kitchen door. "Here are the eggs," she called to Mrs. Johnson, who bustled about the kitchen.

Cookie threw her a glance. "I'll take 'em."

Earlier he had sent her out to collect some for a delicacy he was baking. He had muttered something about "high time for a proper wedding cake."

She had to agree that it was. She and her husband had been married for nearly six weeks. Today was the day for a promised feast.

Ellie watched the older couple, considering that someday, she might ask them to teach her to cook. Then she reconsidered. With Cookie's blessing, she had assumed the medical care of everyone on the ranch. But soon she would have no time to learn any new tasks or take on more responsibilities.

Shouts from the corral drew her attention. Her husband yelled encouragement as Pete clung to a bucking mare. Together they managed to calm the horse. Tripper stood nearby, always the levelheaded gelding who never got excited. Many a time, the men brought him into the corral to help soothe a wild horse. On the other side of the corral stood Pete's wife, watching. Ellie's and her eyes briefly met before the woman returned to eyeing her husband.

Ellie did the same, admiring the way Rhett approached the trembling mare.

Some sixth sense must have told him she watched, because he turned and smiled at her.

Overflowing happiness rose at the expression she saw more and more frequently—an expression of unburdened happiness, as though he were slowly shedding the imprisoning secrets of his past. He left Pete in the corral and strode toward her. As she'd noted many times, he seemed to walk without sound. But perhaps that was because he still favored the soft, knee-high boots.

The sun sparked the blue in his eyes. "What are you grinning at, my love?"

"You." She felt her smile broaden at the endearment he used. Inexplicable tears welled. Mere moments before, she had been brimming with joy. Was it natural for conflicting emotions to both be so intense?

He took her hands, bending his head to peer into her face. "What's wrong?"

"I…" She couldn't go on—delighted, terrified and astounded at the same time about what she had begun to suspect. And because she found no way to say it subtly, she blurted the news. "I think I'm going to have a baby."

His fingers tightened. Then he surprised her by ducking his head and pressing his lips to her hands. When he raised his head, his eyelashes were moist. "I wondered. You've looked…different lately."

Different? The word confused her.

"Better." He squeezed her fingers before releasing them.

She chuckled at his vehemence.

Gentle fingers cradled her jaw. "And more beautiful than ever."

She had to ask. "Are you happy with the news?"

"How could I not be?" He drew her closer and kissed her.

Leaning her forehead on his chest, she sniffed loudly. "I'm sorry. I don't know why I feel like crying and laughing. At the same time."

Rhett tilted her chin up to gaze into her face. "We'll adjust."

They would, as they had for the past six weeks. Many things had changed. So many wonderful events had happened—new ranch hands, new stock, new horses. The Double M had a new, but temporary, foreman as Rhett learned the ropes so that he could one day take over.

"Hey." A yell from across the yard interrupted them. On the porch stood her father, one fist planted at his hip while the other gripped a cane. "How're men supposed to get any work done if womenfolk constantly distract them?"

Laughing, Ellie retorted, "I don't think you mind all that much."

A woman appeared beside him—Rhett's mother, Lillian. Since her arrival several weeks before, she kept finding reasons to delay her return to Cheyenne. Finally she admitted she wanted to stay. Here was her home. As was their daily habit, she and Will visited every afternoon on the porch.

Rhett leaned closer. "Should we go tell them they're going to be grandparents?"

"Now?"

"Absolutely. Together?" He held out his arm.

Rather than take it, she slipped under his arm so that it rested across her shoulder. "All I wanted, from the moment we met, was to be with you."

He squeezed her shoulder. As they walked toward the house, she rejoiced that they would bring both their parents this blessed news. Not only would this give her father another reason to guard his health and life but would give all glory to their Father in heaven who made it possible.

* * * * *

LOVE INSPIRED

Stories to uplift and inspire

Fall in love with Love Inspired—
inspirational and uplifting stories of faith
and hope. Find strength and comfort in
the bonds of friendship and community.
Revel in the warmth of possibility and the
promise of new beginnings.

Sign up for the Love Inspired newsletter
at **LoveInspired.com** to be the first
to find out about upcoming titles,
special promotions and exclusive content.

Get 4 FREE REWARDS!

We'll send you 2 FREE Books plus 2 FREE Mystery Gifts.

The Sheriff's Promise
RENEE RYAN

LARGER PRINT

To Protect His Children
LINDA GOODNIGHT

LARGER PRINT

Love Inspired books feature uplifting stories where faith can guide you through life's challenges and discover the promise of a new beginning.

FREE
Value Over
$20

YES! Please send me 2 FREE Love Inspired Romance novels and my 2 FREE mystery gifts (gifts are worth about $10 retail). After receiving them, if I don't wish to receive any more books, I can return the shipping statement marked "cancel." If I don't cancel, I will receive 6 brand-new novels every month and be billed just $5.24 each for the regular-print edition or $5.99 each for the larger-print edition in the U.S., or $5.74 each for the regular-print edition or $6.24 each for the larger-print edition in Canada. That's a savings of at least 13% off the cover price. It's quite a bargain! Shipping and handling is just 50¢ per book in the U.S. and $1.25 per book in Canada.* I understand that accepting the 2 free books and gifts places me under no obligation to buy anything. I can always return a shipment and cancel at any time. The free books and gifts are mine to keep no matter what I decide.

Choose one:
- [ ] **Love Inspired Romance Regular-Print** (105/305 IDN GNWC)
- [ ] **Love Inspired Romance Larger-Print** (122/322 IDN GNWC)

Name (please print)

Address   Apt. #

City   State/Province   Zip/Postal Code

Email: Please check this box ☐ if you would like to receive newsletters and promotional emails from Harlequin Enterprises ULC and its affiliates. You can unsubscribe anytime.

Mail to the Harlequin Reader Service:
IN U.S.A.: P.O. Box 1341, Buffalo, NY 14240-8531
IN CANADA: P.O. Box 603, Fort Erie, Ontario L2A 5X3

Want to try 2 free books from another series! Call 1-800-873-8635 or visit www.ReaderService.com.

---

*Terms and prices subject to change without notice. Prices do not include sales taxes, which will be charged (if applicable) based on your state or country of residence. Canadian residents will be charged applicable taxes. Offer not valid in Quebec. This offer is limited to one order per household. Books received may not be as shown. Not valid for current subscribers to Love Inspired Romance books. All orders subject to approval. Credit or debit balances in a customer's account(s) may be offset by any other outstanding balance owed by or to the customer. Please allow 4 to 6 weeks for delivery. Offer available while quantities last.

Your Privacy—Your information is being collected by Harlequin Enterprises ULC, operating as Harlequin Reader Service. For a complete summary of the information we collect, how we use this information and to whom it is disclosed, please visit our privacy notice located at corporate.harlequin.com/privacy-notice. From time to time we may also exchange your personal information with reputable third parties. If you wish to opt out of this sharing of your personal information, please visit readerservice.com/consumerchoice or call 1-800-873-8635. **Notice to California Residents**—Under California law, you have specific rights to control and access your data. For more information on these rights and how to exercise them, visit corporate.harlequin.com/california-privacy.

LIR21R2

But he was also about to go visit his brother, Bobby, if he kept his promise to his ailing father. And when she'd heard about that visit, it had been a wake-up call: she shouldn't get too close with him. The fewer chances she had to spill the beans about Bobby being the twins' father, the better.

He came out of the pizza shop quickly—he must have called ahead—carrying a big flat box and a white bag. What would it be like if this was a family scenario, if they were Mom and Dad and kids, stopping for takeout on the way home from work?

She couldn't help it. Her chest filled with longing.

He climbed into her small car, juggling the large flat box to make it fit without encroaching on the gearshift.

She had to laugh at the size of his meal. "Hungry?"

"Are you?" He opened the box a little, and the rich, garlicky fragrance of Pasquale's special sauce filled the car.

Her stomach growled, loudly.

"Pee-zah!" Addie shouted from the back seat.

"Peez!" Emmy added, almost as loud.

"That's just cruel," she said as she pulled the car back onto the road and steered toward Luke's place. "You're tempting us. I may have to order some when I get these girls home."

"No, you won't," he said. "This is for all of us. The least I can do is feed you, after you drove me around."

Her stomach gave a little leap, and not just about the prospect of pizza. Why was he inviting her to have dinner with him? Was there an ulterior motive? And if there was, would she mind?

Don't miss
Finding a Christmas Home *by Lee Tobin McClain,*
available October 2021 wherever
Love Inspired books and ebooks are sold.

LoveInspired.com

LIEXP0921

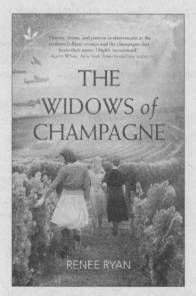